UNLIKELY NEIGHBORS

RENEE DANIEL FLAGLER

 HARLEQUIN

 afterglow BOOKS

ISBN-13: 978-1-335-57494-7

Unlikely Neighbors

Copyright © 2025 by Renee Daniel Flagler

Harlequin Enterprises ULC
22 Adelaide St. West, 41st Floor
Toronto, Ontario M5H 4E3, Canada
www.Harlequin.com

Printed in U.S.A.

Unlikely Neighbors

This book is dedicated to my sister and one of the captains of my cheering squad, Cora Daniel. I miss you deeply.

And to the women who groomed me.
Thank you for your time, talent, treasure and wisdom.

One

Holland Davenport

You're ready for this.

Those words were part of my daily pep talk, reminding me that leaving Florence, South Carolina, needed to happen. It would be the scariest and bravest thing I'd ever done. I wanted nothing more than to do fearless and bold things.

A life bigger than what Florence could offer was finally on the horizon. Florence was familiar and familiar felt safe to me. I was completely over seeing the same people, doing the same things, and going to the same places all the time. Days, weeks, months, and years clumped together into a mountain of sameness.

Thank God my cancer scare wasn't the death sentence I had feared, but I couldn't help thinking, How could I die without ever really living?

Two short toots of a car's horn let me know my cousin Amy had pulled up. This was our last weekend together before my move to Charleston. My announcement last month shocked everyone, especially my adoptive mother. You would have thought I told her I was jumping off a cliff. Ma been an emotional mess ever since.

Grabbing my bag, I braved the balmy heat, knowing Amy would have the air conditioner on ice-cold once I entered the car. Inside, her teary eyes stared back at me.

"Don't start," I said, rolling my eyes and holding my hand up at her.

She pouted. I stared at her beautiful face, marveling how her signature bright red lipstick perfectly contrasted with her espresso-colored skin.

Glistening hazel eyes bore into me as the corners of her mouth turned down and quivered.

"Ugh!" She sniffed. "I don't want to ugly-cry," she groaned. "Who would have thought you would leave this place before me?"

I tasted the salt of my own tears.

"Girl! We have to stop all this crying," I said, wiping my face and flipping down the visor. "We're going to look like raccoons." I laughed through sniffles.

"I know!" She fanned her eyes with her hand, blinking rapidly. "These lashes won't last through the night."

Amy wasn't just my cousin, she had been my best friend, therapist, and bodyguard since I was five. When she walked into a room, she hijacked all the attention. Loved hard and never bit her tongue.

Since childhood, I'd admired her boldness. Now it was my inspiration. Living hours away from Amy and Ma wasn't going to be easy.

Amy squeezed my hand gently and then let go before she slowly pulled into traffic.

"Charleston isn't that far away. What is it? A two-hour drive? I'll be back all the time." I turned to Amy with wide eyes. "Why don't you move to Charleston with me? You've wanted out of Florence for years. Take my second bedroom."

"If Mama's health was better, I'd leave in a minute." Amy's lips turned down again, and the weight of being Aunt Shirleen's sole caretaker since an autoimmune disease rendered her fragile dimmed the light in her eyes. "Anyway," Amy sighed. "That gumbo at Jazz on Dargan is calling my name."

Adele's "Rolling in the Deep" came up on Amy's playlist, lifting the mood. "Oh, girl! That's my song." Amy cranked up the volume. We danced in our seats like life wasn't beating down on us.

"What grade were we in when this came out? Eleventh? Twelfth?" I wondered, snapping my fingers.

We sang along with Amy's playlist until we pulled up to the restaurant. The weight of my secret bore down on me. I'd told my family about the move, but never shared the real reason I felt so strongly about doing it now. Amy had always been my confidant; keeping her in the dark about this didn't feel right.

Once she parked, I placed my hand on her arm before she could turn to get out of the car.

Raising one brow, she side-eyed me. "What?" She always knew when something was up.

"I need to tell you something, but you have to promise to keep it to yourself."

Alarm widened Amy's eyes. "What's wrong, Hollz?"

I took a deep breath. "My doctor found a lump in my breast."

Gasping, Amy clutched her chest. "No!"

"I'm fine," I said immediately and watched Amy release the breath she held. "It was small," I reassured her. "They did a biopsy, and I had a quick procedure to remove it. A small cyst. No cancer. I'm all good now."

Amy went to open her mouth, probably to rip into me but I held my hand up, stopping her.

"I kept it to myself because my doctor assured me there was nothing to fear and that it could easily be taken care of. Ma and Aunt Shirleen don't need unnecessary bad news at their age."

Both women were old enough to be our grandmothers.

Amy shook her head and squinted at me.

"Just hear me out." I rummaged through my brain in search of the right words. "I know it seems incredibly selfish, but I promise you I was thinking of all of you more than me. If it was bad news, I would have said something. And this scare made me think about how much more I wanted out of life. I'm moving to Charleston and pressing the restart button. This is something I need to do for me."

"Normally, I would have a mouthful of spicy words for you, but I get it." Amy shrugged. "I understand."

Amy reached over and hugged me, then pulled back with tears shining in her eyes. "I'm not happy about how you handled that by yourself, but you deserve this move. And! I want daily play-by-plays so I can live vicariously through you. Fly, little butterfly. Fly!" Amy flailed her arms and smiled and we laughed through our tears.

"Let's get inside," Amy said. "Patience is waiting for us and you know how she gets."

Relieved, I exited the car feeling lighter than when I'd entered. Like Amy said, my sister Patience was right inside the restaurant waiting on us. Her striking gray eyes were glued to her cell phone. Some days, an olive-green hue rimmed her irises. Mostly, it depended on her mood, her eyes shifting like a temperature gauge, getting greener when she was sullen and lightening when she was excited.

Long acrylic tips *tap, tap, tapped* against the phone screen at lightning speed. Blond braids cascaded down the back of her hourglass figure, meeting the ragged hem of her cutoffs.

"Hello!" I sang, breaking through her self-absorbed bubble.

Twisting her lips, she rolled her eyes. "It's about time," she teased before throwing her arms around my neck. Patience hugged like every embrace could be her last, tight and lingering. This time I matched her intensity. It was going to be hard leaving her behind.

The energy in the restaurant was electrifying. Waiters and customers hustled and scurried in a well-orchestrated ensemble. Summer Walker's latest hit floated through the speakers.

Amy, Patience, and I pressed through the crowd, waving at friends. We knew almost everyone in there.

"What's good in the neighborhood?" Tony, one of the long-time waiters, said once we sat down. "Your regulars?" he yelled referring to our drinks. We nodded. "Be right back," he said, his voice muffled by the loud music.

Our city wasn't one-traffic-light small, but small enough to know people based on who their family members were. Smaller towns came to us for action.

Patience's attention was back on her phone as we sat. I leaned close enough for her to feel my breath in her ear. "No texting all night. Hear me?" This needed to be said. Patience could live her entire life through her cell phone while the outside world passed her by.

She laid her phone face down on the table and blinked at me. "Why do you have to leave?" she asked for the umpteenth time.

Amy and I snickered when Patience folded her arms across her chest and pouted.

"You are so mature," Amy teased.

"And pouting won't help," I laughed.

"I'm gonna miss you," Patience whined. "Who will fix my life when you're hours away?"

"Just pick up your phone and call me. Phones still function that way, you know. It's always in your hand anyway," I said, rubbing my chest to loosen the lump of guilt that formed there.

"It won't be the same without you here," Patience groaned, her abandonment issues on full display.

Ma had adopted me in time to put me in kindergarten. Patience joined our family a few years later, but her struggle with abandonment never waned. Once she'd learned that I could be trusted, she clung to me. It felt good to go from having no siblings to being the big sister.

"How sweet," Amy teased, pushing her lips into an exaggerated pout. "She's going to miss her big sister."

"Whatever." Dismissing Amy, Patience turned to me. "Why the rush, Holly?" she asked, using my nickname.

I took a breath, preparing to explain my position once again. Patience wouldn't understand that I needed to separate myself from her, Ma, and everything I'd ever known to figure out who I really was, or that after my cancer scare, every question about my medical history was a glaring example of how much I didn't know about myself.

There were so many ways to answer Patience's question. "I have to get settled before starting my new job in September." I kept it simple.

"Are you coming home for your birthday?" Patience asked.

"No," I said, forcing what I hoped was a warm smile.

"No!" Patience jerked her head back. Appalled, she asked, "We can't even celebrate your thirtieth birthday with you? Dang, Holland!" Even in the low light of the restaurant, I could see the light in her eyes dim.

"Of course you can." I reached for Patience's hand. "Come

to Charleston anytime you want," I said matter-of-factly, in contrast to Patience's dramatic response. "It will be fun."

Turning the big three-oh *was* a big deal. My next decade needed to look drastically different from my last.

On my last birthday, I vowed I wouldn't turn thirty in the same town. I didn't take myself seriously until the health scare. Then I made plans to leave Florence, landing a job and an apartment in Charleston within months.

I didn't hate Florence. Fond memories bonded the city to my heart. But none of the things on my life's checklist had happened for me. Upward mobility? No. A husband? No. Possibly a kid or two? No again. There wasn't anything holding me back.

Tony the waiter arrived with our cocktails and set them down in front of us before taking our orders.

Amy raised her glass. "Welp! Here's to a new start."

"To living the life you want... I guess," Patience muttered then grinned sheepishly. "At least you got a job first." Everyone laughed. Patience would have left without one.

I raised my glass to meet theirs. "And to doing it all, scared as hell," I added.

The glasses clinking was the best accompaniment to our laughter.

"What about Sean?" Patience asked, setting her glass back down on the table. "How did he take the news of you moving?"

I took a long sip, then carefully set my cocktail on the table. Suddenly, it wasn't strong enough. I didn't want to discuss Sean.

"It's over."

"Good!" Amy said, before sipping her chocolate martini. "Find a man that will make you a priority."

"*Wow.*" That stung a little.

"Did I lie?" Amy asked matter-of-factly.

She didn't. Admittedly, I allowed Sean's behavior, and it didn't feel good at all to realize that. Sean was the most unfulfilling situationship ever. Following a fun start, whatever we had between us withered after a few months but didn't completely die. It lingered with late-night visits and conversations that vehemently avoided substance.

I had hoped for more. What girl didn't? The freedom of not being pressured worked for Sean and avoiding the direct sting of rejection worked for me, so instead of pinning him down, I acted as if I didn't care when he called less frequently and eventually not at all. Whoever I dated next would have to make me a priority.

Reaching in my bag, I panicked when I didn't feel my phone.

"Amy! Do you see my cell?" I asked, still rifling through my purse.

Both Amy and Patience looked around for it before shaking their heads.

"Ugh! I think I left it at home." I shrugged like it wasn't a big deal. "Waiter." I raised my hand before he could pass us by. "Can I get one of those?" I pointed to Amy's chocolate martini and then gulped the last of my drink, looking forward to the sweet, strong cocktail to ward off the anxiety that fluttered in my chest because I didn't have my phone.

"Sure." He nodded politely.

"So. Are you going to find a new man in Charleston?" Patience asked.

"Nope! I'm going to focus on me," I declared.

Patience cocked her head to the side and tapped her chin thoughtfully. "But what if he has a cute brother for me?"

Laughter bubbled up from each of us, refusing to subside.

"Don't be selfish, Holly. I'm gonna need a husband some-day. Who would I marry here?" Patience asked.

"Cousin Willie," Amy said, guffawing. I covered my mouth to keep the drink from spilling out.

"Exactly!" Patience pointed a finger at Amy, her shoulders bouncing as she cackled.

Through the rest of dinner, we imagined ourselves living bigger lives in metropolitan cities across the South.

"Charleston could just be my first stop," I said, prompting a new list of cities to explore.

It was after midnight when Amy dropped me back home. Martinis swam in my stomach, making me queasy. I dropped two tabs of Alka-Seltzer into a small glass of water and watched them fizz, then downed the contents in one long gulp. Instantly, a belch rumbled through my chest, erupting before I could get my hand to my mouth. "Excuse me," I said into the emptiness of my apartment.

My cell phone sat on the table near the door. I grabbed it on the way to my bedroom to undress.

Ma had left a message about a package I received from New York. I didn't know anyone from up North and won-dered why it had gone to her house. Knowing she would be asleep, I waited until after my fitful night of alcohol-induced sleep to call her.

"Hello," Ma croaked early the next morning. She cleared the sleep from her throat and repeated her greeting.

"Hey, Ma. Sorry to wake you. Your message sounded im-portant."

At the sound of rustling sheets, I imagined her propping herself up on her elbow.

"It's all right. A package came. It looks important. Come on over and get it."

"Okay. See you soon."

When I reached Ma's house, she was sitting at the small, round table in her neat little dining room, sipping on her favorite tea. Steam swirled above the mug. The aroma wafted through the small room.

"Hey!" I greeted her, kissing her cheek and reaching for the priority envelope on the table.

Ma watched me over the rim of her cup. The curiosity behind her eyes made me rip the package open faster, revealing official-looking documents. The contents proclaimed that I was the next of kin and sole heir to the estate of a woman I'd never met.

My heart didn't know whether to beat faster or stop completely. Mindlessly, I circled Ma's oak coffee table, reading slowly, zeroing in on the words that requested my presence at a law office in New York in less than two weeks. I'd wanted to embark on a journey of self-discovery and was getting what I'd asked for. It came in the form of legal documents and an unexpected trip to New York.

"Deep breaths," I reminded myself in a whisper. I closed my eyes. Counting, I willed my breathing to regulate itself. Ma watched me, her expression unreadable. I expected questions but she didn't ask any. Had she somehow known what was in the envelope?

Goldie Mae Williamson. I breathed the name listed in the documents, trying it on my tongue. The papers said she was my maternal great-aunt—my grandmother's sister. Tracing the letters of her name with my fingers was the only way to feel her. I had a biological family member. A living one—until two weeks ago.

I guess I was going to New York.

Two

Noble Washington

Tim: We need to talk.

This text message flashed in my memory like a buzzing vacancy sign at a janky motel. I saw the message from the chairman of my board of directors last night, but it was too late to respond. No greeting. No salutation. Just those four brief words.

I picked up my cell phone to look at the message again. If Tim Billia said we needed to talk, texting wouldn't suffice, but the light of the sun had yet to peek through the darkness.

As close as we'd become, calling Tim at this hour would have been inappropriate without a life-threatening emergency. In the ten-plus years I'd known Tim, he'd taught me more than my dad had in all my thirty years on this Earth. Whereas Tim never let me down, let-downs were the strongest memories I had of my real father.

I told Siri to remind me to call Tim at nine thirty. Facing

the day was inevitable. I dragged myself out of bed, crossed the thick carpet toward the bathroom and turned on the rain-shower system. The cool water woke me up as it did every morning.

I arrived in the office an hour early to give myself time to prepare for my meeting with my leadership team. Mixing tasty concoctions to stay awake through late-night study sessions in grad school had led to the launch of my company, Push Beverages. Thanks to my roommate and friend, Tyler Keen, and his uncle Tim Billia, Push had taken me from a broke kid from the hood to one of the most successful young CEOs on the Forty Under Forty Power List.

Tim became more to me than just a mentor. His support and powerful network of deep-pocketed investors turned what started as a small team of three into one of the fastest-growing beverage companies in the world with corporate offices in the heart of New York City, over a hundred employees, and global distribution. Tim has served on my board of directors since Push's inception and helped me become a respected businessman. I could never have fathomed the life that he and Push had afforded me.

Anxious about calling Tim back, I checked my watch every ten minutes for an hour and a half. I tapped his name in my list of favorites at nine twenty-nine.

"What time can we meet?" Tim asked the moment he picked up. No greeting. No small talk.

My stomach knotted. "Is it that bad?" I asked, swiping my clammy palm down my face.

"Noon good?" Tim wasn't even using full sentences.

"Ah. Sure."

"Let's meet at Nelly's," Tim said, referring to the famed diner on Manhattan's Upper West Side with an ethnic twist. The decor and uniforms were a throwback to the seventies and the large servings of delicious soul food kept people coming back.

"I'll make it happen. See you there," I agreed.

Just as I was about to disconnect, I heard Tim say, "Oh, and Noble?"

"Yeah, Tim?"

"Come by yourself."

"Sure," I said, slow and easy. Tim ended the call without saying bye.

What the hell was this about? I knew Tim was referring to leaving Tyler behind. Besides being his nephew and my best friend, Tyler was also my chief operations officer and right-hand man. Nothing in Push happened without Ty.

I stood up, rounded my desk, and paced my office floor. What did Tim have to say to me that couldn't be said in front of Ty? I sat back down, tapped the keys on my laptop until our financials for the last few quarters filled my screen. We didn't do as well as projected, but were still in the black.

My mind went in every possible direction, trying to figure out what Tim wanted to discuss. His discretion drove my insecurities to the surface. Had I done something wrong? I'd just been nominated to receive another award for the Top Fifty CEOs Under Forty. I swiped my hand down my face and dragged in a breath. To be honest, I've felt uneasy for weeks.

I pushed my chair back and walked over to my favorite corner looking out over downtown Manhattan and tried to gather my thoughts. The view wasn't calming me down like it usually did, so I resumed pacing.

This hadn't started with Tim's email. Life has been firing on all sides for a few weeks, wreaking havoc on my serenity. People on my board with whom I'd become friendly seemed to avoid me. When they were around, they seemed less talkative.

"Mr. Washington." My assistant, Ashley, interrupted my wallowing session.

"Yes!" I answered abruptly at first. I didn't mean to snap at her. "Hey, Ashley. What's up?"

"Um. Your meeting." She raised a brow and then looked at her wrist. She didn't have on a watch. I got the message.

I looked at my watch. It was fifteen minutes after ten. I'd forgotten to cancel the ten o'clock meeting with my leadership team.

"Ugh! Thanks. Can you tell Ty I need him in here, please?" I headed back to the chair behind my desk and let my thoughts run wild again.

Several minutes later Ty knocked and entered my office. I could read the questions in his eyes before he opened his mouth.

I nodded and gestured for him to close the door. He did, then turned to me. "What's up?" he said, his eyebrows creased.

"Something came up with the executive committee, and now I have to prepare for a meeting with Tim at noon. I needed to reschedule our meeting but got caught up and forgot."

"Where are we meeting him?" Ty asked.

"Not us. Me."

Ty lifted his brows. "Oh." An uncomfortable silence expanded between us. "Is everything all right?" Ty finally asked.

"I hope so." I sat back in my chair and repeated more to myself than to Tyler, "I really hope so." We swam in that discomfort for a few more moments. "I'll update you as soon as I get back."

Ty tilted his head and pulled his bottom lip into his mouth. After a deep exhale, he said, "Okay."

The problem with preparing for the meeting with Tim was that I didn't know what to prepare for. Between emails, I watched the clock until it was time to go. I arrived at Nelly's, fifteen minutes early. I wanted to be there before Tim arrived.

I spotted Tim the second he walked in the diner. I waved him over. He wore a look that said "I'm not your average middle-aged man." He was tall and fit, with a salt-and-pepper beard—mostly salt—bright blue eyes, almond skin, and slick, platinum-blond hair cut closely on the sides. He looked like a mature model and was capable of turning the heads of women of every age and ethnicity.

"Noble!"

"Hey, Tim." We shook hands and hugged.

"What are you having?" he asked as he slid into the booth.

"Burger and fries. You?"

"The wife says I gotta watch the cholesterol. I'm gonna go for the chicken salad sandwich. That's better than a burger, right?"

"I don't know, man." I shrugged.

"Ha! Me neither, but at least it has the word *salad* in it." Tim laughed, slapping the table.

His mood seemed lighter than when we spoke earlier. That gave me some relief. I felt like I'd been holding my breath from the moment his text came in.

The waitress came over, flirted with Tim, took our order, and disappeared as stealthily as she had arrived.

"Before we start, how's things with your dad?"

"Okay," I said, genuinely appreciative. Only a few people knew about my father or cared to ask about our "it's complicated" relationship. I didn't like talking about him, but Tim always asked. As much as he was like a father to me, he wasn't mine and didn't want me to forget that I had one, regardless of how we got along. He was the only family I had. "How's the family?" I asked.

"Great. Everyone is great," Tim said.

The waitress placed two ice-cold glasses of soda in front of us. I sipped nervously and sputtered a cough when some of it went down the wrong pipe.

"You know, a wise man once said that a company should change its CEO every ten years. Do you believe that?" Tim looked me straight in the eyes.

I took another sip of soda so Tim wouldn't see that his comment had impacted my breathing. "I don't know. Do *you* believe that?"

"It depends. The thing is, we have some members of the board who strongly believe that." Tim stopped talking. I wasn't sure if he was expecting me to respond. I didn't. I said nothing at all. My mind was too busy trying to figure out where Tim was going with this. "Here's the thing. You've been a great CEO."

"Wait. They want to fire me?" I blurted my question. My temples began to throb.

Tim held his hand up to calm me. "Hear me out. You've been amazing. Our numbers haven't been the greatest lately and it's about time for a change. Several things usually happen at this stage for a company to go to the next level. Here are two." Tim held up two fingers. "They get a new, more seasoned CEO." He put one finger down. "Or sell."

My stomach caved in. Tim's lips continued to move but I heard nothing other than my mind repeating *They're taking your company away from you.* Was I not good enough to take Push to the next level? No one ever asked Bezos or Gates or Jobs to step aside so their companies could be better. Swallowing hard, I pushed down the tightness forming in my throat and studied Tim's mouth. I needed to focus on what he was saying.

Just as I had begun to find words to respond to Tim, our waitress interrupted us with our meals. He dug right in, but my appetite departed when Tim told me two reasons why I needed to go.

Both of Tim's options sounded like I would have to hand my company over to someone else to run it. I didn't want to do either of those. They all sounded like ways to get rid of me.

"Why is this necessary?" I said, hoping I didn't sound like an angry kid. What I didn't ask out loud was *Who was behind this?* Did Tim want this, or was there someone on the board that was out for my job?

"So that Push and you can be greater," Tim said matter-of-factly.

I screamed *Bullshit* in my head. Sitting back hard, my mouth said, "Help me understand this."

Tim put his sandwich down and wiped his hands with a napkin. He looked directly into my eyes. "Push and you are at a crossroads. I need you to think about whether you're more committed to the company's future or your success."

"I thought I was supposed to be committed to both."

"You never want to overstay your welcome. It's important to leave a company while you're still attractive to other companies and your career is at a high."

I dropped my head into my hands.

"I know this feels deeply personal to you."

"Damn right." I slammed my hand on the table, causing my untouched drink to teeter. Heads whipped around in our direction. I lowered my voice. "This company is my life. I started it from my dorm room."

"But now it belongs to the millions of people who drink and invest in Push daily—the shareholders. Isn't that what you wanted?" Tim looked confused.

"Well, yeah." I felt like saying "Duh." Of course I wanted this.

I knew the company belonged to our shareholders once

we had gone public, but Push was my child. I had nurtured it, watched it grow, and loved what it turned out to be. It was my greatest accomplishment and my way of staying out of the poor house.

I hated struggling as a kid and did everything I could to help my mother out after my dad had cheated and left. While my friends played video games that I couldn't afford, I worked in the local bodega and fast-food restaurants to buy my own school clothes and take the burden off my mother. Push became my way out. I dedicated every accomplishment to the memory of my mom. Now they wanted to snatch that away from me?

"What do you want for your future Noble?" Tim asked.

Buying time, I finally sipped the icy soda, hoping to quench the dryness that settled in my mouth. Push was all I had come to want for myself. For the past ten years, while friends were partying, getting married, and having kids, I was building Push. I woke up in the morning for Push. Came home at night to Push. The only true family I claimed to have is the one I gained through Push. In return, Push had given me more than I had ever imagined—something to call my own. Acceptance, approval, respect, and wealth. Extracting Push from my life would leave very little behind.

Instead of answering his question, I asked, "You want me gone too?"

Tim drew in a breath and shook his head. "I want you to win, but you need to define what winning looks and feels like for yourself, and it has to be more than running Push. Ready or not, a transition is coming, and I need you to be just as attractive as Push is when it takes place. Think about what you really want. When the time comes, use the transition to live a little. Hell, go on some dates. Join a board, get involved in community service. Do things for yourself. You have a life outside of Push."

But I didn't. My life *was* Push.

I dropped my eyes to the uneaten french fries I had moved around on my plate. I knew where Tim was going with all of this, but it didn't make me feel better. I felt like I was being gutted.

Tim took a final bite and laid down the remnants of his sandwich, then slurped the remainder of his soda.

"Let me make this crystal clear. This is not personal. The board is pushing for change. Profitability is the name of the game, and a public company's goal is to find the best possible path to the highest revenue. We owe that to shareholders. If a new CEO or selling to the highest bidder offers the possibility of greater profits, that's what the board will pursue. Professionally, I can't stand in the way of that. Personally, when it comes to you, I want to make sure that no matter what, you land on your feet. I need you to be ready. Understand?"

I drew in a sharp breath and released it with a grunt. I understood. Was I ready? That was a different question altogether. I had become synonymous with Push. My company had turned me into someone who people respected. Doors opened for me because I was the founder. Before Push, I was just a kid working my ass off, trying to get as far away from my past as I could. Push gave me a life I never imagined living. Who would I be without my company?

Three

Holland

Noise engulfed me as I stood before the handsome Brooklyn brownstone I'd just inherited. Bathed in a warm reddish-brown hue, it stood tall, like a proud soldier slightly worn from earning his share of battle scars over the years. Despite a crack in the stoop and a few scattered paint chips, the home was an elegant marriage of modern flair and historical charm.

Honking horns, crying babies, skateboard wheels grinding against the concrete, and laughter spilling from the teens whizzing by blended together like a dizzying symphony. A car passed by with rap music playing so loudly I could hear the metal vibrating.

Florence, South Carolina was a whisper of a city compared to Brooklyn, which was as loud and alive as the people who constantly traipsed through the concrete streets. I looked down at the address on the papers in my hand and back up at the numbers above the door. This was it.

Stepping through the wrought iron gate, I pulled out the keys the attorney had given me. "Here goes nothing," I said, sucking in a breath. I was about to walk into the house my aunt had lived in for almost fifty years. My hands trembled and a mix of excitement and curiosity danced in my chest.

This felt like an adventure—a nerve-racking and scary one. What would I find inside? Could I handle it? Was I ready? I had to encourage myself to take the next step. I swallowed the trepidation threatening to lodge itself securely in my throat.

I made my way up the few steps separating the sidewalk from the front of the house, turned the key, opened the creaky door, and stepped over the threshold into the 1990s. Pushing the door closed, I shut out the noise that lived outside and ran my hand across the mustard-colored wallpaper in the entrance, fumbling for the light switch. A low haze illuminated the yellow couch under the front window, which faced a pair of floral wingback chairs, all covered in once-shiny plastic. The bold red-and-yellow print on the wingback chairs matched the drapes framing the bay window at the front of the room. From the door I looked straight through the living room and dining room into the kitchen in the back of the house. Sturdy, worn oak stood strong and thick in the dining room table, chairs, and cabinetry in the kitchen. Every surface was covered with a thin layer of dust.

Besides the slight musty smell, the home was remarkably tidy to have been empty for the months my aunt had spent in hospice. Cancer had put her there. But it was a bout of pneumonia that had ended her life.

Gavin, one of Aunt Goldie's lawyers, talked about what a gem this house was. He said I should keep it and make it my own. That's what Aunt Goldie would have wanted. They said she'd made several attempts to find me and when her end was near, she made them promise they would continue the search.

The other attorney slipped a card for a real estate agent into my hand in case I wanted to sell. Since I wasn't interested in moving to this dizzying place, selling made the most sense.

I walked through the dining room into the kitchen. What would it take to get rid of all the old furniture? I had a big job ahead of me: figuring out how to pack up and prepare this house for sale as soon as possible. I had a new life to start in Charleston and couldn't wait to get to it.

Framed pictures on the wall caught my attention. I walked to the slanted wall beside the staircase.

"Wow!" My mouth fell open. I recognized Aunt Goldie from the funeral program. In several photos, she stood tall, elegant, and smiling next to famous people like Aretha Franklin, Diana Ross, and even Tina Turner. How did she know them?

Aunt Goldie's pretty, round face had large eyes, dimples you could sink into, and skin the color of honey. I ran my finger across the photo and a lump formed in my throat. I wish the attorneys had found me in time to attend her funeral. I'd missed it by two weeks, and would've loved to have seen her face in person, even if it was for the last time.

I had so many questions. What was she like? Did I have any other blood relatives, or was I truly alone now that she was gone? What were my grandma and mother like? I wanted answers more than ever.

Mother. It felt weird calling a woman I never knew *mother.* Patricia was my mother. For some reason, I needed to reconcile that.

I looked back at the gallery of memories. I saw a photo with Aunt Goldie's arm around the shoulders of a woman who looked just like her. She had the same high cheekbones, soft eyes, and robust hips. Her skin was a bit darker. Could that have been my grandmother, Clara? Next was another picture with the same woman carrying a little girl on her hip. Was that Yona, my mother? I had just learned my mother's and grandmother's names at the will reading. Goldie's husband, Jonah, died shortly after they were married. That's where she'd gotten the name Williamson. Her sister, Clara Ann Reeves, and niece, Yona Reeves, were my grandmother and mother.

Another lump lodged in my throat as I traced lines around the frames and faces in more pictures. My tears surprised me as they slid down my cheeks. These Reeves women were my family.

I wondered if Ma had met any of them when she adopted me. How had I gotten to Florence if they all had lived in New York?

I continued fingering the images, noticing more photos with Goldie, Clara, and Yona. There was one with a little girl on Yona's lap, seated on the yellow couch. Her big toothless smile reached through the years and warmed my heart. Yona squeezed the little girl in her arms, pressing their cheeks together. Was *I* that little girl?"

I blinked, forcing back fresh tears. Curiosity led me from room to room in search of more information about these women. After a while, I forgot about the cobwebs, dust, and stuffy scent that clung in the air. They—my mother and grandmother—had walked through that house, slept in those beds, cooked in that kitchen, and ate in the dining room—and I had been there with them. That realization made me want to explore more.

Memories of life before Florence were so faint that it felt like a dream. I was little when I went to live with Ma. I didn't remember anything about my mother and grandmother. Missing someone I didn't know wasn't something I thought was possible, but now I longed for them; to see their faces, hear their voices, and feel the love that seemed evident in their eyes. The void that swelled in my heart felt fresh, like it had only been days since they had departed.

I searched for evidence that the women in the pictures were my mother and grandmother. I found piles of old photo albums under the coffee table in the living room. Sitting on the couch, I opened the first book. Pictures slid from under the plastic. Time had turned the edges of the photo album brown. The adhesive no longer held them in place. There were so many books. I found a picture of a woman in a cap and gown, head tilted and smiling. It read Class of 1989. I flipped the picture over and saw the picture had been signed. "To Aunt Goldie. Thank you for everything. Love, Yona."

This *was* my mother. My hand flew to my mouth. Tears blurred my vision, while air circulated in my chest like a tornado. My hands trembled as I pulled the picture to my chest and sobbed.

When I finally got my emotions together, I flipped through more pictures. The little girl on Yona's lap *was* me. I looked to be around four years old. I took several of the pictures from the albums and put them in my purse.

I stood, needing to do something else with myself for a moment. I moved to see more of what was in the house. I only realized how fast I was moving when I got upstairs and had to catch my breath. I paused, scanning the rooms on the second floor before stepping into the one closest to the front of the house. This had to be Aunt Goldie's room before being taken out by an ambulance.

All the other rooms were neatly kept, except this one. A chunky four-poster bed sat boldly in the center of the small room. A paisley comforter matching the thick drapes was crumpled near the foot of the bed. Pillows had been tossed across the mattress and floor. Dried coffee stains colored the lace doily covering the top of the nightstand. Next to it, a scattering of prescription pills were sprinkled onto the beige carpet below.

I stepped inside slowly. There was an obvious sense of urgency in Aunt Goldie's final moments. The closet door had been left open. I craved the stories these walls could tell me if they talked. I ran my hand across the thick wooden headboard before pulling back the heavy drapes. Sunlight accosted the space, filling the room with a brightness it hadn't seen in months.

I sat on the bed and closed my eyes, imagining the woman on the funeral program moving about in this room only months ago. When I opened my eyes, I noticed another picture of my mother on the nightstand. I was sitting on her lap again. This time, wearing a birthday hat and a huge smile as we sat on the yellow, plastic-covered couch in the living room downstairs. I studied the image closely, recognizing the uncanny resemblance of the child to the mother. The same large brown eyes, high cheekbones, and honey complexion. Squinting, I brought the picture closer and noticed imprints from writing on the back. My heart leaped into my throat. I removed the picture from the frame and flipped it over. "Holland's fourth birthday."

I pressed the picture to my heart and choked on a cry that wracked my body. Covering my mouth didn't stop the sobs. I held the image in my hands until my blubbering subsided to a whimper. I was both extremely happy and incredibly sad. I never expected to become so emotional.

I sat on my aunt's bed until only a sliver of sunlight was left. My stomach growled, reminding me that I needed to get back to my hotel and find something to eat. I finally stood up with the picture still in my hand. I passed the open closet on my way out of the room and tried to push it closed. Something blocked the way. Placing the picture aside, I knelt to see what kept the closet door from closing. I found a large, flat leather bag with papers spilling out of the opening. I carried it to the bed and tried to stuff everything back inside. The words *Death Certificate* caught my eye. The name on it read Yona Reeves. *My mother*, I mouthed, with my hand on my heart.

I dumped the bag and riffled through the contents to find even more documents, letters, bills, and a journal. This was more of a glimpse into my past than I had imagined.

"Oh my goodness," I repeated over and over as I skimmed through the pile.

There was so much information. So many gaps that could be filled. I gathered the papers, put them back in the bag along with the picture from the nightstand, and ran downstairs. I grabbed my cell from my purse and ordered an Uber. I needed to get back to the hotel and look through everything.

I watched the app as my driver drew closer. When he was outside, I locked the door behind me and raced toward the car, crashing into a man I hadn't seen coming.

"Oh!" The bag fell from my hands, hit the ground, and spilled the contents all over the sidewalk. "No!" I screamed, kneeling so fast I bumped my knee on the concrete. I ignored the pain. These weren't just papers. They were pieces of my life.

"I'm sorry. Are you okay?" the man said. The rich timbre of his voice caressed my ears, pulling my attention away from the papers.

I looked up into apologetic brown eyes, hooded by lashes that would make any woman jealous. Skin like smooth dark chocolate, and lips so full they begged to be touched. I blinked, realizing that I'd stared much longer than was reasonable and necessary.

"Let me help you," he said, running after the papers lifting in the slight summer breeze.

"I've got it," I snapped in frustration. I couldn't let this man's gorgeous face cause me to lose focus. These documents were too precious to be allowed in the hands of a stranger. It dawned on me that this little mishap was my fault. I'd been so caught up in what I'd found I hadn't paid attention. I blew out a hard breath. "I'm sorry."

"It's fine. I wasn't paying attention either." He shared the blame and continued helping to pick up the papers.

I dared to look at him again. "I—I—" My words fumbled. I looked away. His strong jaw made me pause. "I…" Embarrassed, I fumbled again. "Thanks. I'll get the rest," I said, averting my eyes. *Stay focused, Holland.* There was no time to be gawking at a complete stranger that I'd likely never see again, no matter how fine he was. My Uber was waiting.

"Here." The man stood, straightening the documents before handing them to me. My skin tingled where his hand brushed against mine. I wondered if he felt that too.

"Thanks." I focused hard on stuffing the papers back in the bag. The driver blared the horn. Holding Aunt Goldie's bag closed, I rolled my eyes. "Coming!"

"Have a nice day," the guy said, walking off.

That voice, full and sexy, had the sultry resonance of an R & B crooner. Was he a singer? This *was* New York. I'd heard celebrities walked around here like it was nothing. If this were Florence, he'd have a mob following him. I groaned. When I dared to look back, he was facing me but moving away as he walked backward. He waved, turned, and kept going. Long legs carried him away in a rhythmic, confident stride.

"Damn." The word slipped from my lips in a whisper as I closed the car door. He. Was. *Fine.*

As my Uber rolled down the street, I watched the house until it was no longer in view. Then I looked for the man I'd crashed into. He was gone.

Four

Noble

Tim: You up? Can you talk?

I grunted when I saw the text message. Lately, messages from Tim made my stomach knot, especially when they came right at the crack of dawn. Usually, I would be asleep this early in the morning, but lately, sleep evaded me.

Me: Sure.

My phone rang seconds after I had texted him back.

"Hey. What's up?"

Tim released a hard breath into the phone. "Clear your calendar. The board wants to meet first thing this morning."

My chest tightened. I tried my best to keep my tone even. "Regarding?"

"Regarding what we talked about the other day. You know I can't say much, so be prepared."

"Thanks for the heads up."

"Of course. See you at nine."

I disconnected, swung my legs over the side of the bed, and rubbed my temples. I refused to speculate about what they wanted to meet about. No matter how calm I tried to be, the fact that they wanted to meet before I started my workday made me anxious.

Reflecting again on my last few interactions with the board, I felt it coming. We used to feel like a group of friends—a team. Now, I felt like an outsider in my own company. That, and the fact that our numbers weren't as impressive in recent quarters had shaken my confidence.

I dressed quickly and made it to the office by eight thirty so that I could mentally prepare for whatever the board wanted to meet about. I spent the better part of that time pacing in my office. Usually, I'd call Tyler and fill him in on everything happening with the board. This time, I didn't. I couldn't.

Tim arrived shortly before nine. Peeking into my office, he announced that several board members were already in the boardroom.

"Are you okay?" he asked.

I wanted to ask him "What the heck do you think?" but I nodded instead, rubbing my sweaty palms against my tailored pants. No, I wasn't okay. My heart beat faster than normal. I could feel every quickened thump. Not knowing what to do with my hands, I fidgeted. "Be right there," I said, trying my best to mask how unsettled I was.

Sighing, Tim said, "See you inside."

I waited until it was close to nine before grabbing my tablet and heading to the boardroom. The knot in my stomach felt more like a brick. Dreading each step, I paused before entering to take one more deep breath.

I straightened my back, held my chin up, and said "Good

morning!" as I entered. I wondered if I sounded as cheerful as I intended.

"Good morning," several members responded as they found their way to seats around the long marble table. I could feel the tension in the room. No one smiled. Each pair of eyes avoided the others.

That brick in my stomach churned. I took my usual seat near the front next to Tim.

Tim pulled out his chair, sat, and looked around the room. "Let's go ahead and get started." He looked at his watch and nodded at the board secretary. "We're officially calling the meeting to order at nine-oh-five." Tim turned to me. "Noble, we've called this meeting to…"

Tim said many words, but they all crashed together in my brain after I heard "…ask you to step down from your position as CEO of Push Beverages."

The room spun. Or maybe it was just my head. I wanted to turn back time. No, I wanted time to stop. I was losing my job. Not just my job. I was losing my *company*. The way I proved to my mother that I could make it without her. She would have been so proud of me.

I squinted and concentrated on Tim's mouth. I struggled to focus on what he was saying. Maybe I could hear him better if I watched the words come out.

I waited patiently for him to finish. Every word felt like a fresh jab.

"We understand that this may be difficult for you, but trust that you understand the reason for this decision…" Tim sounded robotic, as he repeated what he'd told me about wanting the best for me and Push.

When he was finally done tearing my world apart, he asked if I had any questions.

Yeah. I wanted to ask them who they thought they were.

Did they think Push could survive without me? I *was* Push. Instead, I didn't speak at all, because I didn't trust my voice. I wanted to curse—tell them where to put their obligations and their shareholders. I had plenty of real questions. My brain was filled with words. None would pass my lips.

I knew this type of stuff happened at companies all the time. Just the other day, news of a CEO of a major pharmaceutical company stepping down had hit the airwaves. I knew it wasn't her choice to leave. She'd been in the same seat I was now, hearing the same speech. I wondered if she felt like a dagger had been driven through *her* heart.

Tim peered at me over his glasses. The room was quiet. All eyes were on me, waiting for me to respond.

I looked around the large marble table and then cleared my throat. "Um… Wow. This is pretty hard. As you know, I've poured my heart into this company for the past ten years."

"Noble. Please know that this isn't personal," Stew, one of the other board members, said.

Stew was an entrepreneur. Had he ever been fired? Did he know what it was like to feel powerless while something he nurtured with his own hands was being stripped away?

Tim had given me the heads up, but that wasn't enough to get me through this moment without feeling like a knife had been plunged into my heart, leaving behind a gaping hole.

I cleared my throat again, swallowing the emotion threatening to steal all the air from my lungs. "I understand, but—" I paused again to gather my thoughts. I stayed quiet for too long while I took deep breaths and squared my shoulders.

With brows knitted, Tim tilted his head. A concerned look washed over his face as the silence grew wider and more uncomfortable.

"It's hard for this not to feel personal," I finally continued, speaking around the lump in my throat. "While this is all about business to you, this company is very personal for me. I want the best for Push and our shareholders as well." I lifted my chin. "Please let me know what the next steps are."

"Yes." Tim pushed a file toward me. "We'll ask that you review and sign these documents. Feel free to have your attorney look them over. Your package is substantial."

They filled me in on the next steps, which included asking Ty to step in as interim CEO until they found my replacement.

Ty? They were going to ask my best friend to replace me. That felt like another jab.

The rest of the meeting was a blur. Tim mentioned dinner later that evening. I stayed behind as the room emptied. Angst cemented me to the chair. I couldn't bring myself to move. This would be my last few days at Push—*my* Push. The company I started.

When I finally got up from the chair, I went straight to my office, slammed the door shut, and paced hard circles around my office floor. They wanted me to go. Me! I thumped my chest with my fist. Push was my greatest accomplishment. I didn't have children, but I imagined this is what it felt like when a child was snatched from its parent's arms. This was by far the greatest loss I'd ever experienced, next to losing my mother. I pressed the base of my palms to my eyes. I couldn't cry at work. Men didn't do that—especially CEOs.

Someone knocked on my door. I didn't want to talk to anyone but I still said, "Come in." I rounded my desk to sit down.

Tim stepped in, frowning. He closed the door behind him and locked it.

"How are you doing?" he asked, concern etched in his expression.

"How am I doing?" I shook my head and shot to my feet. "How do you think I'm doing?" I spat. Flopping back into my chair, I asked, "How am I supposed to feel?"

"I know." Tim held both hands up. That was his pitiful attempt to calm me.

"Bullshit! Whatever you're about to say is *bullshit*." I marched to Tim with a pointed finger. "You said you were going to have my back." My voice cracked. I was angry but didn't want to completely break down in front of Tim.

"I did have your back. I still do, but I was outnumbered." Tim's hands fell to his side. "I rooted for you. You have to know that. Hell, I wasn't even supposed to warn you, but I did."

I wanted to be disappointed in Tim. I hated that he was the one to deliver the blow, but as the chairman of the board, it was his job to do so. That must have taken a lot for him. Right now, I couldn't be concerned about how this affected Tim. I was the one being fired. *My* life was changing drastically. Not his.

"I don't know anything except that the one thing that made me who I am…the thing that I created with my own hands, was just snatched away from me," I said through clenched teeth.

Tim huffed and dropped his shoulders. Slowly, he walked toward my desk and took a seat. Saying nothing, he let me vent.

When I was done, I stood over my desk panting like I'd just run a marathon. Tim waited a few moments before finally speaking.

"I'm glad you got that out. This is not the end for you," he said.

It *felt* like the end to me.

"Take some time for yourself. Go on a vacation. Date."

What was Tim talking about? Who had time for vacations and relationships when my life was falling apart? I hadn't ever had time to nurture a relationship. I'd been married to my company.

Then I remembered the beautiful, honey-colored skin of the woman I'd bumped into the night before. Where had she come from? I swore I'd felt something when our fingers touched as I handed her the papers I'd picked up for her. I had never felt anything like that before. Not even when I dated Piper, who I thought was "the one."

"Take some time for yourself." Tim's words broke through my thoughts. "Then, we will work on your personal brand—prepare you for what's next."

I didn't want what was next. I wanted what I had.

Five

Holland

"I could barely sleep last night," I said to Amy. "I got dressed and came back to the house this morning to explore more and do some cleaning. Filled up a few garbage bags with old papers and stuff from the kitchen cabinets."

I kept looking out the front window. I was thinking about the guy I'd run into the evening before and wondered if I'd see him again.

"Aunt Goldie was a backup singer for a bunch of stars." I let the curtains go. "I found pictures of her with all these famous people and newspaper clippings of shows."

"That is amazing and insane all at the same time! I guess you got your beautiful voice from her," Amy said.

People often told me I had a nice voice. It was no big deal to me—until now. "I guess," I said, liking the idea of inheriting something from my biological family. I strolled around the square coffee table while talking to Amy. I couldn't seem to keep still. "Then I ran into this man."

"Oh! Do tell," Amy said. I could picture her getting comfortable in her chair, ready to devour every detail. "Was he cute?"

I sat on the couch and folded my legs under me. The edges of my lips curled into a smile. "*F-i-n-e*. And I wouldn't mind running into him again," I joked.

"Mm-hmm!" Amy muttered and then laughed. "I bet you wouldn't. Tell me more."

"There's not much more to tell. It happened so fast. I ran out to get into the Uber and wham! We collided. The bag I was carrying dropped, everything fell out and started flying away in the breeze. He helped me gather the stuff. When he handed the papers to me, I swear I felt something when his fingers brushed against mine."

"Oh, chile! Chemistry? You felt *sensations*?" Amy squealed.

"Girl!" That one word was confirmation. A complete sentence. Amy and I melted into giggles.

"When are you heading back to Charleston?"

"Tomorrow morning. I changed the date for the movers to come so that I would have time to take care of things here and get back. The attorney told me there were some bank statements and other documents I needed to close some of my aunt's accounts. He said the sooner I did it, the better. I have a little over a month before I start my new job. I'll use that time to close out as much as possible and get this house on the market."

"Are you sure you want to sell, Hollz?"

Amy's question gave me pause. I thought about all the things I had found and the feeling I got walking through the same house that my mother walked through. "New York isn't for me. It's so far from home."

"Nothing a bus, plane, or train ride couldn't fix."

"True, but I have my mind set on Charleston and they al-

ready have my security deposit. Ha!" I didn't admit that something about the house was already pulling at my heartstrings.

"Hello! Hello!" A nasal, high-pitched voice sailed through
the slightly opened window followed by a series of knocks.
"Hello!" the voice said again. More knocks.

"Hold on, Amy." I scrunched my nose. "Someone is at the
door." Puzzled, I tiptoed to the window, trying not to be seen.

"Girl, don't you open that door. You're in New York. It
could be anybody."

I peeked through the heavy drapes and saw only a portion
of the small frame on the front porch.

"You still in there?" the woman asked.

I reared back from the window. Who was this woman and
how did she know I was here in the first place?

"I'm Ms. Elsie," she said, as if she'd heard my thoughts.
"Goldie's friend and neighbor. You Goldie's family?" Ms. Elsie
said my aunt's name as if it had an *a* at the end, like we did
down south.

I still hadn't answered, but somehow, Ms. Elsie knew I
could hear her. I figured I might as well open the door.

"One moment, please," I finally said. Pretending not to be
there wasn't going to work.

"Who is it?" Amy whispered through the phone as if Ms.
Elsie might hear her.

"Hold on!" I giggled.

"You're gonna open the door?" Amy asked with incredulity.

"Yes. I'll be fine. It's an old woman."

"Keep me on the phone in case she's crazy. I can be your
witness. Put me on speaker. Let's do FaceTime so I can see
her creepy ass."

My giggles blossomed into full-blown laughter. I kept the
sound low as I turned the lock and pulled the door back, revealing a petite woman in a black tracksuit with silver se-

quined panels down the sides. Even her tennis shoes sparkled. She topped off her look with bright eyes and a dazzling smile.

She was holding the door open as I unlocked the screen and stepped inside before I invited her.

"Oh. Hi!" I said, blinking. "H-how can I help you?"

Ms. Elsie walked in easily, like she'd done this all the time. I stepped aside, making space for her. We filled the small entryway.

"Hey, honey! I'm Ms. Elsie. I believe Goldie was your aunt, right?" She widened her eyes quizzically.

"Yes, ma'am. My great-aunt." Despite this woman's boldness, I remembered my manners. I only gave her a slight side-eye.

Ms. Elsie's lips curled into a happy smile. She tilted her head to the side. "Oh, child." She nodded. "Goldie would have been so thrilled to see your face." She parked her hands on her hips and added, "And you look so much like your mama. Mm-hmm. Just as pretty too."

Her words melted my side-eye and rigid posture. "You—you knew my mother?"

"I shole did, sugar. And your grandmother too. Me and Goldie moved in around the same time, almost fifty years ago. Both came up here from down south," Ms. Elsie said proudly. "We grew to be the best of friends. I'd watch her place when she went out on tour. You know she was a singer, right?" I assumed the question was rhetorical because Ms. Elsie didn't pause long enough for me to answer. "Your aunt was beautiful inside and out. Mm-hmm. Shoh was." Ms. Elsie nodded, agreeing with herself. "She helped me with my kids after my husband died. We looked out for one another."

Ms. Elsie stopped long enough to study me for a moment. She tilted her head. Her gaze was soft. Tears pooled in her eyes, which she quickly wiped away with worn, copper-skinned hands. "I know she would have done anything to be able to rest her eyes on your pretty face again," she said.

"Thank you, Ms. Elsie." I felt my eyes moisten. Several silent moments ticked by.

"Oh. Were you on the phone?" Ms. Elsie asked.

"Huh?"

Ms. Elsie pointed to the phone in my hand.

"Oh. Yes. One moment, please." I lifted the phone to my ear. "Amy?" She was still there.

"Sounds like you're safe, girl. Call me when she leaves, okay?"

"I will," I promised, and ended the call.

I felt compelled to officially invite Ms. Elsie inside. I'd known her for five minutes, and I liked her already. She was sassy, but there was also a warmth about her. Plus, she'd whet my appetite with her comments about my mother, grandmother, and aunt. I was hungry to hear more of what she knew about my family.

"Please. Come in." I turned and walked toward the couch.

Ms. Elsie followed behind. She sat, looked around, and rubbed the couch cushions beside her. She dragged in a breath and wrung her hands.

"Oh! I have a key," she said. "I'll bring it next time I come over. We kept keys to each other's houses. I tried to keep the place tidy while she was in hospice. These old fingers and bones only allowed me to do so much." Ms. Elsie splayed her fingers wide, then closed them into fists.

"I'm sure she appreciated that," I said. And I did too. This place could have looked much worse when I arrived.

Ms. Elsie sighed again and looked around the living room. She was hurting. Pain flashed in her glistening eyes. She'd lost a close friend. I couldn't imagine losing Amy.

"She would have done the same for me. The one room I couldn't bring myself to go into was her bedroom." She sniffled.

"Why?" I wanted to move closer to her—hug her. I stayed put on my side of the couch.

I needed to hear everything—anything this woman could tell me.

"That's where I thought I almost lost her," she said after a few raw moments. "We always went to church together. It was a Sunday morning. She wasn't answering her phone. I called and called. When she didn't answer, I searched for my key and came inside. I yelled her name a few times. I knew she was home. When I got to her room, I found her slumped halfway off the bed. Lord!" Ms. Elsie squeezed her eyes shut. She took a moment to collect herself. When she opened her eyes again, tears rolled down her cheeks.

"She went to the hospital that day and never came back home. Ended up in hospice a few weeks later. Stayed there until the Lord called her home three weeks ago."

"Wow." The word escaped in a breathy whisper. My heart crashed into my stomach and I winced at the thought of such a narrow miss. I had only been three weeks shy of meeting my aunt. Why hadn't I searched for my family before? Why hadn't I pressed Ma for more information? Why didn't Aunt Goldie's lawyers find me sooner?

I don't know how long I sat there listening to Ms. Elsie. Her voice became distant even though she was right in front of me. The pounding of my heart and rampant thoughts trampling through my mind drowned out her words.

She paused, studying me for a moment. With a gentle touch, she placed her hand over mine. I nodded and she continued telling her story. I needed to hear all of it. Her considerate gesture showed that she knew the impact her words were having on me.

Ms. Elsie paused again. Patted my hand this time. "You

okay, baby?" The way Ms. Elsie called me *baby* made me feel like she carried me in her loving arms.

"Yes. Please continue."

After telling me about the day she found my aunt, she shared stories about their friendship. Those tales made my heart smile. I was getting to know my aunt through Ms. Elsie's memories, imagining her pretty face as she came alive through her reminiscing.

The bright slivers of sunshine that beamed through the blinds when we first sat down turned into a yellow-orange haze. So much time had passed. I didn't mind, though. Ms. Elsie's stories were rich and colorful. Her favorite word was *shit*. She stretched the word into multiple syllables ending with a *d* instead of a *t*. Every single time she said *shiiid*, I giggled.

"When your aunt wasn't singing, she was cooking. Let me tell you, baby." Ms. Elsie hooted. "That woman cooked like she was feeding an entire army. Everybody loved her food. Most people thought she cooked that much just because she loved cooking, but I knew better."

I drew closer to Ms. Elsie, wondering what she knew. She pursed her lips and nodded like she had a big secret.

"Her cooking brought people together. Made her feel like she had a family, but nothing could replace the family she'd lost, or the one she always wanted but never had." Shaking her head and wagging her finger, she said, "Mm-mmm. Never could."

My aunt had longed for family as deeply as I did.

Right in the middle of Ms. Elsie's story, she placed her hand across her stomach and announced, "I'm hungry." She stood and headed toward the door, marking our conversation's abrupt end. I laughed, appreciating how no-nonsense elders were.

I didn't know how old Ms. Elsie was, but if she was close in age to my aunt, that meant she was a spry and spunky eighty-something-year-old, just a few years older than my adoptive mother.

I walked Ms. Elsie out, taking two of the large garbage bags with me to throw in the trash can. She hugged me tight at the door and insisted we exchange cell phone numbers.

"I'll keep watch over the house until you get back. Call me anytime, ya hear?" Ms. Elsie held my hand and smiled. "Okay, sugar. You let me know when you come back. I'll cook you a nice meal."

Smiling, I said, "I'll be back in a few days."

She passed through the gate in time to open her arms and embrace someone passing by on the street. He lifted her small frame in the air with one hand and held a basketball with the other.

"Boy, put me down," she giggled.

Carefully, he set her back down like she was a porcelain doll.

She swatted him playfully and tugged on her sparkly jacket to straighten it out.

Watching them interact, I couldn't help but smile. Assuming it was one of her grandsons, I looked closer and froze. It was the guy I'd bumped into the day before. Something electrifying shot through me. With eyes glued to his long, taut frame, I tensed and watched his muscles move under his smooth, nut-brown skin. His perfect face was framed by a freshly cut fade and divinely decorated with a neat goatee around the plumpest set of lips I'd ever seen on a man. He turned his head in my direction in what seemed like slow motion, giving me a full-on view of his gorgeous face, brooding eyes, and dimples so deep I could fill them with water and take a swim in them.

He looked finer today than he had yesterday. His white tank did nothing to hide the muscles that rose and fell like hills and valleys over his taut arms and chest. Black basketball shorts gave way to sculpted thighs, leading to equally sculpted calves. A slight sheen of sweat glistened across his forehead. My breath caught when he looked my way. Time continued to stretch, moving slowly as his sexy lips spread into an inviting smile, revealing a set of even, pearly white teeth. Resisting the urge to swoon, I wondered, was this how all New York men looked? Had I not been paying attention?

"Oh! Noble, baby. This here is Ms. Goldie's great-niece. Ain't she pretty?" Ms. Elsie said, mischief sparkling in her eyes.

Noble held his hand out. I stepped close enough for him to take my hand in his for a gentle shake. That electrical thing happened again. Did he feel that too?

"Your aunt was an amazing woman. Nice to meet you, uh…"

"Holland," I finished for him. "Thank you. Nice to meet you too."

That voice. Deep and sexy. His face. Chiseled and fine. Those eyes. Smoldering and penetrating. His…everything. *Damn.*

Realizing he still held my hand, I gently pulled away. His touch left me tingling.

"Well," I said, wiping my clammy hands on my leggings. Thank you for a lovely talk, Ms. Elsie. I will definitely let you know when I get back. Good night."

"You gonna let me know too?" His sultry voice should have been registered as a lethal weapon.

Was he flirting with me? "Are you flirting with me?" I asked in a high voice that I didn't recognize.

"Maybe!" He raised one of those thick, beautiful brows, and winked. His perfect lips curled upward at the corners of his mouth. "Nice meeting you, Holland. Have a good night."

"You too. Don't hurt nobody, okay?" Nobody, as in me.

"Take care, Ms. Elsie." He leaned his tall frame forward, kissed her on her forehead, and spun on the balls of his feet like he was on the basketball court.

"Behave yourself," Ms. Elsie said. "Aw hell. It's more fun when you don't behave. Shiiid!" Her laugh was infectious.

Ms. Elsie took her time climbing her steps. I watched to make sure she made it inside. Noble watched too.

Once she was safely inside, he turned to me.

"So. Ms. Goldie was your aunt, huh?"

"Yeah." The smile wasn't planned. I couldn't help myself.

"She was loved around here." He tossed the basketball he was carrying into the yard next door.

"You live there?" I asked. "Next door?" I added, as if *there* didn't offer enough clarity.

"Yeah. By the way, I'm sorry for your loss."

"Thanks."

We quieted but no one moved. I wanted to reach out and touch his smooth brown skin.

"You moving in?" he asked.

"Me?" Immediately, I felt silly. Who else was he talking to? Something about him made me feel girly, knocked my reasonable thinking off-kilter. That had never happened before. "No. I plan to put the house on the market as soon as I get it cleaned out."

"Too bad. It would have been nice to have you as a neighbor."

"Is that you flirting again?" I asked, adding a little sass.

"Maybe." His chuckle eased into a perfect smile. I avoided his eyes and tried not to stare at his lips. "I'd be happy to help you get it ready. Ms. Goldie probably wouldn't have it any other way."

"Oh! Don't worry. I'm sure you have plenty to do. I take it you knew my aunt well?"

He seemed lost in a fleeting nostalgic moment. "Yeah. She looked out for me. Treated me like her own grandson."

"Then I should be saying sorry for your loss too."

His eyes dimmed a bit. "We miss her around here."

I smiled, fighting back a tinge of jealousy.

"May I?" he said, pointing to the stoop.

Confused, I didn't know what he was referring to.

"Sanitation comes tomorrow."

I stepped back as he opened the gate and sauntered past me. My eyes were pinned to the muscles maneuvering under his tank and I suddenly felt the urge to lick my lips. Noble picked up the two trash bags, put them in one of the large cans sitting beside the stoop, and carried them to the curb. I remembered Aunt Shirleen saying *The kind of man who takes out the trash is the kind of man who will take good care of his woman*, which never made much sense until now.

"I'll bring them back in for you after sanitation comes in the morning and check to see what else you need help with. I'd be happy to help Ms. Goldie's beautiful niece."

Did he just call me beautiful? I blushed, feeling heat spread across my cheeks. "There you go flirting again. But thanks for offering. I should be fine though."

Noble winked and flashed that sexy smile. "I'm right next door. Come to me for whatever you need," he said, sending the flirtation meter off the charts, and I was here for it.

"Oh, you're not even trying to hide it now," I chided.

We both laughed.

"Seriously. Just knock on the door if you need anything," he said. "I mean it."

I dipped my head in appreciation. "Thanks."

We studied each other openly for a few brief moments, letting the tension tornado between us. The interest was blatant on both sides and the banter was enticing.

"Have a good night, Holland." I liked hearing my name on his lips.

"Good night," I replied and whipped around. I jogged up the stoop, feeling his eyes on my back.

Not only was he sexy, he was accommodating. I already liked being in his presence, but nothing could come of our obvious attraction. My time here was limited. The work I had to do in the few short weeks I was scheduled to spend here didn't allow enough time to get into any entanglements with the man next door, no matter how electrifying it felt to be near him.

Besides, this was my season to focus on myself.

Six

Noble

The rumble of the sanitation trucks woke me. I jumped out of bed and threw on a T-shirt and sweats to grab the empty cans from the front of my house. While I set Holland's cans back in her yard, I thought about how refreshing it was to talk to her. I'd tried not to let her catch me checking out her smooth skin, pretty face, and perfect curves. I was a breast man, and she had more than enough to entice a brother like me.

I'd discovered that idle time was the hardest part about being unemployed. Without a specific agenda for the day, I climbed back into bed and scrolled through Instagram, swiping away the messages appearing at the top of the phone. When the messages didn't stop, I rolled over and covered my head with the pillow. I didn't want to talk or text. I didn't want to get out of bed. I didn't want my current reality. The truth was, I felt useless.

Growing up poor made me believe money could solve every issue. Now I had more money than I could spend in my life-time, and life still wasn't problem free.

No matter how hard my mother worked, we often came home to a dark house, scraps in the fridge, or lines on the cable box indicating that our service had been cut off. My mother would negotiate with the utility companies to get our services restored. I knew the money I made from my odd jobs after school only helped a little, but it was better than nothing.

Going to college wasn't optional if I was ever going to make enough money to take care of my mother and myself. I fantasized about putting her in a huge house and gifting her luxury cars. She was going to do anything and everything she could to make sure I made it through college. And I vowed to do everything I could to make sure we'd never be broke again. Becoming a finance major would guarantee that.

Now I knew better. Being well-off didn't make my relationship with my estranged father better either. It didn't even help in the romance department. And it certainly wasn't helping to maintain my confidence.

Tim had said this move was good for both me and the business, but the messages my self-esteem struggled with was "They don't want you anymore" and "You're not good enough." I'd hadn't battled rejection this strong since my dad walked out on us. Rejection had sucker punched the wind out of me.

The phone dinged again and again. The notifications wouldn't stop. I rolled onto my back, sucked in a deep breath, and stared at the ceiling awhile.

"Ugh!" I sat up and grabbed the phone to see who the hell kept texting me. Tim. Ty sent a screen full of texts with links. Then my dad. There were missed calls from each of them and one from Ms. Elsie.

I opened Ty's texts first.

Ty: Did you see this????

I clicked the link and sat straight up when the headline displayed across my screen.

Ty: And this???

Another link. Another article.

Ty: Call me...

Ty: Bruh... Call me!

Ty: Bruh! You good?

Ty: Here's another one. Damn.

Ty: Answer your phone!

Each link led to articles about me. "Noble Washington Out as CEO of Push Beverages." "Famed CEO Washington Gone After Shake-Up at Push Beverages." "Push CEO Ousted!"

My stomach caved along with my confidence. I didn't think feeling lower was possible. The articles were endless. Every newspaper, blog, and news channel had its own version of the story—each besting the other with provocative headlines, using phrases like "forced to resign" and "sudden departure." I tossed the phone aside and lay back, listening to my heart thump wildly and feeling my pulse throb in my ears. I tried to calm my breathing. Nothing worked.

What was I supposed to do now? What company would want me to be their leader after I'd been *ousted*? Was I going to have to cover my face in public like Kanye and his wife? I groaned and jammed my fists into the mattress.

I didn't want to continue reading the articles, but I couldn't stop myself. Endlessly scanning each text, I clicked on all the links and read all the reports. I needed to know what they were saying about me. It was torture, but I was insatiable.

The cursor blinked at the end of my name in the Google search bar. My finger hovered over the return key while I debated whether I should go further down this rabbit hole. I did it, filling my screen with pages of images, videos, and news. The weight of a brick fell into the pit of my stomach.

How many different news outlets had published an article? Where did they get their news from? Had Push released anything to the press? Someone could have prepared me for this.

I pressed my temples, trying to ease the banging in my head. I went to the company website to see if anything was posted there. Nothing.

Bang! Bang! Bang! Bang! Bang! I jumped out of the bed. What the hell? I grabbed my phone to check the app for my security system. It took a second for the image to load. When it did, Ty's full face was right in the camera. I touched the mic icon on the app. He was yelling right into the security camera.

"Noble! Open the door! It's me, Ty."

"Okay, hold on."

In bare feet, I jogged down to the first floor and pulled the door open. Ty rushed past me and paced circles around my living room.

Hands flailing, a barrage of words tumbled out of him. "Who told the media? We didn't approve anything for publication. Where did they get this information from?"

Ty rambled as he wore down my wood floors. I sat on the couch with my elbows parked on my knees, my head cupped in my hands. I had the same questions and wanted answers.

Finally, he stopped talking and moving. The only sound coming from him was harsh breathing, like he'd just finished a run. My eyes closed. I heard the thud of his feet as he walked toward the couch where I sat. The cushions sank when he sat near me. We wallowed in silence for the longest time.

"How are you doing?" Ty asked after a few moments had passed. Inhaling slowly, he then let the air out in a rush. "It's not the same without you." His voice was low. "I didn't want this. I would never have wanted this."

"I know." I opened my eyes and looked at him. Ty looked worn. Like he hadn't slept in days.

"I don't want you to think—"

"I know, Ty," I said, cutting him off. "You don't owe me an explanation. There's no better person to step in as interim CEO. You've been there from the beginning."

"What if they—"

"Asked you to stay?" I finished his thought.

A beat passed before he dragged in a breath and nodded.

"Then you take the position."

Ty opened his mouth. Held his hands in the air. Closed his mouth and let his hands fall into his lap.

"I'd rather you than someone else."

Ty took another deep breath and asked, "How are you?"

Sitting back on the couch. I found a semblance of solace in the way the soft material felt against my back. I shook my head slowly and thought about how to answer. How was I? How I felt changed from day to day—more like, from one hour to the next.

Today was a bad day. I felt like I'd failed. I was ashamed to tell my father, but I'm sure he knew now from the number of missed calls and texts. Outside of football season, he watched three channels, all delivering news around the clock. I kept thinking about everything I could have done differently to get better results out of Push. So, how was I doing? Not well at all.

"Not good."

"I can understand that," Ty said. "I'm sorry it went down like this."

"How's the staff?" I changed the subject. I didn't want Ty's pity.

"Sad. Confused. Angry."

They cared that I was gone. My fake cough forced down the lump in my throat. I already missed the camaraderie and the bad jokes Ty told around the office.

Weddings, bat mitzvahs, and BBQs had made us even closer. I had made sure we added tuition assistance for staff members trying to get through college. I was all too familiar with those struggles.

Grief had depths. This didn't feel as dismal as when I lost my mom, but it still bore a hole in my chest that threatened to swallow me whole. I wasn't the crying type. Instead of tears, angst rammed into my chest, cutting my breath short. I drew in a shaky breath and huffed.

Without looking at him, I sensed Ty studying me. In my peripheral I felt the intensity of his gaze, peeling back the layers of me, trying to discern how hard I was taking this. Avoiding his eyes, I let my head fall against the back of the couch and stared at the ceiling.

"How's Tim's plan coming along?" Ty asked, breaking through my mental pity party.

"He has a board for me to join," I swallowed thickly. "An organization called Chosen Alliance, an agency that works with youth in foster care and adoptions. It'll give me something to do." Giving back to kids always made me feel good and right now, I desperately needed to feel good. "Tim says it will be a good look for me. We have other things in the works to keep my brand attractive and marketable," I said, hoping Tim's plan worked after all this news. "I just don't know if these headlines will have an impact."

"Hopefully not."

We sat in silence.

"Tim told me I should take a vacation. Get away for a while." I stood up, no longer able to just sit still.

"You should."

Stuffing my hands in my sweats, I shrugged. "Maybe." But with who? Ty had a lot on his plate as the interim CEO, and I didn't think Tim understood how distressing this was for me. All he wanted to do was fix it with PR spins, board appointments, and making sure I looked good for the next job. I didn't want another job. Besides, running away wasn't going to change anything.

Ty stood, wiped his hand down his face, and walked to the window. Several moments passed with us steeped in weary silence. After a while, he asked, "Any updates on the house next door? I still can't believe Ms. Goldie is gone."

Mentioning the house made me think of Holland. She was gorgeous in a natural and effortless kind of way. Thoughts of her big brown eyes, full lips, and hair and skin the color of honey were a welcome distraction.

"Nah. No updates. I met her niece though." A vision of Holland's beautiful face flashed across my mind's eye. I grinned at the remembrance of her curvy hips and the sweet melody of her southern lilt. There was a warmth and lightness about her, unlike many of the women I'd met in New York City. No disrespect to the women of my city—their edge was required—but something was refreshing about this woman.

"Holland. Yeah, that was her name." I pretended to forget. I liked the way her name felt on my lips. *Holland*. Thinking about her eased some of the anguish from the week. "Not sure what she's doing with the house, though. I can ask."

Having that much temptation right next door could be distracting.

"That place is a gem. Good for rental income. I'm sure it needs a lot of work. I'd be interested in buying it if she's selling."

"We're cool, but I don't know if I want you to live that close to me," I teased.

"Ha! We'd get into too much trouble," Ty added and we laughed together.

"Kidding aside, I'm sure Ms. Elsie will be able to tell me what she's planning," I said, though I'd much rather ask Holland myself. I'd use any excuse to speak with her again. To get close. Feel the sizzle like static when her skin brushed against mine. That had never happened before.

Silence nestled its way into the conversation again.

Ty finally said. "Maybe a getaway would do you good."

"Maybe."

"I know this isn't easy for you, but it can give you a chance to live a little," Ty added.

"I have a life," I snapped, feeling stung.

Ty twisted his lips and side-eyed me. "When's the last time you had fun, hooked up, or went out to the Spot?" he asked, referring to one of the lounges we used to frequent.

I opened my mouth and closed it, having to think. Had it really been that long since I'd gone anywhere besides the office?

"See what I mean?" Ty said, shrugging. "There's more to life, bro. Push was a major accomplishment. I applaud you for it all. For the life it afforded you and me." Ty pointed between us. "But dude, look around. What else do you have?"

Ty's words landed in my stomach like a gut punch. I sat on the couch stewing, jaw clenched and throbbing. I wanted to ask Ty who the hell was he talking to. Tell him to get out, but he was right. I could always count on him to crash my pity party with a hard dose of reality.

What else did I have? My home. Money.

No mother. A complex relationship with an occasional father. No siblings. No girlfriend, wife, or children. Besides Ty and Tim, I was alone—decidedly alone. I was asset rich, yet bankrupt.

Enamored with making poverty a distant memory, I gave Push my all, vowing to never be poor again. With every accomplishment, I told myself I was making my mother proud. What I had really done was toss all my happiness eggs in the Push basket. Now I had nothing.

"Bro!" Ty stood in front of me. I lifted my head, slowly. "Fuck those headlines. You're Noble Washington. It's time to have some fun."

But did I even remember how?

Seven

Holland

When the last of the movers left, I closed the door, turned around, and scanned my new apartment from one side to the other. Smiling hard, I covered my face with my hands, stomped my feet, and squealed. I did it! No music played, but I danced, waving my hands and moving to the happiness that strummed in my heart. I stopped to catch my breath and turned on some real music while I unpacked boxes, thinking of this new journey and the life I'd left behind. I hoped Ma was proud. I wanted her to be happy with me.

I pulled the thin plastic off my couch and flopped down. It would take days, maybe weeks, to get through the city of boxes stacked throughout the living room. Unpacking major items would have to wait. My flight back to New York was leaving in a few hours. I was only in Charleston long enough for the movers to deliver my things. After a few weeks, I hoped to have my aunt's house cleaned out, painted, and sold so I could return to Charleston to start my new life, and celebrate my birthday. It was a good thing I'd planned my move with some extra time to get settled—only now most of that time would be spent up north.

Ma cried so hard when I left—her small body jiggled with each sob. I promised to call her every morning and every night.

I folded myself on the couch and swiped through my phone until I got to her name.

"Hey, Ma."

"Hey. Everything came in one piece?" she asked, referring to my furniture.

"So far."

"Good. When do you think you'll come back to visit?"

"I'll be home for Thanksgiving and Christmas."

"At least you're not moving to New York. I don't know what I'd do if you did that," Ma said. "You be careful out there," she said through sniffles.

She'd always had a special disdain for New York. I always wondered why. Perhaps the pace was as dizzying to her as it was to me.

"What's so bad about New York?"

At first, she didn't answer. "It's just far," she finally said, her voice lower than it had been minutes before. "I don't like it there. Those people—" Her sentence fell off.

"How many times have you been there? When was the last time?" I didn't remember her ever going while I was living with her.

"Once…a long time ago." She was curt.

"Was I with you?" I asked, ready to calculate the years in my head. What if she was there around the same time my mother and grandma were alive?

"I don't remember. Stop asking me questions," she said, irritated.

"I just want—"

"What difference does it make?" she interrupted, clearly agitated. Her voice squeaked the way it did when she had enough of our pressing. "You're making my head hurt. I had a long day."

"Ma!" I scolded, but she said nothing. "Well, whether I'm here or in Florence, I'm still your baby," I said to comfort her.

"That you are," she said, sounding less agitated.

I was glad to have broken through her sadness. "Want me to bring you something nice back from New York?"

"And wait all the way until Thanksgiving to get it? No thanks."

I chuckled, though I still felt a little guilty. Ma was up in age, never had a husband, and foster kids flowed in and out of her life constantly. Patience and I were all she had to hold on to, and now I was leaving. I needed to do this for myself.

We talked for a few more minutes before I promised to call her when I landed.

Ma doted on me like a delicate flower that needed special care. No sleepovers, no sleepaway camps. Nothing. She hardly let me out of her sight. Friends could come to my house but I couldn't go to theirs. Patience wasn't bound like I was.

I knew this move to Charleston was going to be hard for her. She didn't have to worry about me moving to New York. Unlike Charleston, living in Brooklyn would be too stark of an adjustment. That place was a whirlwind, spinning wildly and threatening to sweep me up in its wake. The sheer volume of the city was alarming. The place never truly quieted, not even through the thick of the night. There were too many people, and half of them didn't sleep.

But it wasn't all bad. New York crackled with energy. The blend of cultures created a mesmerizing tapestry. The people were so interesting that watching them was a sport. Brooklyn was a character in and of itself—loud, bold, edgy, and confident. And then there was the house and all its history—*my* history—a new discovery in every crevice. Being there made me feel like I belonged, even if it was temporary.

I thought about Aunt Goldie, wondering what it could have been like had she been able to get a hold of me sooner. I would have given anything to see her face, feel the warmth of her embrace, or sit at her feet listening to her reminisce about times shared with my mother and grandmother.

Then there was Ms. Elsie and Noble. If I kept the house, Noble would be my cute next-door neighbor. I chuckled, thinking about the way he shamelessly flirted the night Ms. Elsie introduced us. I hoped to run into him again, since I was staying at the house instead of a hotel this time.

Thinking about Noble reminded me to call Ms. Elsie. She insisted I remind her when I was coming back.

"Hey, baby," she sang into the phone.

"How's it going, Ms. Elsie?"

In her usual fashion, she recapped her day, offering way more information than necessary. "Enough about me, what time are you getting in?"

I shared my travel details with her.

"That's just in time for dinner. I'll have something good for you to eat when you get here. You should be good and hungry after all that traveling."

"Aw, thanks, Ms. Elsie," I said, looking forward to her delicious food. There was no use saying no to her, even if I wasn't hungry. I hadn't known her for long at all, yet I looked forward to seeing her again. "See you soon."

I showered away the sweat from unpacking in the oppressive Carolina heat then threw on a tee shirt and leggings. Then, I twisted my bushy hair into a messy top bun, grabbed a light sweater for the airplane, and ordered an Uber to the airport.

Once I got through security and settled in my seat, I was sure I'd fall asleep before the plane left the tarmac.

As expected, my eyes fluttered open when the wheels skidded on the runway at JFK. I dragged my overstuffed luggage off the carousel and maneuvered through the endless sea of people inside the terminal. Exhausted, I found it hard to keep my eyes open on the Uber ride to the house.

I grew tired just thinking about the past few days—flying from Florence to New York to Charleston and back to New York again. Not to mention the physical exertion and emotional gymnastics. I was spent and couldn't wait to eat some of Ms. Elsie's food and climb into bed.

The driver had to wake me, to let me know we'd reached my destination. Thanking him, I lugged my tired body from the back seat, the familiar buzz of Brooklyn filtering through my Air Pods. By the time I'd exited the car, the driver was rolling my suitcase toward me. I looked up at the stoop and groaned, not looking forward to dragging my suitcase up those steps.

Then the space around me crackled like lightning. My stomach fluttered. I felt him before I saw him. Noble. His scent—bold, rich, and woody—tickled my nostrils.

"Let me get that for you." His voice, deep and masculine, slid through me. I wanted to close my eyes and drift away.

A smile teased the corner of my lips as I turned, letting my gaze wash across his handsome face and sexy grin before we locked eyes. Suddenly, I remembered that I was a hot, tired, stale-breathed, barefaced mess and was immediately mortified. My hand flew to my top bun, which was most likely lopsided from ugly-sleeping on the plane and in the car.

"Oh…uh. That's okay. I got it," I said, wanting to disappear, I reached for my luggage and his hand grazed mine, sending shockwaves up my arm. Flinching, I yanked my hand away, disconnecting the current. "Oh. Sorry. I mean. I got it. Thanks," I sputtered.

Noble's crooked grin suggested he was enjoying the way I squirmed in his presence. It also suggested a hint of confidence on his behalf. Maybe even arrogance.

"I was taught better than that." Noble winked, grabbed my luggage, and effortlessly carried it up the steps, setting it in front of the door. The perfect gentleman.

"Thanks again," I said as I reached behind me to close the back door of the Uber before realizing he'd already driven off. It was just Noble and me. No one to distract me from studying his full lips.

"You're more than welcome."

My cheeks warmed. All he had said was that I was welcome. Why was I blushing?

"Welcome home, baby!" Ms. Elsie's voice broke through, cooling the heat rising in my cheeks and other parts. "Good to have you back."

"Thanks, Ms. Elsie. Good to be back."

She swallowed me in her arms. Today, she wore a lime-green sweat suit with fabric so soft I wanted to bury my face in her jacket.

"Dinner is ready. Go on and put your stuff down and come get you some of this good food." She turned to Noble. "You're such a gentleman," she said, pinching his cheek. "You eating with us tonight?"

"Anything for you, Ms. Elsie." Noble winked. "I'd be happy to join you." He responded to her, but his eyes burned a sizzling hole in my back as I fumbled with the keys in the door.

Noble lifted my luggage over the threshold and backed outside. "See you in a few?"

"Yeah." That came out breathier than I'd intended. "I just

need a few moments to freshen up. You know, wash the travel off of me."

"You look pretty fresh to me." That crooked smile was so damn sexy.

"Ah! Here you go again." We laughed.

"Shameless!" His self-deprecating teasing tickled me. "I need to be more subtle when I flirt."

I giggled into my shoulder like a teenager. How embarrassing.

Releasing me from his magnetic hold, Noble jogged down the steps and out the gate toward the delectable aroma escaping Ms. Elsie's open window.

As soon as I cleared the doorway, I flipped my suitcase open, grabbed a cute little sundress, and dashed upstairs for a quick shower. I dried and spritzed my skin with a light floral spray, fixed my hair, lined my eyes, brushed on some mascara, and slid a vibrant, shiny pink gloss across my lips.

I was ready for Noble and enjoyed the attention he lavished on me. Might as well have fun while it lasted, because once I headed to Charleston in a few weeks, I'd probably never see him again.

Eight

Noble

Dinner with Ms. Elsie and Holland last night was the boost I needed. Holland's playfulness was refreshing. Her laughter—weightless. Her smile—pretty. And her body—curvaceous. Ty had reminded me that I needed to learn how to have fun again. Laughing with Holland reminded me how good it felt. I still had a smile on my face when I finally laid my head on my pillow. But that all changed when I woke this morning to remnants of the news about me leaving Push. New headlines had pushed my story down a few notches, but not far enough to be forgotten.

Being in the press never bothered me until now. Phrases like "Successful Young CEO" were much more affirming than the speculation around me being ousted. Now I knew what it felt like to be on the receiving end of unfavorable press. In a word—horrible. I hadn't expected it could bring me down so much, but I can't remember another time in my life where my confidence had been so tested. This didn't feel good at all.

I wanted to stay in bed. A new day was another reminder

of what I no longer had—my company. Social media taunted me as much as my favorite news channels. Every negative comment was like a hot dagger shot point-blank toward my self-esteem.

Tim told me to ignore the media. That seemed impossible. He also said that Push didn't define me. I begged to differ. I *was* Push. Push was me. Everything I had was because of Push, including my father's respect—finally.

Before my company took off, I was a broke student on a scholarship with a mother working two jobs to make sure my greedy ass had money for books and food to eat when the cafeteria closed. Cynthia Washington couldn't have her baby starving. Push rendered the grad degree I'd pursued unnecessary. Wasn't that why people got MBAs? So they could be successful in business? Did that. Push was what I had to show for my hard work.

No MBA. No wife. No kids. Now, no Push.

I slid the covers back but didn't get out of bed. Instead, I stared at the ceiling. I thought about calling my father. I'm sure he knew I was avoiding him. I wasn't ready to talk. His military background had stripped him of empathy. His extended absences stripped us of a relationship. Still, I was part him and part my mom. He'd act. She'd feel. I did both. Right now, I needed to feel. I knew well enough to give heartbreak room to breathe.

I had the urge to get out of the house. I jumped up and got ready for a late-morning run. Adrenaline and endorphins always made me feel better. When I opened my front door, I caught sight of Holland getting out of an Uber with two large bags of groceries. Suddenly, my morning didn't suck as much. She was the perfect distraction.

"Good morning," I said, jogging down my stoop. "Let me help you with that."

We reached the front of her brownstone at the same time.

"Oh. You don't have to." When she smiled, the sun got jealous and shined brighter.

"It would be my pleasure," I said.

Following her up the steps, I noticed how her gray leggings hugged her frame. She wasn't slim. She wasn't chunky. Holland was just right. Her black sweatshirt hung low on one side, revealing the smooth caramel skin of her shoulder. I wondered if it felt as silky as it looked.

"Here we go," she said when the locks finally clicked. The door groaned as she pushed it open.

"These older wooden doors get tricky on hot days. Mine does that," I said.

"It's such a beautiful door. All these front doors are gorgeous." She looked up and down the block. "Ours don't look like this in South Carolina."

I carried her heavy bags over the threshold and followed Holland inside. "That's the accent I detected," I said. "Reminds me of my grandmother."

"Was she from South Carolina?" Holland put down her keys and plopped the large tote onto the couch.

"Columbia," I said.

"Oh! I know Columbia." She took the suitcase from me and rolled it toward the staircase. "That means we're probably not related."

I laughed. "I remember going down south in the summers to see Grams as a kid. It seemed the whole town was our family. Whenever we went somewhere, Grams would point at people and say, 'You know that's your cousin?' One day I asked, 'Who isn't my cousin?' Grams said, 'That's a good question.'"

"Ha! It's like that in Florence too, but not as bad as the smaller surrounding towns. We always joke about knowing

who you're dating so you don't end up marrying a cousin.
Were you born in Columbia?"

"Me? Nah. Just Grams and my mom. My mother moved
to Brooklyn in the seventies. I was born here."

"Is your mother in Brooklyn?"

I waited a beat while a blast of grief spread in my chest,
piercing my heart like shrapnel. It always took me a moment
to say she had passed. It's like I had to fix the words in my
mouth before pushing them out. "My mother died years ago,
but sometimes it still feels like she just left me last week."

Pity flashed in Holland's pretty brown eyes. "I'm so sorry."

I nodded.

Holland walked to the kitchen. Flicked on the light.

"Uh! I would offer you something, but I'm still getting settled," she said after a few thick moments of silence.

"Ah!" I waved away her concern. "I got plenty. I should be
offering you something. Did you eat?"

"No. Don't worry about me."

"I've got skills in the kitchen. I haven't had breakfast yet
either."

Holland shook her head. "I wouldn't want to impose," she
said.

I wanted her to say yes. That way, I wouldn't have to be
alone with my thoughts.

"You do eat, right?" I raised a brow. Hit her with my pat-
ented The Rock look.

"Ha! Of course. Do I look like I miss meals?" Her laugh
was sharp.

She looked like every morsel she'd ever eaten settled in all
the right places. I couldn't say that, so instead I said, "You
look great to me."

"Aw, thanks."

Silence.

"How about French toast?"

"I love French toast," she said.

"Consider it done."

I scanned the house. Dim blades of light passed through the windows, casting dull shadows around the furniture. It had been a year since I'd been inside regularly. Gone was the airy atmosphere that popped of light and life when Ms. Goldie was there. Always a sweet scent emanating from one of those old Glade air fresheners or something delicious baking in the oven, unless she was traveling. Ms. Elsie and she had been like the mother and grandmother I'd lost.

"Your aunt looked out for me. Always made sure I had a meal. Taught me a few things too. She was like another grandmother."

"You must miss her too." Holland's voice was as soft as her gaze.

I did. Instead of answering, I cleared my throat, maneuvering the emotion congealing in there. Watching her slowly diminish from a bold, charismatic, loving woman to a withered shell of her former self was brutal. I visited weekly, even after she retreated into her mind and barely knew who I was.

She and Ms. Elsie had praised and fed me—shared wisdom that guided my decisions and even asked when I would get married and give them some kids to spoil. I clung to those women.

I didn't say any of this to Holland. What could I say to the woman who had Goldie's blood running through her veins? If she was anything like me, she probably wished she'd had a connection with her aunt the way I wished I had had one with my father. Yes, I missed Ms. Goldie. More than I could admit.

I clapped, bringing my thoughts out of the past. "Let's go eat."

With eyes squinted, Holland angled her head at me, knowing I'd wandered off in my thoughts. For a moment, I thought she would ask more questions. Instead, she dragged in a breath and said, "Okay. Give me a little bit. I want to freshen up."

"Cool." My emotions were quicksand lately—threatening to pull me under. I needed to climb out and get back on solid ground. "Feeding Goldie's pretty niece is the least I can do." I felt the smile slide across my face.

"You flirting again?" Holland gave me a side-eye.

"Maybe." I winked. "See you in a few."

Mischief sparkled in her eyes and she shook her head. Her laugh followed me to the door. Making a swift departure, I jogged down the stoop. I hadn't known her long, but I knew I liked being around her. If she was anything like her aunt, she was good people. More than that, she was beautiful and I could ogle her all day. Leaving was better than being weird.

Several pairs of shoes and sneakers lay haphazardly at the door in the same spot where I'd stepped out of them, and the floor needed sweeping. Skipping my run, I headed back inside to clean up the mess I had let accumulate over the past few days. After tidying up, I sprayed an air freshener and opened the window to allow fresh air to flow in with the warm breeze. Pausing, I wondered when I last had a woman in my house.

I headed for the kitchen, cranked up a playlist, and pulled out the ingredients for my gourmet French toast. I'd been in a bad mood all week. These moments with Holland lifted my spirits.

By the time I laid the French toast in the frying pan, the trill from my security camera floated through the house. I wiped the egg off my hand and grabbed the door.

"Welcome!" With a sweep of my arm, I waved her in as if I were announcing her royal presence.

I felt the corner of my lips curl up at the sparkle in her eyes

and the sound of her giggle. I liked the sound. Liked that I
caused it. Liked how her breasts filled the blue T-shirt and
how her hips packed the jean shorts she'd changed into.

Holland gasped. "Wow!"

"What?" I said, concerned.

Awestruck, she spun slowly, taking in the entirety of the
first floor. "Your home is…beautiful. It's so different from my
aunt's. So…modern."

"Thanks!" My chest puffed. I felt it. I was proud of my
home, but more excited about impressing Holland.

"Come on back to the kitchen." I pushed the door closed.
Holland followed my lead toward the kitchen, savoring every
inch of the open-floor plan from the dark wood floors to the
stark white walls filled with art.

"It's like an art gallery had a baby with HGTV." She giggled. "It's gorgeous." Leaving her to admire the decor, I
headed into the kitchen. "My goodness." She studied a paint-
ing I'd commissioned, hovering in front of it as if she were
compelled by an unseen force. "This canvas is as tall as me!
It's breathtaking."

"Oh yeah. That's a Foster Blake piece. He's one of my favorites. I can introduce you to him if you'd like. He has a
show coming up in downtown Brooklyn."

"You know him?"

"Yeah. I've got several of his paintings."

I turned my attention back to the banana I was cutting
while she continued taking in the art.

"May I?" She finally made her way to the kitchen. I nodded, and she ran her hand across the granite on top of the island. "Did you decorate this place yourself?"

"Me?" I reared my head back. "Nah. A friend did it for me.
I can refer her to you."

She hopped up on one of the stools on the opposite side of the island from where my ingredients were laid out.

"No. That won't be necessary. I'm cleaning up and selling as is. She'd probably be too expensive anyway."

I held my sigh. Didn't want to show my disappointment.

"You don't want to keep the house?"

She did that shoulder thing again. "I just got a new place in Charleston. I'm kind of starting over."

"Starting over?" Was her reason for a reset anything like mine? "What makes you want to start over?"

Holland hesitated. "It's time." She shrugged, lowered her eyes to the counter and fingered the veins of the granite. "I've lived in a pretty small town all my life and I'm ready for something different."

"You didn't like it there?" I wanted to know as much about her as possible.

"I do." She didn't sound convincing. "But..." Holland twisted her lips and looked toward the ceiling. Seems like she was deciding how much she wanted to reveal. "I'd always wanted to know what it was like to live somewhere else. As a kid, I used to imagine living in places I'd seen on TV. This past year, I decided it was time to explore. Home will always be home, right?"

"True."

"My aunt's house is amazing, but updating it would be a lot of work *and* a lot of money." She fingered the granite again. "And a move to New York...that's a huge change. I don't know anyone here. I'd have to find work." Holland rattled off all the reasons she had against staying, but never said no.

"You know me and Ms. Elsie."

She smiled sheepishly. "Well, yes, I do."

Again I tried not to let my disappointment show. "When

are you thinking about putting it on the market?" I asked, flipping the French toast.

"I'm hoping to get as much done as possible while I'm here this time. Maybe before I leave."

"How long are you staying?"

"Almost four weeks. That should be enough time to get everything done. Then I'll head back to my new life in Charleston. I can't wait." Holland put her elbows on the counter and rested her chin in her hands.

"Oh." That at least gave me a little time to get to know her better. Anything could happen in four weeks.

I let the music fill the silence while I plated the French toast, spooned the banana compote on top, sprinkled on confectioners' sugar, and drizzled raspberry sauce across as a finisher. Then I poured two glasses of orange juice and heated up a cup of maple syrup.

"Wow!" Holland looked down at her plate. "Fancy. Where'd you learn all this?"

"My mom." I pulled up a stool and sat next to her at the island.

"She taught you how to cook?"

"She insisted I learn to cook. Said it was a life skill. She didn't want me to be the kind of husband that sucked the life out of my wife, lest she send me back home to her."

"Ha! Seriously?" Holland chuckled.

"Her words!" I laughed. "Hope you like it."

I dug into the French toast with the side of my fork. Holland gently stopped me, placing her hand over mine.

"You mind?" Holland bowed her head and closed her eyes. I followed her lead.

Holland opened one eye to make sure I obliged. We laughed. Then she shut her eyes again, said a quick grace, and smiled before removing her hand from mine. I missed her touch immediately.

"Thanks," she said.

"I'm cool with it. Me and the Big Dude talk sometimes."

She chuckled. I swear it sounded like music.

Holland poured syrup over her mound of French toast and bananas. I watched her cut into it and bring a forkful to her mouth. Her eyes fluttered closed as she moaned. I liked the sound of her pleasure and thought about other ways I could coax those sounds from her. Bliss washed across her pretty face. Smooth caramel skin glowed in the light bouncing off the white granite countertop. I watched her as she chewed, jealous of the sweetened bread, wishing I could know how she tasted.

Holland dropped her head back. Her twists bounced against her neck in all its honey-colored glory.

"This is *sooo* good." Eyes still closed, she groaned over the mouthful. The long line of her neck teased me. My fingers itched to trace her skin from there to the center of her chest. Heat spread across my groin.

This woman had no idea how her delight affected me. Shaking her head, she slowly opened her eyes. Caught me staring and froze. In that moment our eyes locked. Sultry music wrapped around us. Her neck bobbed as she swallowed. My gaze followed the movement and I suddenly felt the urge to kiss her neck.

Blinking, Holland broke the searing gaze binding us and cleared her throat. "This might be the best French toast I've ever tasted," she said, pointing the fork at her plate.

My chest swelled with pride. "Of course it is." I exaggerated my response to cover any sensual overtones.

Holland covered her full mouth with her free hand and giggled. She looked at me, playfully rolled her eyes, and shook her head. Damn, this girl was beautiful.

"Just kidding. I'm glad you like it."

"What else are you good at?" she asked.

I put my fork down and looked at her with a wry smile. "You're making this too easy."

"Ha! You're so bad. I'm talking about cooking, silly."

"Everything. You?"

"I'm pretty good around a stove myself. I'll return the favor and cook something for you one day. What do you like?"

"It's probably easier to ask what I don't like."

"Okay. I'll surprise you."

"Sounds like an invitation to me." I was here for it. I took in a bit of toast, thought of something, and hurried to wipe my mouth. "We could do a cook-off. Show off our best dishes."

"Now that sounds like fun," she said, pointing her fork toward me.

Holland's cell phone rang. She looked at the display, muted the ring, and returned to her food. I wondered who'd called her. Why didn't she answer? Was it a man? Did she have a man? I didn't see a ring or a tan line, but that didn't mean she wasn't spoken for.

The conversation started to flow easily between us. We fell into a comfortable rhythm as she asked more questions about her aunt.

And as I answered, Holland closed her eyes, breathed deeply, and settled into the peaceful smile on her face. She stayed like that for several moments. I watched, not wanting to disturb her moment. Instead, I concentrated on her beauty. Flawless skin, gorgeous hair—natural, coiled, and perfectly unruly. Plump, heart-shaped, kissable lips with a hit of gloss. I could imagine what those plump lips felt like against mine.

She exhaled. Her eyes fluttered open, glistening. Seeing

me watching her, she tilted her head. "Thank you for that,"
she said in a soft whisper. "I wish I was able to get to know
her for myself." Holland folded a napkin and dabbed her eyes.

I smiled back, keeping my eyes locked with hers. I studied the pain in them. Knew how palpable a loss like that felt.
The feeling of having just missed something. All the what-if
moments you played over in your head, wishing things were
different. What if I had gotten to Mom's house a few hours
earlier? I didn't know her what-ifs, but I knew she had them.

I kept my eyes locked on hers. Tried to let her know her
feelings were safe with me. No matter how much she wiped,
tears pooled in her beautiful hazel eyes. I felt privileged that
she was comfortable enough with me not to hide her emotions. I touched her arm. She looked down at the counter.
Cleared her throat.

"This…breakfast was amazing. Thank you. I better get
back." She slid off the stool. Holland cleared the remnants of
food from her plate into the garbage and went to wash the
dish in the sink.

I held my hand up. "I got that." I stood and met her at the
sink. "Listen. I'm around most of the day. I can help you get
your house in order."

"Oh no, no!" She held both palms up and shook her head.
"You've done more than enough. I really appreciate it."

"Okay. Call me if you need anything." I pulled out my cell
phone and thumbed through the icons to pull up my contacts.
I handed Holland the phone so she could add her information. She did.

Holland went to hand the phone back to me but pulled
back. "Wait." She called herself from my phone. "This way,
I'll have your number too."

"Yeah. That's cool." My lips quivered, trying to hold back

the big smile threatening to spread across my face. *Yeah, boy! You got her number now.*

"Thanks again, Noble."

I followed her to the door, said my goodbyes, and watched her leave. Breathing in slowly, I savored the sweet floral scent that lingered. I needed to figure out when I could see her again.

Nine

Holland

After leaving Noble's house, I looked around my aunt's brownstone. With a few steps, I'd walked from one time period into another. Noble's place was airy and contemporary with a bright white kitchen and a huge center island. Varying blues in the stools, sofas, and decor made it chic but masculine. Walls full of art made it look more like a gallery than a private home, but it somehow felt cozy.

My aunt's house was cluttered, with heavy drapes, bulky, worn furniture, and years of stuff accumulated in every corner, but felt like a big ol' hug. The more I did, the more I had to do. The clean-up process was never-ending. I wish I knew what things held sentimental value. I didn't want to toss anything that had meaning to my aunt, but there was no way for me to tell.

I plugged in my speaker and selected a playlist on my phone. Wine was always a perfect companion to cleaning days. I didn't have any, so I'd have to clean dry today. After wrapping a headscarf around my twists and snapping on some rubber gloves, I dug in. Grabbing the boxes and extra-large trash bags I'd had delivered before my arrival, I labeled everything, writing down the destinations I intended to send the filled containers: storage, Goodwill, and Charleston.

Despite all the work I'd done on my first visit, it took four hours to get through half of the first floor. I filled up eight of the large trash bags. Exhausted, but still motivated, I kept cleaning and rummaging. Going through my aunt's things was like playing dress up in a time warp. I learned about my aunt—her style, taste, and that she loved elegant things like fur coats, jewelry, crystal, lush fabrics, and travel. Trinkets and picture frames from all over the world topped the furniture, filled the deep bays of the window sills, and lined the walls. Most of all, she loved her family, who she displayed alongside some of her famous friends. She had class pictures of my mother for every year of school.

As exciting as it was, it saddened me that I didn't get to know her myself. So many of the smiling pictures included me—playing in the backyard, in dresses and bonnets on Easter Sunday, and sitting on Santa's lap at Christmastime. I wanted to remember so badly, but my mind hadn't stored those memories anywhere.

Her picture collection was massive, existing everywhere—in albums, boxes, on the walls. I flipped through a few in a box and stopped when I saw a picture of my mother lifting me in the air. My smile was big, my eyes wide and full of joy. My mother's smile was as big as mine. We wore matching pink dresses. A rush of emotions swelled in me, lying heavily on my heart and stealing my breath. Why didn't I remember her?

I couldn't stop the tears. I sat cross-legged on the floor while my heart yearned for the mother I couldn't remember—for these women who shared my blood. I banged the base of my palm on my head, trying to jog my memory. I wanted to see her in my mind. To remember her touch, her voice. *Nothing.* I sobbed, grieving her loss like it had just happened, weeping for the lost moments I wish I could have had.

The air inside became too thin. I shot to my feet, bolted through the house, and out the front door, gasping for air. I reached the front gate before crashing to my knees. I rolled over, sat with my head in my hands, and cried. It didn't matter that the block was teeming with people, like any other hot summer Saturday.

"Holland." His soft voice, ripe with concern, broke through the sound of my sniffles.

I looked up through watery eyes. Noble entered the gate. There wasn't anything for me to say. I buried my head back in my hands. I felt Noble's body settle next to mine. He sat right beside me. Right there on the ground. Just sat there. No words. I wasn't ready to move, so I didn't.

He stayed.

I sat until my chest stopped heaving. Until my eyes dried and my legs felt strong enough to hold me. I attempted to get up. Noble's strong arms guided me to my feet. He waited for me to move, and when I finally felt like I could, he followed me toward the stoop, where I plopped down. Wiping away the remnants of my tears, I looked up at him again.

"Grief is like that. It hits you out of nowhere. One minute, you're okay. The next…you're not."

Noble's words plucked a chord in my heart. I closed my eyes, releasing fresh tears. I nodded. He was right. Why was it so visceral? It had to be the house. I needed to hurry up and get it ready for sale so I could return to Charleston. I had to get away from it. And yet, I didn't want to. I felt my mother there.

"I…" My voice croaked. I cleared my throat and repeated myself. "I was cleaning up." My voice was fuller now. "Then… I saw this picture. I looked at the picture and couldn't help myself." I sighed. "I'm usually not the emotional type. That's my sister. She's the dramatic one." I chuckled awkwardly. I missed Patience. I wanted to lay my head in Ma's lap, like I had when my first boyfriend broke my heart.

"No explanation needed," Noble said.

I smiled. I didn't know Noble well, but I was glad he was there.

"Thanks."

"Anytime," he said.

I watched his full lips when he spoke. Looked into his beautiful eyes and remembered. My hands flew to the scarf covering my head. I was covered in dust. "I look a mess," I said apologetically. I shouldn't be worried about how I looked to this man, but I did every single time.

"Is this what a mess looks like on you? I can only imagine what you think beautiful looks like."

I smiled but gave him a hard side-eye.

Noble held his hands up in surrender. "Not flirting this time. Just telling the truth."

I smiled harder. Couldn't help it. This gorgeous man showered me with compliments and I ate it up. Was that New York swag at work? Was he playing me to draw me in? I didn't know, but I liked it.

"Hey, sugar."

I looked up to see Ms. Elsie letting herself in the gate.

I stood to hug her, thought again, and halted. "I'm dirty from cleaning." I brushed at the dust on the front of my shirt.

"Girl, come on over here and hug me. I ain't scared of no dirt," Ms. Elsie said, releasing her hearty laugh into the humid summer air. The sound of it infected my tired spirit, giving it a jolt, and I laughed with her, feeling better than I had moments before.

Ms. Elsie's hug covered me like a warm blanket. She let me go, looked into my eyes, and squinted. "You okay, baby girl?"

I nodded.

Noble bent his tall frame over and swallowed Ms. Elsie in his arms.

"Y'all ate? I'm about to fry some fish," Ms. Elsie said, not waiting for an answer. "Want some?"

"Ms. Elsie! What kind of question is that? Have I ever turned down your fish?" Noble teased.

"Boy, you never turn down anything! Y'all give me about an hour. I'm moving a little slow today. Back been bothering me," Ms. Elsie said and then looked back at me. "You eat fried fish, right?"

"Yes, ma'am. But I'd hate to impose. You said your back hurts."

Ms. Elsie waved off my concern. "I'm fine. You don't get to this big ol' age without tolerating a few aches here and there. It's no imposition at all." She turned to leave. "Oh, sugar." She turned back to face me. "You been up to your room yet?" she said with a huge smile.

"My room?"

"Yeah!" She reared back as if she were surprised by my question. "It's the same as you left it," Ms. Elsie said, with her head at a soft tilt, her lips spread into a warm smile.

My heart pounded in my chest. I felt my pulse thumping in every part of my body. "Wha—" I had walked through the house when I was there before, but never went to the third floor, thinking it was the attic. I planned to tackle that space last. Was *my* room there?

"Let me get home and start this fish." Ms. Elsie turned to leave. "Your aunt knew you'd be back one day. She said it. Sure did," Ms. Elsie continued as she approached the fence. "She tried so many times." It seemed Ms. Elsie was talking to herself

more than she was to me. "See y'all in an hour." She waved
and moved through the gate, pushing it closed behind her.

I didn't respond. I couldn't push words past the lump in
my throat. I couldn't string together an intelligible sentence
with all the thoughts swimming in my head. "She…tried…"
What exactly did Aunt Goldie try?

Ms. Elsie was still talking, walking away from my gate,
through hers, and up her steps. "There was a cute little chest
in there. I wonder if it's still there?" Her words reached me
from her stoop.

My head swiveled in her direction. The ground moved
under me. Ms. Elsie's revelations made me dizzy. A chest?

Ms. Elsie continued walking. "I'll let y'all know when the
fish is ready." She disappeared inside her house, leaving me
paralyzed.

When she slammed her door, it jolted me out of my trance.
Noble's hands cradled me. I felt him holding me up. The closeness of his skin against mine felt like electric currents sizzling
across my skin. I couldn't enjoy the effect he had on me after
Ms. Elsie dropped this new bomb. A puff of air could have
blown me over. I had a room. There was a chest? Aunt Goldie
had waited for me to return.

"Noble." I turned to face him and looked into those gorgeous eyes. "Thank you for today."

"You're welcome."

"I need to get a little more done before Ms. Elsie's finished
frying that fish."

Noble slowly backed down the steps. "You definitely don't
want to miss that."

When he reached the bottom step, Noble stood for a moment, eyes connecting with mine. I didn't look away. Neither
did he. It seemed he didn't want to leave. I didn't really want

him to, but I had a room and a chest to explore. I wanted him to stay, but needed him to leave.

I tore my gaze from his. Focused on the doorknob. "See you in a few," I said and walked inside.

I looked at the staircase for a moment before racing to my room. Taking steps two at a time, I barreled up both flights of stairs. On the third level, I faced three closed doors, wondering which led to my room. Picking the door nearest to me, I touched the knob, paused, and dragged in a breath.

My heartbeat thumped like a bass drum. I closed my eyes, took another breath and pushed the door open. My hand flew to my mouth. I whispered, "Wow," while turning and taking in a panoramic view of the space. It was a playroom haven. Baby-pink wallpaper covered the walls. A canopy bed dressed in pinks, whites, and lace-covered decorative pillows with the letter *h* stitched in the center. One small white dresser with clear drawer pulls stood on the opposite side. A rainbow area rug sprawled across the center of the floor.

I walked to the bed and rubbed my hand across the comforter and the matching curtains. Pushing them aside, I looked out the window down at the front gate and the people walking past the house. I closed my eyes and imagined the little version of me counting the stars at night.

When I finally moved from the window, a white picture frame caught my eye. I lifted it off the dresser and peered at the image of the little girl in a yellow dress and white bonnet holding an Easter basket with a huge smile. Thick ponytails bent at the sides of her head. I touched my hair. I hadn't outgrown those thick black tresses. The corners of my lips turned up. I couldn't help the smile spreading at how happy she—*I*—looked.

I cradled the picture frame in my arms, closed my eyes again, and imagined myself playing in the room. I opened my eyes, moistened by emotion and noticed it immediately. The chest. I walked over and traced the horse carved in the top, running my hand in the grooves. My chest heaved. I reined that emotion in and opened the chest.

Teddy bears, dolls, coloring books, and a diary with a little lock and key were inside. I turned the key in the lock and opened it, but there were no entries. I reached in and put the diary back and found a book with a tattered leather cover. I took it out, opened it, and the writing on the first page took my breath away.

October 30, 1997

Today was Clara's funeral. Mama, Yona, and now Clara have all gone on to be with the Lord. It's just me and Holly left. I know Clara's in a better place. No more pain for her. But I miss her, my sister. I'm all alone now. Ain't got nobody left but me. How am I supposed to go on without them? Who's gonna love me like they did? This hurts so bad. I hope she knew how much I really loved her. How hard I tried to show her in the best way that I could. I put her away really nicely. Lord, please help me get through this. I have to be strong for Holly. I need you more than ever.

The entry for that day ended there. The words blurred and wet splotches stained the pages as I sat cross-legged on the bed. Closing the journal, I had to pause myself from reading more. My heart broke for Aunt Goldie. Her pain lived in her words. I couldn't imagine experiencing those losses one after the other the way Aunt Goldie had.

I don't know how long I sat holding that journal. When my mouth grew dry, I ran downstairs, grabbed a bottle of water from the fridge, drank half, and paced the old kitchen. Despite the parts that were hard to read, I was drawn to every word my aunt had written. Her notes gave me more information than I'd imagined possible, filling in the blanks like puzzle pieces. The more I read, the more I learned about the women I came from. I was getting to know me.

Finishing the water, I went back to the journal. I needed more. After the funeral, Aunt Goldie went on tour. Her account painted vivid pictures of the cities and trials she encountered on the road with some of the country's biggest stars. It read like a memoir—joy and drama mixed in with a little scandal of who was loving who back then. She also mentioned the dolls and toys she'd purchased and planned to give to me when she returned home.

Closing my eyes, I pictured a younger, glamorous Aunt Goldie, showing up with dazzling clothes, shades like saucers, and a British accent, showering me with kisses and exotic gifts from her travels. Giggling at my imagination, I couldn't explain why I associated everything fancy with a British accent.

Minutes ticked away as I read and read and read until my mouth fell open and the journal slipped from my hand.

I covered my gaping mouth with trembling hands. Heaviness crashed in my belly, launching a tornado that left me gasping for air. It took several moments to recover. What had I just read? I picked up the journal and read the words again—to confirm that I wasn't hallucinating.

Working all those long hours with grief heavy on my heart took a toll on me. I was exhausted and I couldn't wait to get home and hug my little Holly. I hated having to leave her so soon after the funeral. I needed the money, knowing it would cost more to care for her now. In the summers, I could bring her with me and pay someone to watch her when we did gigs at night. It was a good thing I had Patricia to care for her while I was gone. I hope she loves the beautiful scarves I brought as a token of my appreciation…

Aunt Goldie left me with Ma?

It couldn't have been the same person. Ma would have told me she knew Aunt Goldie.

The doorbell rang, and I could hear Ms. Elsie calling my name through the window. I quickly gathered my scattered emotions and went to the door.

Ten

Noble

I filled my belly with Ms. Elsie's delicious golden-fried fish, homemade coleslaw, tartar sauce, and sweet tea and said my goodbyes. As I jogged down her steps, I noticed someone at my front door.

"Can I help you?" I asked, wondering who decided to come by unannounced.

"Noble Washington?" a young redhead with a face full of freckles asked.

"Who's asking?"

"Oh!" He shoved a hand in his backpack and retrieved a card. "I'm Bill Halperin from—"

I took the card from him. He worked for *Enterprise Insider*, a weekly business journal that prided itself on bringing readers behind the scenes of the most prominent businesses and professionals.

He nodded at me as if my taking the card was enough of an answer. Tim would have said "Control the narrative." I could hear his voice in my head.

"How can I help you?" I asked again, wondering why he was evading my question.

"Mr. Washington?"

I sucked in an annoyed breath. "What do you want?"

"Your side of the story," the guy said, pulling out a small microphone. "There's a lot of speculation out there about you leaving Push—or being pushed out." The tail end of his statement sounded more like a question. "This is your chance to get your version out there."

"My version?" I was confused. What speculation? He was baiting me. I took a deep breath to swallow the anger.

"No comment," I said, stepping around him. I shoved my key in the door and paused. Turning back to him, I asked. "How did you know where I live?"

I didn't like the way he smiled.

"I can't reveal my sources, sir. This is your chance, Mr. Washington. I can help you," he said, insinuating I should be grateful that he showed up on my doorstep, unwelcomed and unannounced.

I felt my lip curl in disgust. He flipped a switch on his microphone.

"Was it your performance that caused them to fire you? A situation with an employee? You can tell me."

I respected his audacity, but he needed to go.

"Get off my porch." I pushed the door open, stepped inside, and shut it behind me.

The heat followed me in. Despite leaving the air conditioner on, sweat beaded on my forehead. Adrenaline rushed through my veins, making it impossible for me to stand still. I marched back and forth from the front of the house to the back. Who gave that guy my home address? What speculation was he referring to?

I tapped my way to the internet on my cell phone and

searched my name. I shouldn't have. Tim said not to pay attention to the media. My curiosity didn't care what Tim said. I kept scrolling. Today, the media had focused on why I had been ousted, drawing their own conclusions ranging from performance issues, rumors of mergers, and possible workplace scandals. The more I read, the harder I marched through the house.

How had they come up with these stories? What if they ruined my chances of a new job or the board I was joining? The more Tim mentioned the board, the more I liked the idea of joining something meaningful. This organization helped kids, reminding me of a time when I needed support and people like Oscar, the owner of the bodega in my old neighborhood who had given me a chance when I needed to make extra money.

I called Tim.

"How ya doin', Noble?"

"Not good!" My tone was sharper than I intended.

"What happened?" I could hear the concern in Tim's voice. I told him about the reporter and all the information I found online.

Tim groaned. "Did you tell him anything?"

"No!"

"Good. Don't talk to any of them. We'll control the narrative and post pictures of everything coming up, like the award ceremony. Also, I spoke with the chair at the organization I told you about. They're excited to have you on the board and can't wait to meet you. You've got a huge week coming up. Don't worry about the media."

I wanted to believe Tim when he said don't worry about the media, but the reporter had rattled me. Hearing that the chairperson was excited to have me on the board made me feel a bit calmer. This was something that would have made my mother proud.

"Who are you bringing to the awards gala?"

I hadn't thought about that. "I don't know," I said. The truth was, I had no one to bring. When I first got nominated, I planned to bring my leadership team at Push.

"Call up one of your lady friends. Buy her a nice dress and let me take care of everything else. If you have any additional names you want to add to our table, send them to me by Monday morning. In the meantime, chill out, get ready for your big day next week, and plan a vacation or something. Get away for a while. Do anything but torture yourself following all this crazy media, okay?" Tim didn't seem rattled at all.

I huffed. "Okay."

"Enjoy your weekend."

I nodded as if Tim could see me. "Yeah."

I put my phone on the island, sat on one of the stools, and held my head in my hands. The award ceremony was days away. I had a tux in my closet, but other than what I'd wear, I hadn't given the event much thought. A table of ten came with my recognition, and I had no one other than Tim and Ty to invite. Normally, I'd invite board members, my assistant, and other staff members, but now that I wasn't at Push, inviting them felt awkward. I didn't even have a potential date.

With my head buried in work, I had put dating on the back burner. If you heard Ty tell it, I had put my entire life on the back burner. I felt empty now. I tried to recall the last time I'd been even semiseriously involved with a woman. My brow creased at the realization that it had been over three years since I'd dated Piper Johnson, the pedigreed, double-ivy beauty who grew up summering in Martha's Vineyard. Her business-mogul father and honorable-judge mother didn't think much of my self-made empire, and the fact that my last name didn't ring any bells in their prestigious social networks. Six months in, Piper's resistance to their idea of a suitable prospect fizzled along with our budding relationship.

Three people at a table of ten would look really sad. Ms. Elsie would probably love something like this, but bringing her as my plus-one would look pathetic.

I thought about Holland. She may not have a dress, but we could easily fix that. The question was, would she go with me? I could already see her thick curves wrapped in an elegant gown as her honey-streaked coils bounced against the silky smoothness of her shoulders. It would be great to spend more time with her before she left. Once she sold that house, I might never see her again.

I picked up my phone to call her. I closed my eyes, took a deep breath, and cursed when my father's number lit up the screen. His timing was the worst. I didn't feel like being interrogated about losing my job. He'd called several times this week when news of my resignation first came out. In fact, he'd called more this week than he had in the past several months.

What did he even want? Money again? We'd barely spoken until Push took off. When he finally reappeared in my life, he told me the words that I'd waited my whole childhood to hear, "I'm proud of you, son." Only by the time he said them my chest didn't swell with pride because I no longer desired to impress him. I was satisfied with showing him I had succeeded despite his abandonment.

Communication between us became an awkward dance of trying not to verbally step on each other's toes. It was overly cautious, lacking depth and intimacy. Deep down, I wanted him to just take the reins and be the father I needed even as an adult, but too much had transpired, and I sensed that even he didn't think that mantle rightfully belonged to him after so much time had passed.

The relationship I had with Tim was the closest I'd had

to anything shared between a father and son. It would have been nice to have that with my father, but that wasn't the hand we'd been dealt.

The phone stopped ringing and started again. He never called back-to-back. Curiosity nudged me to tap the answer button. "Hey, Pops."

"Noble!" A woman's tearful voice made my breath catch. "It's...your father!" Tanya, my dad's wife, stammered before her words melted into thick sobs.

My stomach knotted. "Where are you?" My heartbeat quickened.

"The house..." she whimpered. "The amb...ambulance is here. Oh Lord!"

"Which hospital are they taking him to?" I found myself pacing, breathing like I'd just run a race.

"LIJ." She referred to the hospital like most people in Queens and Long Island did, despite them becoming part of Northwell Health years ago.

"I'm on my way." I grabbed my car keys from a drawer in the kitchen and fumbled them twice before taking a deep breath and heading to the door.

I felt bad for not answering the first time. If I had, I would have been several minutes into the forty-minute drive already. The bigger issue was the distance that existed in our relationship. All the moisture in my mouth had been sucked dry from fear of losing my dad. Our relationship wasn't the best, but I wasn't ready to lose him. The emptiness that I'd been living with already felt like it would swallow me up.

I had to get to my father, fast.

Eleven

Holland

As much as I enjoyed Ms. Elsie's visits, I couldn't wait to leave so I could get back to my aunt's journals. Noble already left and now, not even the savory sweet potato pie could tear my attention away from the words that plagued my thoughts. Her colorful stories couldn't drown out the loud hum of questions buzzing in my head.

"Okay, honey. Let me know if you need anything else," Ms. Elsie said, walking me to the door.

"I will. Thanks again Ms. Elsie.

Back at the house, I stared at the book, circling it like an animal sizing up its prey. I reached for it but pulled my hand back as if it would scorch my fingers. I needed to know about my aunt's connection with my adoptive mother, and at the same time, I was afraid of what I would confront between those pages. Ma never mentioned knowing Aunt Goldie, yet her name appeared in her journal. My pulse quickened and throbbed in my ears.

Before I could reach for the journal again, my phone rang.

Mama's image smiled back at me. I dragged in a breath, trying my best to sound composed. "Hey, Ma."

"Hey, baby." Her tone was sugary sweet. "I hadn't heard from you."

"Sorry. I've been busy cleaning out this house. There's years and years of stuff here." Forcing myself to sit, I flopped on the bed. The nervous energy coursing through me found an outlet through my bouncing leg. I wanted to ask how she knew Aunt Goldie but needed to know what the journal said before saying anything.

"Okay. Are you eating?" Ma asked.

"Um. Yeah. Just had dinner with Aunt Goldie's neighbor."

"Oh…" Ma paused a long while. In the silence, I stood, paced a few steps and sat back down. "Okay," she finally said.

"Ma." I paused, thinking about how I wanted to ask my next question. "How did you know Aunt Goldie?" She said nothing. I thought the call ended. "Ma. You still there?"

"Yes. I'm here." Her tone flattened. Gone was the tender, soothing timbre she reserved for me. "I knew she was your grandmother's sister."

She had never mentioned my grandmother before either. "You knew my grandma?"

Tentative silence expanded on the line, dissipating when she finally said, "Yes."

My heart plummeted to my stomach. I shook my head. Had I heard her right? Ma admitted knowing my grandmother too. There was so much I wanted to ask. Of all the words jumbled in my mind, "How?" was the only question I could get past my lips. She didn't respond. "How come you never told me you knew them?" There was no response. "Ma!" I yelled. She seemed to remember she was on the phone when I yelled her name.

"I… I'd help her out sometimes." Her voice had lost its luster. "I looked after you." She cleared her throat. "When you were young." A few more silent beats pulsed by as I waited impatiently. "And—" another long pause "—I helped them out when I could. That's all. Why are you asking me this stuff?" Ma's voice cracked. Then she snapped. "Where are all these questions coming from? Forget it!" she added before I could respond. "I'm not feeling well. When are you coming home? I need you."

"Patience is there!" I snapped. "She can help you with whatever you need. Just answer my questions."

"I did. And it's not the same. When can you come home? Just put that old house on the market and come back, please. I need you here!"

I pulled the phone from my ear and looked at it. Torn between what I wanted—no, *needed* from her—and the fact that she sounded so desperate and delicate.

"Ma." I couldn't go to her now.

"What?" she spat.

Surprised at how her tone changed. I asked, "What's going on?"

"Nothing. She left you money, right? You can book a flight. *Please.*"

I didn't know what to make of her sudden change in demeanor. "Where's Patience?"

Ma started crying. Her sniffling pricked at my guilt for leaving in the first place. This erratic behavior was alarming. She knew I didn't like to see her upset and that I would acquiesce when her emotions flared. This time, I couldn't bring myself to simply submit. Standing my ground, I let her cry for a few moments without comforting her.

"Hold on. Let me get Patience on the phone."

"No! Just forget it." Her voice turned harsh again, like the tears had suddenly dried up. "I love you, Holland. You have always been my baby girl." Ma hung up the phone.

I blinked repeatedly, looked at the phone as if answers to my mother's strange behavior would come from the screen.

I dialed Patience. She picked up on the first ring. "Hey, sis," I said, keeping my voice steady. I flopped on the couch and folded my legs under me. "Are you home?" I asked, worried.

"Yeah. I'm in my room. Why?"

"Ma was acting strange and then hung up on me."

"Last I checked, she was in her famous chair watching Netflix and chilling!" Patience cackled. "Let me go see if she's still there." Humming as she walked, I could hear Patience's music decrease as the volume of Ma's television show increased. "Ma, are you okay?"

"I'm fine." I could hear through the phone that her tone was still sharp.

"Okay," Patience said to her and then whispered to me, "Dang. She just snapped at me. Did you make her mad or something?"

"She'll be fine." I didn't feel like going into details.

"Okay. I'm heading to my boyfriend's house. I'll call you tomorrow."

"A new one?"

"Just for tonight!" Patience's bark-like laugh startled me. I wanted to laugh with her, but only had the energy for a light chuckle.

"Don't have too much fun," I warned.

"I will," she giggled. "Love ya, sis." She ended the call with a kissing sound.

After the call, I sat there puzzled. Shock, confusion, anger, and denial tangled and tightened in my chest and wrestled with the guilt of being over six hundred miles away. Ma's behavior was telling.

I needed answers. Dealing with her over the phone wasn't going to work. A face-to-face conversation was inevitable. That would have to wait until I got back down south. For now, all I had was the journal. I wanted to see if Aunt Goldie mentioned Ma again. As I grabbed the journal, an alarm sounded on my phone. It was time to put out the bags of clothes I'd set aside for the donation pickup. My raging curiosity would have to wait a little while longer.

With just over three weeks in Brooklyn and the first day almost over, I wasn't sure how to get all three floors cleared out before leaving. I kept finding stuff I wanted to keep for myself.

Once I set the donation bags on the porch, I fixed a cup of tea, grabbed the journal, and sat cross-legged on the couch. Flipping through the pages, I found my way to where I'd left off just as my phone rang. Groaning, I rolled my eyes, but still looked to see who was calling and grabbed the phone when I saw Amy's name and image.

"*Amy,*" I moaned, releasing a rush of frustration. She was just the person I needed to hear from. The sound of her voice always made me feel better.

"You okay, girl? I'm just checking in on you. Did you eat?"

"Yes, I did. My mother just asked the same thing." I'd tell Amy everything I'd learned later. I had more information to gather.

"Because you forget," she said.

"I don't forget. I get busy and push it off, that's all."

"Until you're ready to pass out!" That was her way of scolding me. "Make sure you eat and don't be a homebody while you're there. New York has great food, and there's so much to see. I've always wanted to visit. Make these few weeks count. Who knows when you'll ever get back there."

"I'll try," I said, already feeling calmer. She'd been my safe place since we were little. "There's so much for me to do.

Anyway. Let me tell you about my latest findings. You won't believe this." I told her about the journal but kept the part about my mother to myself.

"Oh my goodness," she squealed. "Is it scandalous?"

More than you could imagine. "Some of what I've read so far. I'm about to read more before bed."

"Okay. Call me and tell me about anything juicy. With all that traveling around with celebrities, I'm sure there are some scandalous stories."

"Hey!" I chuckled. "This is my elderly aunt we're talking about," I teased. "But I'll let you know what I find." Both of us laughed at how quickly I folded.

"Was she wealthy?" Amy asked.

"Not as much as you would expect. The attorney handling her estate took care of her medical bills. Cancer almost bankrupted her. The house is most of what she had left."

"Wow," Amy said, slow and long. "I'm glad you're learning so much about your family. That's really great."

Amy was right. I smiled. "Me too." I wanted to know it all. The good and the bad. The only information missing was details about my father. None of the information I'd found mentioned anything about him. No pictures—nothing. Was he even living? I wondered how I could find out more information about him. "Okay, girl. I want to read more before I get too tired. Love ya," I said to Amy.

I never imagined the journey to step out of my comfort zone and live would lead to all of this. In about a week, I'd gone from feeling like a lonesome outsider to discovering intimate details about my family. I was insatiable now, needing to know everything—enticed by this scavenger hunt to find myself.

After Amy said good-night, I grabbed my still-steaming cup of chamomile tea and turned on the television for background noise. The journal read better than any novel I could remember until I had gotten to the parts that mentioned my mom. I debated whether to pick up from where I'd left off or get Ma back on the phone so she could plead her case. Deep breaths and a few false starts gave me the space to ready my heart and mind for what I'd find buried in the pages next.

I read a few pages and had to close the book. My poor aunt went through so much. Losing her husband to a tragic accident without realizing she was pregnant, then losing the baby. Wanting a family so bad, but never being able to have one. And then there was my mother and grandmother. The compounded sense of loss was staggering. I see why she clung to Ms. Elsie and Noble so much. They were the family she chose.

I covered my mouth, feeling my aunt's pain, and fought back the urge to cry. I kept reading. Several pages later, I sat up straight, almost knocking the cooled cup of tea into my lap. I blinked, scanned the words again, and felt my chest tighten. What had I just read? I didn't want to believe the perfect script in front of my eyes.

March 12, 1997

I can't get in contact with Patricia. She hasn't called me back. And now I'm getting a message that the number is no longer in service. No one in Aiken has seen her for weeks. It's driving me crazy. I haven't been able to sleep since I got back from the tour. Please, God, don't let anything bad happen to my baby niece. I just had her room fixed up nice.

I'm heading south first thing in the morning to make sure Patty and Holland are okay.

I hate it there. Too many bad memories, but I have to find Holly. She's the only family I have left. Help me find her, Lord.

A distant memory of Ma and me leaving a small white house flashed in my mind. Florence became the only home where my memories remained vivid. My heart caved into my stomach.

Twelve

Noble

Dad's eyes finally fluttered open.

"Oh! Gerald, baby!" His wife, Tanya, ran to his bedside and gently took his hand in hers. She kissed his forehead.

Dad lifted his head off the pillow, focused on Tanya, and squinted. Swiveling his neck left to right, he settled his gaze on the IV, ogling the tubes leading from his forearm to the bag of liquid hanging on the metal stand. His eyes narrowed a bit and then landed back on Tanya.

"Honey!" Tanya's words rushed out of her. She blinked back tears. "You passed out. I *had* to call the ambulance."

The way she said *had* made me think he would have objected had he known she was calling them.

Dad dragged in a shaky breath and laid his head back on the pillow.

"Noble is here," she whispered but somehow managed to sound cheerful.

That made me wonder how he felt about my being here. Still, I had to come. Dad's brows furrowed. He lifted his head again and winced. I stepped closer to his bedside. My father nodded and then turned away. Every muscle in my body tightened. Did he not want me here? Regret formed a tight knot in my stomach. Why had I come?

"Let me give you two a moment," Tanya said and left the room before I could protest. I'd rather be the one leaving.

While my father avoided eye contact with me, I focused on his limp body lying in the bed. It seemed to swallow him up, and my anger subsided. He must have shed thirty pounds since I'd seen him last. His once-smooth caramel skin had lost its glow and now clung tightly to his high cheekbones, making him look gaunt. His formerly strong jawline, which deemed him handsome, now jutted out like a caricature.

The man I remembered was tall, sturdy, and good-looking. Women forgot their manners around him. And one day, he forgot he was married. That's how he ended up with Tanya. My mother had had enough and sent him and ten garbage bags full of clothes back to "the whore he'd come home smelling like." After my mother passed, I expected to have my father back, but that didn't happen. The bottle won his attention, leaving Tanya and me in the shadows.

This frail remnant of my dad pulled on the heartstrings of the little boy who longed for his attention. The one who wanted to make him proud. The one who saw him as a hero no matter how long his absences spanned, until he just didn't come back anymore. Maybe it was time to lay down my grudge. I wasn't that little kid anymore. I was a grown man who understood that people made mistakes that were hard to come back from. They pushed people aside in search of things that could never give them what those same people offered willingly. People like me. Seeing my father this fragile allowed me to see all of his vulnerabilities.

I realized I didn't even know what was wrong with my father. Though we spoke occasionally, he never mentioned being ill. Had drinking finally gotten the best of him?

The weight of our estranged relationship settled in the room like thick smoke.

"Hey." I finally spoke.

He still didn't look at me. "I called you," he rumbled in a low croak and cleared his throat.

"I know." Guilt blossomed in my chest. I bit the inside of my lip and swallowed the lump budding in my throat.

"Lost your job, huh?" It didn't sound like a question. He still didn't look at me.

I didn't need my father, of all people, making me feel worse about my situation. "Yeah."

"That's too bad."

"What happened to you?" I asked.

"Just some stomach issues," he said, finally turning toward me with glassy eyes.

"Looks like more than stomach issues." *Or is it because your stomach was full of liquor?*

"Yeah. It's no big deal. I don't know why Tanya called the ambulance or bothered to call you. If you had called me back…" Dad looked hard at me. Several fleeting emotions flashed in his eyes before he turned away again. Regret flashed brighter than the rest, and I wished I had answered those calls.

Standing straighter, I said, "I've just been busy."

"Yeah. I know. Like always."

My teeth clenched. This is why I didn't want to talk to him. His words always felt like digs, as if I was the one who broke up our family. I pulled my bottom lip in and gnawed on it, trying to be careful about my words. "I run a company," I said, as if he needed reminding. *Ran a company.* I chose to stand down. Keep the peace for now. "What made you call?"

"Saw the news and thought I should check on you. Losing a job never feels good."

"Thanks." My clenched jaw loosened. Maybe he wasn't judging me.

"I'm fine now. You can go back to your busy life."

Both hands balled into fists. I bit back the response, choosing not to go down this road with him, and trying to see this for what it was. Dad didn't want me to see him as weak. He never was good at managing his emotions. Regardless, I was pissed at putting myself in a position to be insulted by him once again.

I now knew why he called, and why he was in the hospital. What else were we supposed to talk about? How many insults would it take before I walked out the door? I hated that our communications were so strained. I watched his chest rise and fall and listened to the low whistling of his labored breathing, and it reminded me that I no longer had a mother and could eventually be fatherless too.

He was difficult, but all I had. I was used to being alone, but as long as he was around, I wasn't by myself in this world. The thought of being entirely alone without him seemed all-consuming, and the timing couldn't be worse. How could I stand to have anything else taken away from me?

I pulled my bottom lip in and held it between my teeth. My chest tightened, and I felt myself begin to unravel.

Tanya peeked her head in the door just in time. I pulled myself together. Despite how I felt about their relationship, I could tell she was scared by the knit of her brow and the look on her face. I felt bad for her.

Tanya entered the room slowly, curling herself around the door and then gently pushing it closed.

I looked at my dad with his eyes set on the nothingness of

the stark white walls on the opposite side of the room. Then I looked at Tanya, who seemed to be on the verge of tears again.

My chest tightened. The muscles in my shoulders, neck, and back were rocks under my skin. Suddenly I needed more air than the room allowed.

"Thanks for calling me, Tanya. Please keep me posted." I left.

I heard Tanya call my name and stopped just outside the hospital room door. Stepping out, she closed the door behind her.

"Your father misses you."

I stuffed my hands in my pants pockets. "It's hard to tell."

"It's why he drinks so much. Much worse than he used to, and now it's affecting his health. Ruined his stomach and esophagus." She paused a moment and placed a hand on my shoulder. "Noble, I know this isn't easy and he won't tell you himself, but he loves and needs you."

My teeth gritted involuntarily. I could believe that when he said it out of his own mouth.

I walked away, leaving Tanya where she stood, not stopping until I was out of the hospital and several blocks away. I coughed out the breath that was causing my chest to hurt, pulled out my cell phone, and paced with a slew of emotions stirring in my heart. Instead of going home, I drove to a bar a few blocks from my house.

I didn't want a drink. Seeing my dad in that condition made me not want to drink ever again, but I needed a place to go besides home. A place that didn't remind me of everything that I faced. Hours later, I'd drank them out of ginger ale and decided it was time to go home.

"Hey." Holland's soft voice was an instant salve and felt like a warm caress. Sitting on her stoop, she glowed even in a scarf, tank top, and sweatpants.

"Hey," I said back. I tried not to sound conflicted. "You're out late." I checked the time. It was almost midnight.

"Yeah."

"Want some company?" I wanted to be with her more than sitting at home alone.

"Sure." She inched over and patted the space beside her. "Come on," she said with a smile. "Heck of a day today." She sighed. "I couldn't sleep, so I came out here to look at the stars."

"Wanna talk about it?" I asked, figuring listening to her woes could help me temporarily forget about mine.

Holland dragged in a deep breath and released it with a groan. "How…" She twisted her lips and tried again. "I just…" Holland looked up at the sky and then directly at me. "How do I find myself, when all I seem to come up with are more questions about my life?"

"I get that." How could I possibly help her when I had the same questions?

"I came here to settle my aunt's estate, sell her house, and return to the new life I finally had enough courage to start. I'm supposed to be on my journey of self-discovery. Humph." Holland threw up her hands and let them fall limply back to her lap. "This is the craziest detour. I'm getting answers to questions I didn't ask and discovering questions I never imagined needing answers to."

"That's deep, but I feel that."

"I'm…" Holland seemed to search for the right word. "Conflicted."

"Why?"

She stood and hugged herself as she paced the walkway in front of the stoop. Her skin glistened from the leftover heat of the day still clinging to the night.

"I'm starting to feel…connected here…to my past…to this house," Holland said, as if she was searching for the right words. "Living in New York had never crossed my mind." She shrugged. "I'm not sure I want to leave now."

"Then stay," I said before thinking about it. "Or at least keep the house. You can visit when you want. Maybe rent it out." The words tumbled out before I could rein them in. I felt less alone when she was around and wanted her to stay.

"I can't." Holland looked at the sky and huffed, and then turned to me and smiled. "How was your day?"

I told Holland about my father. Her hands flew to her mouth.

"I'm so sorry. Here I am, dumping my issues on you, and your dad is in the hospital. Is he okay?"

"I hope so," I said, and I meant it.

"Aw. It's my turn to be there for you."

Holland came to me with her arms open. I stood, stepped into her embrace, and wrapped my arms around her. She felt so good in my arms, I didn't want the hug to end. Warmth permeated every part of me. I wondered if she felt it. Her hands rubbing up and down my back felt more sensual than comforting. My imagination fed me the kind of touch I desired from her.

I felt like I'd been unraveling since I stood beside my father's hospital bed. One touch from Holland put me back together again. I looked into her soft eyes and then down at her full, beautiful lips and wanted to kiss them so badly. Holland looked up at me. Desire flashed in her eyes. Her gaze slid down to my lips and back to my eyes again.

I leaned forward and paused, waiting for her invitation. Holland tilted her chin toward me. I leaned in, stopping a hair's breadth from her plump lips. I didn't want to misread her. My intentions were clear. She'd make the final decision. Still standing in my embrace, her body was close enough for me to feel the heat enveloping her. My hands found the small of her back and I wondered if she could feel the feverish heat emanating from my palms, ready to burst into flames.

Holland leaned closer, eliminating the distance between us. She slid her tongue between my lips. Opened herself up to me. Everything felt right until the kiss grew urgent, then it burned so good. Holland's hands roamed my back and chest. I loved the way she touched me. Hungry for more, I drew closer. We peeled ourselves away from one another long enough to catch our breath. The break was brief. We went back for more, kept kissing, kept tasting each other over and over again, until we heard someone whistle.

Holland and I looked at each other and dissolved into laughter. Desire hung heavy in the space around us.

Still giggling, Holland stepped back, putting distance between us. She shrugged her shoulders, looking embarrassed. "I forgot we were outside."

I wanted her to invite me inside. "It's okay. We're grown. We can kiss where we want." I caressed Holland's kiss-swollen lips with my thumb.

Holland laughed and stepped back again, putting more distance between us. "Yeah, but maybe we shouldn't be putting on a show for the neighbors." She looked around for more prying eyes.

"You've got a point there." I wagged my finger playfully.

We stood melting in hot desire.

"Um. I guess I should go inside and try to get some sleep." She giggled again.

Invite me in. "Yeah. You should."

Neither of us moved.

Her hands were in mine. It felt natural like they belonged there. She looked down, slowly removed her hands, and hugged herself again.

"I guess, I'll see you…" Holland paused pensively.

"In the morning? Breakfast again? I can make sure you have fuel for all the work you need to get done," I offered.

"Sounds nice." She licked her lips. Maybe it was voluntarily, maybe not. Either way, it lit a new fire in my groin. "This has been a long day," she said as I watched each word fall from her pretty lips.

"Yeah."

"Yeah," Holland repeated and cleared her throat.

Holland backed up toward the stoop but kept her eyes on me. She smiled before turning around, traipsing up the steps, and disappearing through the carved wood door.

I waited until the locks clicked and the living room light went out. Then I went home and showered. I lay in bed, hand in my boxers, stroking away the desire, running my tongue across my lips, remembering the taste of her—sugar and chamomile.

Thirteen

Holland

Noble and I were in the air, sitting on clouds, flirting and cuddling. He touched my nose, and I threw my head back, laughing, drowning in bliss, and loving every moment. He looked into my eyes, and my cheeks grew warm. Just as he was about to kiss me, the phone rang, startling me.

I sprang upright, blinked away the haze, and realized I was alone in the center of my bed, wrapped in a soft pink sheet and comforter. No clouds. No Noble. Just the dim light of dawn slicing through the vertical blinds. I touched my lips and remembered our kiss. Fireworks exploded in my head when Noble's lips touched mine last night.

There was that ringing again. I grabbed my cell phone off the small white nightstand with clear drawer pulls that looked like large diamonds.

I flopped back against my pillow. "Hello!" I croaked, cleared my throat, and repeated myself.

"Open the door," Noble said.

I pulled the covers back, climbed out of the frilly twin-size bed, and tiptoed to the window. Noble stood on the porch holding a bag. I opened the window. "I'll be right down," I said, still holding the phone. "Actually, can you give me a few minutes?" I yelled, not wanting him to see me looking like I just rolled out of bed because I had.

"Sure," he said and sat on the stoop. "Take your time."

I washed my face, brushed my teeth, and put a bra on under my tank top.

As much as I'd wanted to do way more than kiss him last night, resisting was the right thing. I'd known this man for about a week. I was on my journey to find me and live out loud. The last thing I needed was to get involved with a man and complicate things. Besides, why get caught up just to leave? My time here in New York would be a small blip on my timeline once I got back to Charleston and started my new life.

That's if I made it back to Charleston. New York was growing on me. Regardless, I wasn't here to get involved with any men. I had to curb the raging desire that had me ready to trample over my inhibitions. Noble Washington was dangerous.

"Good morning," I said, opening the door and making room for him to step inside. I still felt flushed by our kiss and my dream, and hoped he couldn't see the desire behind my cordial smile.

"I hope I didn't wake you," Noble said. "I wasn't sure if you were going to church or something, and I wanted to get your breakfast to you before you left. You seem like the type to go to church on Sundays." Noble handed me a warm covered dish and followed me to the dining room table.

"What makes you say that?"

Noble held his free hand up. "Nothing bad. You have a beautiful spirit and seem so grounded."

That made me blush. "Is that so? I guess it's the Southern

charm." A vision of us kissing on the clouds in my dream flashed across my mind and my nipples pebbled. I looked down at my breasts. *Down, girls.* "And you pegged me right. I *am* a church girl and proud of it." My smile spread wider. "I planned to go to Bedside Baptist while I ate breakfast."

Noble's brows creased.

"That's what I call church when I stream from my bedside instead of going to the house of the Lord in person. Get it? Ha!"

Noble laughed and the rich timbre of his voice, cute curl of his lip, and cavernous depths of his dimples made my knees wobble.

"Have a seat," I sat to save myself from the embarrassment of unreliable knees and then patted the chair next to me for Noble to join me.

"Glad I could make you smile this early in the morning." Noble presented me with the food he was holding.

My eyes landed on the bag in his hand.

"Your breakfast," he said, as if he'd just remembered why he came.

"Thanks." I carried it to the counter and grabbed a fork from the drawer. "Are you going to join me?" I'd never been this forward with a man before. Noble's presence released a boldness in me.

"I already ate, but I'm happy to stick around for a bit. I like watching people enjoy my good food." His wink and sexy smirk were magnetizing, pulling at me like he'd reached across the room and grabbed hold of me.

"You sound pretty sure of yourself."

"I've got skills." Noble raised one brow like The Rock. "Nothing wrong with admitting that."

"Ha!" My short, sharp laugh was shaky. Something savory wafted to my nose when I opened the dish. A happy distraction from the sexiness oozing off this man so early in the morning. Showing up right after my dream only made things worse. At least in the dream, I relished the feel of his plump lips against mine.

"Mm. Smells delicious." My mouth watered.

"It's a Greek egg frittata with grilled avocado, tomato slices, and honey maple bacon."

"Wow. Fancy." I took a forkful, closed my eyes, and moaned. "Oh my goodness, Noble," I said, chewing behind my hand. "This tastes amazing."

"I told you." Noble popped the nonexistent collar on his T-shirt. "I've got skills. A brother can burn."

That cracked me up. "Burn?"

"Y'all don't say that in the South? That's New York slang for cook. A brother can cook."

"Ha! I told you, you're not the only one who can burn. We'll see who really has skills," I said around a mouthful of food. "Sorry. I promise I have better manners than this," I said, chuckling.

Noble looked around. "Get a lot done yesterday, huh?"

"Ugh!" I rolled my eyes toward the ceiling. "It seems like the more I do, the more there is to be done."

"I'm happy to help you out."

The way those muscles of his tangoed beneath his shirt, it sure would be fun to watch him lift heavy things.

"No, thank you. I really appreciate the offer." I thought for a moment. "Actually, there may be a few things you can help me with, if you don't mind. Do you know of someplace I can donate furniture to?"

"Sure! There's a spot that's not too far from here. They'll come pick up the stuff too."

"That's great, thanks."

Noble was quiet while I ate. I could feel his eyes on me—that alluring pull of his closeness that made my stomach flutter.

"Listen. Uh…" Noble started.

I looked up from my plate, connecting with his gaze. We locked in, unblinking. Desire burning between us again. His eyes were beautiful, with lashes most women would envy. He licked his lips, and I had to collect myself. This man was gorgeous—and maybe a bit arrogant and I liked it.

"Yes?" I replied when it seemed like he wouldn't finish his sentence.

"About last night… I…"

"What about last night?" I gave him my coyest smile then looked down at my plate—and stuffed a piece of bacon in my mouth. "Really, it's okay. No big deal," I lied. "We're grown, remember?"

"Huh! That we are." Noble nodded and laughed. "I don't want you to think I was… I didn't want to take advantage…"

"Noble," I interrupted. I placed my fork aside and put my hand on his. "I *wanted* to kiss you." I didn't mean for my words to sound so breathy.

His lips eased into the sexiest smile I'd ever witnessed. "I wanted to kiss you too."

I stared directly into Noble's beautiful eyes. He stared right back. The temperature rose several digits higher. I finally looked away and moved the fork around my plate, though I was no longer hungry for food. "It's just that now is not a good time for me to get involved with anyone. A lot is happening in my life right now."

A fleeting look of disappointment flashed across Noble's face. But then he threw his hands up in surrender. "I respect that. Anything you want to talk about, I'm a vault."

"Thanks. But I'm okay."

"I wanted to ask you something." Noble's gaze narrowed.

"I know you're only here for a short while. I have this awards dinner that I'm attending on Tuesday evening, and I have an extra ticket. I was wondering if you'd like to go with me. I know you've got a lot to do around here, but it would be great if you got to see more of New York.

"It's black tie, but don't worry about an outfit, I'm happy to help you find something. I'd hate to see this ticket go to waste."

I closed my mouth when I realized it had been hanging open. I'd never attended a black-tie event before. There was never a reason to. I did want to see more of New York, but I wasn't sure about letting him buy me a dress. "Me?" I asked.

"Of course. Would you be my plus-one?"

"Oh! Um…" I tried to find an excuse. Being around Noble was becoming dangerous—had me acting in ways I'd never acted before and again, I liked it. A lot. "I don't know."

"Say yes. Don't worry, you'll be at my table with several friends and colleagues. It won't be just you and me. I promise you'll enjoy yourself."

I thought about it for a few moments and remembered why I'd left Florence in the first place—to live. "Okay. Y-yes." I should have said no. There was no reason to get tangled up with this guy. I had nothing to wear to a black-tie event—not here in New York, or even back home.

"Great! We can get you a dress tomorrow."

"Oh." I waved my hand. "You don't have to do that. I'll figure something out."

"I insist. I'm the one who sprung this on you at the last minute. Let me do this for you."

What could it hurt? But also, what was I setting myself up for? I'd never see Noble again once I was done with Aunt Goldie's house. What would Amy or Patience do? Both of them would definitely have said yes. I thought about Amy telling me to live.

"Okay." I couldn't believe this was happening.

"Great. Where would you like to go to look for your dress?"

"I have no idea." I shrugged. "And now I'll really need your help getting this place cleaned out before I leave."

"No worries. I have a few shops in mind, and I'm happy to help you out here."

"Remember you said that." I pointed my fork at him.

We sat in silence for a few moments. The idea of getting all dolled up and going out with him made me giddy.

"Find anything interesting here?" Noble asked, looking around the house.

"Plenty." I shared a few of my findings with Noble. "I understand my aunt's voice was beautiful. They said her trill was like the sweet sound of a blackbird. At least that's what they said in one of the newspaper articles I found." I also told Noble about how Aunt Goldie wrote in her journal about how she would sneak out with friends at night and sing at juke joints deep in the woods. That's where a blues band discovered her. "My great-grandma threw her out. Told her she wasn't having anyone singing the devil's music in her house."

"I can believe it." Noble shook his head. "Lots of singers started in the church and had similar stories."

"Aunt Goldie practically lived on the road and finally 'set down roots,' as they say, in Queens and then here in this house. Apparently, lots of blues, R & B, and soul singers lived in an area called St. Albans."

"My dad lives in St. Albans," Noble said.

I gasped. "Really? That's pretty cool."

"On the way to his house, we pass the St. Albans Greatest mural under the train station with celebrities who lived there, like Billie Holiday, Lena Horn, Ella Fitzgerald, James Brown, Miles Davis, John Coltrane, and even Jackie Robinson."

My mouth dropped wide open. "Wow!"

"Yep. W.E.B Du Bois lived there too. I can take you by the mural and show you the houses they lived in before you leave."

"I'd love that. I can't wait to show my cousin pictures. She just knew I would spend every moment in this house and never see any other part of New York."

"I'd be happy to show you around my city. There's a lot to see."

"Why not?" I shimmied. "I guess I could spend at least one day sightseeing." I was already excited. Amy would be proud of me.

The second I showed Noble out, I called Amy.

"Girl! You will not believe this." I shared everything with Amy.

"Yeeeesssss! Fly, butterfly! It's about time you started to live. Wait! I need a picture of this Noble guy. So if you go missing, I can tell the police what he looked like."

"Amy. Please stop watching *Up and Vanished*."

"I still need a pic. Take one tomorrow when you go to get your dress. That way it won't seem suspicious. Then text it to me right away. I'm already tracking you on the app, so I'll know where to find you."

"Lord." I slapped my forehead. "Really, Amy?"

"Serious as a heart attack. People are crazy out there!"

I doubled over laughing until no more sound came from my mouth. It was funny to me, but I knew Amy was serious. She laughed too.

After our call, I worked the rest of the day while listening to Aunt Goldie's album collection, developing a new appreciation for the music of her time. After a while, I could pick out her voice in the background. Ms. Elsie came by with more food.

By sundown, I was exhausted in the best way possible. I climbed into my childhood bed in the room that looked like a box full of pink crayons had thrown up. Like a kid on Christmas Eve, I was too excited to fall asleep but too tired to stay awake. Noble was like my Santa Baby. I lay on my back, thinking about him and hoping he'd visit me in my dreams again, allowing thoughts of him to take me away from the issues with my mother.

Fourteen

Noble

Watching Holland taking in the city through the back seat of the Uber made me smile on the inside. I paid the driver a few extra dollars to make the ride scenic so I could see the joy in her eyes.

Holland had both hands splayed across the window at one point, looking out in wonder like a kid at Disneyland as we rumbled across the Brooklyn Bridge, through downtown, and past the Empire State Building on our way to Saks Fifth Avenue.

Not used to the erratic techniques of New York drivers, Holland white-knuckled the back of the front passenger seat a few times. She even yelped when a car came dangerously close, cutting us off in traffic.

"Did you see that?" She spun in my direction, her mouth agape in disbelief.

"And you guys are completely unfazed," she said incredulously. Holland shook her head and turned back toward the window. "I could never drive in New York."

"We're here," I said, presenting Saks to her with a sweep of my hand. "Ever heard of this place?"

"I'm a small-town Southern girl, but I've heard of Saks before. We used to have one in Myrtle Beach."

"Oh. I didn't mean to…"

Holland waved away my concern. "No explanation needed. We didn't have *this* Saks. This is the flagship store."

"Let's go get you an outfit fit for a black-tie queen."

We walked around Saks for a while before I led her to the private styling suite where I'd booked her an appointment with a stylist.

"Let's go. It's time for your session," I said, pulling her along.

"Session? What session?"

"Just follow me," I said, excited to give her this experience.

"Okay." Holland tilted her head but followed my lead up to the private suites where we checked in with a short man with striking blue eyes and a sharp navy suit.

"I'll let Alyssa know you're here, Mr. Washington." His tone was jovial but professional.

"Thanks."

Holland looked at me with pursed lips, raised brows, and mouthed, *Mr. Washington.* "Pretty fancy," she said, chuckling.

A young, thin blonde with a sharp bob rounded the corner and greeted us.

"Hi, I'm Alyssa, your stylist. I've got your suite all prepped for you. Right this way," she said.

With brows knit tightly, Holland looked back at me before following Alyssa into a suite the size of a large bedroom, with a rack of dresses, sparkling wine, and refreshments set up like a tea party.

"I understand you're attending a black-tie affair?" Alyssa

said, nodding. "I pulled a few things for you to get started, okay?"

While I waited, Alyssa gave Holland 100 percent of her attention. Skilled at gauging size and knowing what looks good on any body type, Alyssa styled Holland from head to toe in several looks before Holland became smitten with a formfitting wine-colored gown with a trumpet hem. Alyssa added black shoes, a sparkling evening bag, and dangling earrings.

I knew Holland was beautiful, but I hadn't expected her final look to drain all the language from my brain and air from my lungs. I was speechless when Alyssa presented her final look. My breath stuttered. Stunning wasn't strong enough to describe how gorgeous Holland looked. Feeling pulled to her, I stepped closer, fighting the urge to caress the sexy lines of her smooth, neck before kissing her nape.

"You look amazing," I finally said after fumbling through brain fog to find words. Circling Holland, I admired how the dress seemed to be crafted perfectly with Holland's curves in mind. She was a natural beauty wrapped in the perfect combination of sexy and elegant.

"She does, doesn't she?" Alyssa's agreement cut into the rabid thoughts about Holland running through my mind. She turned to me. "Would you like this on the usual account?"

I nodded without taking my eyes off Holland—bottom lip in my mouth. I bit back the desire to moan, but that didn't prevent the tightening in my groin.

"Can you give us a moment, please?" Holland asked Alyssa.

With a polite smile, Alyssa spun on her heels and left the room. When Holland was sure she was out of earshot, she turned to me with wide eyes. "Noble!" she said with a sharpness I hadn't expected. "Did you see these prices?" Her mouth opened, but nothing came out. She tried again. "I can't let you spend this much on me. This is insane," she said, pulling on the price tag.

"It's not insane," I said calmly.

"To you, it's not. The cost of this dress, these shoes, this bag—" she pointed at each item as she mentioned them and shook her head "—it's more than my rent and car payment combined. I—I can't let you do this. We can go somewhere else. You guys don't have Ross around here?"

"Who's Ross?" I asked.

"Ross is a store, silly. Like Marshalls or TJ Maxx. I could easily find something suitable there."

I held my hands up. "Holland, please. Let me do this. It's no trouble at all. I invited you. I said I'd cover the expense of your outfit, and that's what I will do. End of discussion."

Holland tossed me a sharp look and curled her lip. "End of discussion?"

The feisty side of Holland reared its head. I matched her energy. "I'm buying the dress," I said definitively.

Holland blew out a hard sigh and rubbed her temples. She opened her mouth again, and I held up a hand.

"It's already done."

"Noble!" She sighed dramatically. "This is crazy. It will take forever to repay you."

"I didn't ask you to pay me back." I turned away. "Alyssa," I called. "Can we get everything wrapped up? Thanks."

Without looking, I could feel Holland's eyes on my back. She was upset. I was amused. I let a smile slip across my face. Her twisted-lipped glare melted into a defeated grin. I won.

Before leaving the dressing room, I spun back around to face her. "Are you hungry? I am." I left the suite and shut the door behind me.

Moments later, Holland emerged from behind the closed door wearing her regular clothes and a serious look of defeat.

Alyssa carefully bagged her items and bid us a wonderful afternoon.

Holland didn't speak much once we stepped out onto Fifth Avenue. I understood. I'd grown up poor. The prices at Saks would seem obscene to any average person. Until I became wealthy, I hadn't fathomed that people made salaries like mine or had shopping experiences like the ones at Saks.

I tested the temperature to see if Holland was still hot about the purchases. "What would you like to eat?"

She sighed. "It doesn't matter."

"Have you tried New York pizza yet?"

The hard angles of her face softened a bit. "My treat," she commanded.

"I won't object to that. Some of the best pizza is right in our neighborhood."

We caught a taxi back to Brooklyn. I watched her as she watched the landscape whir by.

I racked my brain to find the right words to describe what being around Holland felt like. She was unlike any other woman I had dated. From the way she lavished me with her full attention when we were together, making me feel seen and exposed at the same time, to the way she appeared comfortable in her skin whether she wore leggings or a four-thousand-dollar gown. Holland was an intriguing combination of soft and bold. No pretense, inherent entitlement, or gold-digging tendencies. Her effortless beauty, the rhythmic swing of her curvaceous hips, and the bounce of her ample breasts were the icing and cherries.

I knew she was reconciling the money that was spent. She had to know I wasn't looking for anything in return.

I watched Holland take in the noisy hustle at Gino's, our neighborhood pizza shop. Her eyes ping-ponged along the narrow restaurant, which was teeming with customers sitting, standing, coming, and going. The family that owned and ran it navigated the organized chaos, yelling out orders, stacking boxes, slipping slices into the mega-hot ovens, and tossing dough high in the air.

"Wow," she said under her breath.

"Yo, Noble." The owner's son nodded my way.

"What's up, Tone?" I said.

"Who's your lady friend?"

"This is Holland. Holland, meet Tone. She's Ms. Goldie's great-niece."

"Oh! Pleasure to meet you. My condolences. Whatever you want today is on me."

"Oh, thanks." Holland waved off his offer. "You don't have to do that."

"I…" Tone looked at his father. Gino nodded. "We insist. We loved your aunt. Wanna try her favorite?"

"Um…" Holland turned to me.

"Go for it," I encouraged.

"Sure," she said.

How could a smile be both sheepish and sexy? Somehow, Holland managed that.

"Cool. One grandma and one regular slice!" Tone yelled over his shoulder. "Staying?" he asked Holland.

"Yep."

"To stay," he tossed over his shoulder to complete the order. "And for you, bro? The regular?"

"Yes, sir," I said.

Tone yelled over his shoulder again. "One veggie, one buffalo!"

Snaking sideways through the mass of customers, I parked our bags at one of the small red-and-white-checkered tables near the back of the bustling restaurant, grabbed some drinks, and plopped down in the chair. The sound of car horns, hissing of bus brakes, and random voices from outside floated inside and mingled with the noisy collection of voices. Holland and I had to practically yell across the small table to hear one another.

Moments later, Tone's brother, Sal, brought us four plates of steaming hot pizza.

"Bon appétit," I said, biting into my veggie slice first. "Be careful, it's really hot," I warned Holland.

Holland pinched a piece of the grandma slice, blew on it, and popped it into her mouth. "Mm." Holland nodded. "Utter deliciousness." She picked up the full slice to bite into it.

For several moments, we both ate in silence.

"What's a buffalo?" she said over her last bite of the grandma slice.

"Pizza topped with chicken tossed in buffalo sauce."

"Oh. I've heard of that before. Sounds tasty. I'll have to try that before I leave."

"Here." I held the pizza to her mouth. "Take a bite."

She did, and quickly wiped away the oil dripping down her chin.

"That's really good," she said around a mouthful.

Holland took another bite and eyed me pensively.

"What?" I asked, downing a gulp of grape soda.

"Mind telling me about what you do?"

"Nothing illegal."

Holland twisted her lips. "That's not what I was thinking."

I flashed my best grin. "Just messing with you. I run…" Air swelled in my chest. I took a deep breath. "I *used* to run a consumer goods company."

"Used to?"

"Yeah."

"Why'd you leave?"

I didn't want to talk about this. The sting of being asked

to leave was still fresh. And what would Holland think of a person who'd been asked to resign?

"I didn't choose to leave. I was asked to step down from my role as CEO." I'd said it. What would she think? I resisted the urge to dive into explanations about the reasons corporations fired CEOs other than bad performance.

Holland reared her head back. "Oh! I'm sorry to hear that. Can I ask what company?" she asked, brushing crumbs from her hands.

Many of the women I had dated in the past pretended not to know me at first, but then dropped clues that they'd already checked out my net worth. Holland's interest seemed organic—her curiosity wasn't driven by potential gain.

Holland studied me. I dropped my eyes to the half-eaten pizza on my plate and took another bite just to give me something to do. I didn't want her to read anything that I wasn't ready for her to see. I hated having to say Push was no longer mine.

"You know what, never mind," she said. "I'm sorry if that was too personal."

"It's okay. My comp—the company was Push Beverages."

Holland's eyes widened. "You were the CEO of Push? Oh my goodness! My sister loves those drinks. They get her through long days."

"Same. Thanks. I started the company back in grad school." I told her my origin story and enough about the last ten years to hopefully curtail more questions.

"Wow. Congratulations on such amazing accomplishments. Your mother would have been super proud of you. By the way, how's your dad?"

Another sore subject. "The idea of making her proud motivates me every day. I like to think she's looking down at me, smiling."

Holland tilted her head. "I'm sure she's super proud."

"Thanks. And my dad's fine," I said, telling a small lie. The truth was, I hadn't spoken to him or Tanya since I left the hospital. I want things to be different between us, but I don't know how to *make* them different. He was still stubborn, even after diminishing to a shadow of his former self. Two stubborn people at odds didn't make reconciliation easy. And I didn't feel like I was the one who should make the effort. I'd done that before and it hadn't gotten me anywhere. Years of yo-yo letdowns made it hard to believe that we could be more than what we'd been in the past. But something had to give. I couldn't lose him this way.

I could run a whole company, but couldn't figure out how to have a normal conversation with my dad.

"Good. I hope he continues to get better quickly," she said, bringing my focus back.

"Thanks." There was nothing quick about his condition.

Holland put the last bite of pizza in her mouth, sat back, and rubbed her belly like she going to ask three wishes of herself. "That was good. Now I can tell my cousin I had authentic New York pizza." She sat up and looked directly into my eyes. "I have to admit, I still feel guilty about the amount of money you spent on me today."

I opened my mouth to object.

"But!" She halted me with both hands. "I want to thank you for a wonderful experience. I enjoyed myself. And this pizza…knowing it was my aunt's favorite made it extra special." She reached across the table and took my hand. "Thank you."

Holland's sincerity took some of the weight off.

"My pleasure. I have to take good care of Ms. Goldie's niece. She wouldn't have it any other way. That woman was good to me." A flood of memories flashed through my mind, bringing the dull ache of loss. I'd spent many holidays at her table. Ms. Elsie and I were part of her chosen family—her words.

After a few quiet moments, I asked her, "Are you ready to go?"

She nodded.

We gathered our oil-stained paper plates and tossed them in the trash. I said goodbye to Tone and the family and stepped out of the pizza shop into the balmy evening. I tried to control the pace of our walk. We were just around the corner from home. Dreading every step, I slowed, not wanting to get there too fast. Why did I crave her presence so much when other women struggled to pin me down for more than a few hours?

I walked her to the door, wishing I could kiss her again. For a moment, I thought my wish would come true as we stood suspended in each other's presence. We'd been doing that a lot lately, connecting visually. Words weren't needed. I knew what I felt, and I knew she felt it too.

Holland broke our gaze when she looked down at her keys, cleared her throat, and offered a soft "I guess I'll see you tomorrow." Still, she didn't move. Was she waiting for me to make my move? Had she been any other woman, I would have. After buying the dress, I didn't want her to feel like I was expecting anything more than for her to be my plus-one, but this resistance was painful. I beat back the urge to run my tongue across her pink-tinted lips.

Her eyes bore the reflection of my desire. The pull was mutual. Holland wanted me as much as I wanted her. I stepped back, placing a foot on the lower step, wishing for a breeze to cool whatever this thing was that sizzled between us.

"Yeah," I finally said, our eyes connecting again. She swallowed. I watched her neck bob, imagining how soft and salty that sun-kissed skin would feel against my roving tongue.

My lips suddenly needed moisture. When I licked mine, she licked hers. *Invite. Me. In.* "Tomorrow," I repeated, hoping we could reconsider that timing. "Looking forward to it," I said, hoping I wouldn't really have to wait.

After several hours together, I still hadn't had enough of her.

"And you promised to help me finish clearing this place out, now that you're cutting into my schedule." She wagged a finger at me, bursting the bubble of tension surrounding us.

Smiling, I said, "I will."

Holland's beautiful smile was her only response. Sufficient enough for me.

"Let me know when you want to see the mural in St. Albans."

"As soon as we get this place cleaned out."

"Sounds good."

We did that gaze-locking thing again. Finally, I leaned forward, kissed her cheek, and backed out of the gate as I watched her enter the house safely. Another cool shower awaited me. I'd lived alone for over a decade, but this night, when I entered my home it felt especially empty, and I wondered what Holland was doing next door all alone.

Holland was the best distraction, but I had to get to work on my profile as a prime leadership candidate while I could still be considered a commodity. Thinking of anything else while she was around took extreme focus. Landing on my feet, or at least appearing to land on my feet, was critical. I was done sulking.

Money wasn't an issue. I had plenty of that, and the golden parachute the board had approved set me up for this life and the next. I certainly had no objections regarding their severance package. I could have remained unemployed if I wanted, but that wouldn't work well with my ego.

Holland would be leaving soon. I wasn't ready to let her go, especially when there was no guarantee I'd ever see her again. I needed time to explore the magnetism between us. I don't remember being this drawn to any woman, even the ones I thought would last. Holland's presence was a salve, soothing and dulling the ache of my circumstances. I'd never understand how she'd gotten so far under my skin in just a matter of days.

Fifteen

Holland

For the past two days, I'd desperately tried to survive the sweltering heat in a house that lacked adequate air conditioning. I cranked up the old heap of metal and it buzzed so loudly I flinched and turned it right back off, thinking it would explode. Instead, I turned on every ceiling fan in the house, hoping an occasional breeze would slice through the humid air. They only creaked and wobbled, and I prayed they didn't fly off their bases.

I pulled my hair up at the top of my head, wrapped a band around it, and then swept the edges sticking to my temples toward the haphazard bun. No matter how vigorously I fanned myself with my hand, there was no relief. Removing my bra and trading my leggings for a pair of shorts didn't keep me from sweating through my shirt. Sweat rolled from under my boobs like tears. I headed to the basement to clear out all the old stuff stored there, hoping it was cooler. It smelled of neglect and mildew.

Realizing I hadn't eaten, I headed to the kitchen and popped a piece of leftover pizza in the microwave. It would have tasted better in the oven, but I wasn't about to make the house any hotter.

I'd been back to the pizza shop twice since Noble took me the other day. Antonio never took my money, and would always let me choose from the endless variety they had so I could try different ones each time. I loved the regular cheese pizza, and the chicken Caesar salad slice—topped with mounds of romaine lettuce, delicious strips of grilled chicken, and a drizzle of creamy dressing—made my tastebuds happy. Pizza like this didn't exist in South Carolina.

The young family across the street came by to introduce themselves and offer their condolences. Jackson and Niquel were their names—the quintessential doctor-lawyer couple that gentrified neighborhoods were made for. Their rambunctious pre-K twins, Remy and Aiden, chased their cute little dog around their parents' legs while they expressed how much they loved and missed Aunt Goldie. Now the boys yelled "Hi, Ms. Holly-and" every time they saw me outside. This neighborhood, which had seemed so crowded and cold, started to feel cozy and friendly.

Seeing Jackson and Niquel with their adorable kids reminded me yet again that I was approaching thirty and nowhere near having a family of my own. I wanted that for myself so badly, but not yet. Once I finished figuring out who I was, then I could think about marrying and having children—in that order. My children would grow up knowing and living with both their mother and father.

Speaking of family, Ma and I typically never went more than a day or two without speaking. But after our last conversation, neither of us called. She was upset with me for asking questions she didn't want to answer. And I was upset with her for evading my questions. I refused to wait any longer. I deserved the truth.

So I called.

"Ma."

"Holland." She sounded so formal. "How are you?" Her voice was void of its usually nurturing tone.

"Fine," I said, matching her energy. I rolled my eyes, grateful that she couldn't see me.

"How's the house going?"

"Fine. Can you stop being so cold?"

At first, she said nothing. "You know I love you, right?"

"Of course. I just want you to answer my questions without getting upset. Learning about my r—" I paused, not wanting to say *real*, because Ma *was* my real mother even though we didn't share the same blood. She made the same sacrifices to raise me as any mother would. "—biological family doesn't take away from the love I have for you. It's important for me to know about them."

"Holly!" she snapped.

I groaned and waited for her to protest. Why was this so hard for her? I closed my eyes and counted, but it did nothing to stop my head from throbbing. "I deserve to know."

"It's not that simple," she said. "You can't believe everything you hear."

"That's the problem. I haven't heard anything from *anyone*." I flopped onto the couch. Ma and I didn't have many disagreements. Even as a teen, I'd been pretty mellow, but her behavior grew more bizarre every time I asked her about my aunt. For years, I didn't push when it came to getting information about my family. Now I wanted answers. "No" or "Not yet" was no longer acceptable. I wanted to scream in frustration.

"Just answer me."

"Why now? Huh, Holly? Where are all these crazy questions coming from?" Now Ma raised her voice. "Just…come home. Please? We'll talk in person."

The throbbing in my head intensified. Palming my forehead, I willed the ache to stop. "I'm meeting with the agent this weekend. The earliest I can come home is next week."

"I can't do this." I heard her sniffle before she hung up the phone.

I stared at my cell in disbelief. Most times, she'd call right back and ask "Are you done?" Either this was harder than I thought for her, or there was something she didn't want me to know. I hoped she hadn't intentionally done anything bad. The things I'd read in my aunt's journal raised more questions than I already had. I needed to hear what Ma had to say about everything. Maybe a trip home would get things settled.

"Ugh!" I pushed myself up from the couch, feeling the soreness that had crept into my muscles from dragging and carrying bags and boxes full of stuff. Thinking I had lots of time to get ready, I looked at the time on my phone and realized I only had an hour to prepare for the gala with Noble.

Getting my emotions together was first. I paced, taking deep breaths and willing my heart to stop thumping in my ears. Then I popped two painkillers to arrest the dull throbbing in my temples and the aches in my arms and shoulders. Lifting my arms, I sniffed my pits, took in a strong whiff of onions, and reared my head back so hard I almost gave myself whiplash. Hopefully the shower would wash away more than sweat and stink.

Upstairs, I tossed the phone onto the bed, traipsed to the bathroom, and stood under the old showerhead, letting the hot, pulsing water chop into my shoulders to pound away the stress. Time was slipping away so quickly.

Moments later, I stepped into my dress and folded my hair into a semi-elegant bun. With my fingers, I curled tendrils on either side of my face and let them hang. My simple version of a made-up face was mascara, liner, and gloss—a far stretch from @BeatFaceHoney and their Instagram tutorials.

Despite my lack of beauty skills, I was satisfied with my finished look. Alyssa was a genius, or maybe it was all in the dress and earrings. Never before had I looked into a mirror and considered my reflection stunning, but that was exactly what I saw. Me. Stunning, sexy, elegant.

I'd never been to a gala before. The fanciest events I'd attended were our annual church anniversary dinners. Even though I hardly posted, I snapped a mirror pic and posted it to my Instagram and Facebook stories and wrote #firstgalaever.

Seconds later, the doorbell rang. I hurried downstairs to greet Noble.

"Just give me one more moment," I said. I pushed the screen door open and turned right back around. "I left my evening bag ups—"

"Wow." The word slid out of Noble's mouth on a whisper.

When I looked back, Noble stared, mouth agape, and head tilted.

In that moment, I felt beautiful.

"You," he sighed. "Look. *Incredible.*"

That was a first. I'd been told I was pretty—beautiful, even—but words like *stunning* and *incredible* were new to a chill Southern girl like me who rarely made a fuss of things. "Thank you. Now let me get my bag so we can go."

"Um, sure," Noble stammered. I giggled at the effect I had on him. Noble shook his head like he was trying to shake off the awe.

Rest assured, I hadn't missed how incredibly handsome Noble looked in his black tux with the wine-colored bow tie that matched my dress exactly. He'd cleaned up extremely well, looking freshly shaven. His dark eyes sparkled. On a regular day, Noble's touch sent electrifying currents crawling across my skin, and that was in basketball shorts and jerseys. I wasn't sure if I could survive the wattage of his touch on a night like this.

Noble helped me into the car he'd ordered for the evening. We waded through thick traffic all the way to the Plaza Hotel, until finally our driver rounded the car and opened the door for us. We exited to pops and flashes of multiple cameras as we walked the red carpet to the entrance. Noble paused several times, gently placing his arm across my lower back for pictures. I had no idea what I was supposed to do, so I just smiled.

Inside, I'd never seen a venue so opulent. At the check-in table, a hostess pinned Noble with a badge displaying his name and company with a banner underneath that read Honoree. Then, we were escorted to a private cocktail reception with the other honorees, and someone Noble said was the publisher of the business magazine hosting the awards.

I couldn't keep myself from gawking at the domed ceilings and grand chandeliers. When I wasn't looking up, I stared in wonder at the scores of people milling about. Women seemed to float by in elegant perfection, dressed in dazzling gowns. Their perfect posture made me straighten my back. The men looked sophisticated and polished in their tuxedos. If rich had a look, these people had it down.

Throughout the event, dozens of people offered Noble congratulations and took selfies. Many suggested they "do lunch" and promised to have their assistants set it up. Noble introduced me to a dapper, white-haired gentleman named Tim, who had an infectious personality and looked like he could have been a mature model. I met Ty, his close friend and the one who had helped him get Push off the ground. Everyone at Noble's table was super nice. When Noble went onto the stage to receive his award, we all cheered obnoxiously loud.

"Yeah, boy!" Ty yelled, pumping his fist in the air. "That's my dude!"

I cracked up laughing, not realizing that kind of behavior was suitable in this environment. The cheering squads for many of the nominees were as boisterous as we were.

Once the last honoree was announced, the emcee declared that it was time to party. The DJ put on line dancing music, and throngs of people rushed to the floor.

"You know this one?" I asked Noble.

"I know it. The question is, can I do it?"

"Come on!" I kicked off my shoes and dragged Noble to the dance floor.

He struggled through the Wobble, Cupid Shuffle, and the Electric Slide before giving up.

I bent forward, holding my stomach, laughing. Noble couldn't catch the steps. His jerky, uncoordinated movements tickled me to my core.

"All right, already," Noble scolded, laughing just as hard. "I've got rhythm. I just don't have that much coordination."

The DJ switched the music to old-school pop and R & B. Noble and I returned to the dance floor. His moves were way smoother—downright sexy. Dormant parts of my body awakened and tingled as we swayed together. Our bodies molded together—moved like they were already familiar with each other. Like we'd danced a thousand times before. I felt more alive than I had ever remembered feeling.

Noble's arm fit around my lower back like it belonged there. Our torsos were drawn together like magnets. The temperature rose, and I knew the heat didn't come from the thermostat.

Lazily, I wrapped my arms around Noble's shoulders and rocked to the DJ's rhythm. Noble led with his hips. I followed every sway. We seemed to be the only ones in the room. Drunk on Noble's presence, I closed my eyes and felt like I was in a trance. His body against mine felt so good. So right. I was floating high above the dance floor.

Noble's lips pressed against my neck, setting my skin on fire. My eyes popped open. I found myself pinned under his penetrating gaze, and I liked it. A lot. Desire crackled between us like lightning. I lifted my chin. Noble descended, covering my lips with his. When he kissed me, fireworks went off in my head. Pulling me into him, Noble kissed me deeper. My knees threatened to give out and send me crashing to the floor, but Noble held me tight.

Being in his arms was like releasing a pressure valve. Pressure from moving, Ma, belonging—all of it melted away. I could stay in his arms forever.

The song ended. Reluctantly, we finally released each other. Gasping for air, Noble rested his forehead against mine. Around us, people were oblivious to us, laughing and dancing while my whole world spun deliciously. Cameras flashed, but it all seemed miles away.

"Ready to go home?" Noble's voice was a breathy whisper.

"Yes." My response was more air than words.

Fifteen minutes later, we were kissing, tugging, and touching our way across the Brooklyn Bridge. We exited the car, righting our wrinkled clothes. Again, Noble pulled me to him. His breath delicately feathered my face. We stayed like that for a long, sweet moment.

"Invite me in," I said what we both wanted. Desire made my voice husky.

"You sure?" Noble brushed the palm of my hand across his lips and then kissed it.

"Yes." I was breathless.

"Say less." Noble whisked me off my feet and carried me up his front steps.

He put me down long enough to fumble for his keys. Then he kicked the door open and carried me to his master suite.

Sixteen

Noble

I laid Holland's beautiful body across my bed and vowed to take my time. She deserved to be savored. I just hoped I could last. My body craved her badly, and my erection was a brick threatening to burst a hole through the front of my tuxedo pants.

I couldn't kiss her sweet, swollen lips enough. Holland explored my chest through my tux. I ripped the jacket off and pulled at the buttons on my shirt to feel her touch unfiltered. Tossing the clothes aside, I kissed her again, breathing in the floral essence of her.

Pulling her bun loose, I ran my fingers through her fluffy hair, then traced her nose and lips, working my way down to the center of her chest. I palmed the fullness of her breasts through the dress.

"Take it off," she said through spurts of breath.

Reaching around her back, I unzipped her gown and then pulled it down in the front, relishing in the bounce of her bountiful breasts. Shimmying the dress past her sexy hips, I tossed that and her undergarments to the floor.

I paused to admire her flawless amber skin, running my fingers along the length of her body, and dipping them into the inferno between her legs. I didn't think I could get harder, but I managed it. I was a rock. Holland removed my belt, slid her fingers inside my pants and worked them down until they fell to the floor. I stepped out of them, kicking them aside. I reached into my nightstand drawer, grabbed a condom, and handed it to her.

As Holland began to open the package, I covered her hand with mine. "Wait," I said.

I needed to taste her first. I blazed a hot trail of kisses from her neck to her toes and everywhere in between. Holland squirmed and moaned when I buried my face between her legs and sucked until she drove her fists into the sheets.

"Now," I whispered.

Holland wrapped her soft hands around my erection and tugged gently before covering it with the condom. "Mm."

I didn't want her to let go and at the same time, I couldn't wait to feel her. The anticipation was dizzying. Without breaking our kiss, I climbed over Holland and entered her soft center. Grunting, I was blindsided by how immediate, intense, and nearly crippling the pleasure was. Every molecule in my body was abuzz. There was no way I was going to last. I focused on giving Holland as much pleasure as possible before exploding.

Holland's moans were a symphony of decadent delight, making it hard to control myself. She moved her hips with me, meeting every stroke, thrust for thrust. I was coming undone, unraveling, layer by layer, into a pool of euphoria.

Holland cried out, and her soft walls tightened repeatedly, sucking me in with each greedy spasm. I tried to hold in my groan. Tried to maintain steady strokes. Tried not to lose myself completely as I watched her orgasm beautifully contort her body, claim her senses, and then release her. I failed. The warm flow of Holland's juices washed over me, sending me over the edge.

I pushed into Holland one last time. A groan rose from my gut. Tiny explosions rippled through me, quickly building into one massive eruption. I howled as life spilled from me, emptying me out physically and figuratively in a way I'd never experienced with any other woman.

I rolled over and pulled Holland to me. She rested her head in the crook of my arm. Our chests heaved. Sweat trickled in every crevice. We lay there, hugging, talking, caressing, until night yielded its velvety starlit sky to dawn. Then we slept, cradled in one another's arms.

I blinked against the natural light bathing the room, shielding my eyes from the sun, which was on full blast. I sat straight up in the bed, discombobulated—unaware of time and space, yet feeling sated. Then I noticed that Holland was gone. Was it all a dream? I was naked, lying across the bottom of my bed. I could still taste her. It was definitely real.

"Holland?" There was no answer. I called her again. Still nothing. I checked the bathroom and downstairs. Holland was gone. The realization made me feel empty. Yet the memories from last night put a smile on my face.

I jumped in the shower, feeling better than I had in over a week. I called Holland after getting dressed, but got no answer.

I hoped she didn't feel awkward about our night together, because I sure didn't. Just thinking about her had my nether parts standing at attention. I wanted to do it all over again. Next time, I would savor the sex, instead of acting like an anxious teen wielding an inexperienced dick, trying his best not to explode prematurely.

I remembered Holland's smile. It was something to behold. Maybe it was the accent or the sweet Southern flair. The unencumbered way she moved. Whatever it was, it grabbed ahold of me and I didn't want to let go.

I made a quick breakfast and carried it to my home office for my meeting with the chair of the board I was joining. We hit it off well. I loved the agency's mission, which focused on supporting foster children through adoption. I looked forward to meeting the rest of the board members. Life was looking better by the moment.

It had been days since I felt useful. Perusing my email and social media, I came across pictures from the awards ceremony. It looked like I got a lot of great buzz. Photos of me holding up my award made some of the business media's social pages. I zeroed in on one picture with Holland and me on the dance floor and grinned at the memory of Holland in my arms. It felt like she'd always been there. Even from the picture, I could see that we were lost in each. I screenshotted the picture and saved it to my photos.

My next meeting was with an executive recruitment firm, although I hoped my next job would come from one of my warmer contacts. I wore a shirt, tie, and blazer with my basketball shorts. The recruiter seemed infatuated by me, which was good. It restored a small bit of my confidence. It lessened the feeling of having let my mother down. Staying unemployed would mean that I'd failed, and I couldn't afford to fail. I couldn't go back to being poor. Call it PTSD, but the trauma of poverty motivated me. The reason I worked so hard was because I never wanted to go back. Every day, people get rich and then lose it all. I vowed to never take my wealth for granted.

The media had moved on from speculating as to why I was

ousted to a report about a real corporate scandal that sent that company's stocks plummeting. I didn't have to worry about controlling the narrative anymore, but until I landed another position, I still had to spruce up my personal brand. I wasn't sure what I wanted to do next. I hadn't planned on being jobless. I cupped my head in my hands and groaned. How could I control narratives when I couldn't control what was happening to my life?

I checked a few more emails and came across one requesting that I speak at a leadership conference. I clicked out of the email and shut the computer down. What could I possibly tell a room full of employed leaders?

My LinkedIn profile still said I was the CEO of Push Beverages. I hadn't had the heart to update it. Not a day passed when I didn't think about Push, my staff or Ty.

I got up from my desk and went down to the kitchen. I opened the fridge, realized I wasn't hungry, and closed it again. It wasn't yet noon, and I'd run out of ways to stay sane. I had no idea what to do with idle time. My whole life was wrapped up in Push, professionally, personally, and socially.

I texted Tanya to see how my father was doing.

Tanya: He's okay. Back home and still stubborn.

Me: Thanks.

Tanya: You two need to talk.

Me: Yeah.

I knew my response was noncommittal, but it was all I could give. It felt like too much to deal with my job situation and my father at the same time.

"What now, Noble?" I asked, as if I could give myself an answer.

The best part of this past week had been Holland. And not because she filled a void, but because she was an amazing woman, unlike any I'd ever dated. She was magnetic, drawing me in with her drawl and inviting energy. She wasn't trying to impress me, nor was she impressed by me. She didn't try to size up my credentials to decide if I was worthy of her time. She even got upset about how much I spent on her dress for the gala. None of the women I dated before cared about how much I spent on them. Several of them kept their hands permanently out in expectation. Holland was a comfort to be around, effortlessly sexy and laid-back, yet able to knock my socks off in a ball gown. She was...refreshing. And in bed, she was incredible.

An hour later, I was caught up on emails and meetings and was completely over scrolling through social media. I checked my watch and looked out the window again, hoping to see Holland return.

I was horrible at being bored. There were things I could have done, but didn't want to, like talk to my dad. Even though our relationship was complicated, I felt like I'd failed him too. He'd always said a respectable man held down a job. I needed to get my life back.

Seventeen

Holland

Noble had called a few times as I cleaned out a room Aunt Goldie had turned into a closet. I wasn't ready to speak to him.

I knew people had casual sex all the time, but I'd never slept with a man after only knowing him for a week before in my life. I wasn't that casual about sex. Amy would be surprised. Patience would be proud. And dammit, I felt elated but still embarrassed.

Sex with Noble was crazy good. He made me feel like anything I'd done before him was purely child's play. Noble stroked me into a stupor, making me come so deliciously and thoroughly and hard that I thought my back would crack in two. Once I came to my senses, I was embarrassed by the way I'd trembled and screamed. The way I cursed over and over when the fiercest orgasm I'd ever felt shook me, seizing my muscles and sensibilities. Cushioning me in his arms, Noble had absorbed the aftershocks rippling through my body until the quaking and whimpering subsided.

What the hell. There had to be something in the water in New York.

What if any of the neighbors heard us? I reminded myself that I was a grown woman, had consented, and wanted to feel the high of him in me again.

I knew I wouldn't be able to avoid him for too long. Our brownstones shared walls. And I had questions. Plenty of questions. After our shopping spree and the awards gala, my curiosity skyrocketed.

Noble wasn't working, but he could afford to spend almost four thousand dollars on an outfit for a woman he'd known less than a month. I knew nothing about that kind of life. And the way people doted on him at the gala, full of admiration and respect, made me want to know everything about this gorgeous man. I knew I was out of his league. As amazing as last night was, I'd already credited it as an anomaly. Noble and I were from two different worlds.

Noble called again while I rummaged through enough clothes, shoes, and costumes to fill a consignment shop. It had been a while since his last call. I stared at the phone and finally answered just before it went to voicemail.

Taking a deep breath, I flattened my tone to sound casual and unbothered. My "Hi" was too high-pitched. Cursing, I squeezed my eyes shut. Why couldn't I be normal when it came to Noble?

"Hey. How are you?"

"Okay." The squeak was gone.

"Cool. I just got a call from St. Paul's to confirm the pickup today. They'll be here by two. I can come over now to help get ready for them."

The clock said it was just past noon. I needed help, but my body was still emitting random aftershocks from last night. Having him around was too tempting.

"Okay." Single-word answers were all I could manage.

I'd forgotten that Noble had taken care of that for me. St. Paul's took donations of furniture, clothing, and household items and sold them at their thrift store. They used the money to help families in need. He said it would save me a ton of time.

"Good. You eat yet?"

"No." I had been gorging myself on flashbacks of us in bed. Food was the last thing on my mind. *Down, girl.*

"I was just about to go to the bodega and grab a bacon-egg-and-cheese sandwich. Want one?" The way my stomach growled at the mention of those ingredients was obnoxious.

"Um, sure," I said, unable to deny that I was starving.

"Roll or bagel?"

"Huh?"

"You want it on a roll or bagel?" he repeated.

"Roll. With salt and pepper." I felt like a New Yorker saying that.

"Okay. See you soon."

Noble ended the call. I put the phone in front of me on the round wood table and stared at it. Noble sounded the same as he did before we had voracious sex. I debated whether I would tell Amy about this, and quickly admitted that I would. The timing just had to be right.

I'd barely packed another box when Noble arrived with the sandwiches and two bottles of orange juice, looking sexier than ever, and a tiny explosion went off in my core. After closing the door, I followed him to the kitchen, admiring his wide shoulders, strong gait, and tight ass. We sat across from each other at the round oak table.

My mouth watered for both him and the sandwich when he sat down and opened the foil and wax paper. The smell of the bacon wafted into my nose and was met with a hefty growl.

Shame widened my eyes. I slapped my hand over my stomach and looked at Noble. His smirk unraveled me. Chuckling, I looked away.

I'd had my share of bacon, eggs, and bread for breakfast, but there was something about that combination in New York that made it extra tasty.

"Good, right?" Noble nodded, smiling.

"Mm-hmm," I mumbled, covering my chewing with my free hand.

He pointed at the sandwich. "There's a joke about how we New Yorkers say it. We smash it into one long word, making it sound more like 'baconeggandcheese' and then we add 'on a roll or bagel.'"

"That's exactly how you said it on the phone!" I laughed. "Well, I love this New York staple. This and the pizza both get a thumbs-up from me."

"Can't wait to show you more. There's a lot to see here."

For some reason, that made me blush. It didn't seem like he thought any less of me after our night together. I felt a layer of anxiety melt away.

"I look forward to seeing more of the city before I go. And thanks for helping me out with the donations. That's going to free up so much time. It's been hard trying to do all of this myself. Aunt Goldie had so much stuff."

"Of course. Right now, I have the time. I'm happy to help."

We gnawed on our sandwiches and drank our orange juice. I hesitated before speaking again. "Noble."

"Holland," he teased, saying my name in the same nervous tone.

I swatted his shoulder playfully.

"Can I ask you a question? Actually, I want to ask a few questions."

"Sure," he said, wiping his mouth with a napkin. "What's up?"

Why I felt so timid after laying all my goods in front of him less that twenty-four hours ago, I'll never know. "Have you always lived in your house alone?" I pushed the question past my lips. Suddenly I was concerned about the other people in his life. Namely the other women. "It's a lot of house for a single person."

He dragged in a breath. "I've been there about five years. I had hoped to have a family one day." Noble looked directly into my eyes when he spoke.

Me too, I thought. I averted my eyes. Noble's gaze was a stun gun, intense and electrifying.

"Oh. Okay." I paused a few moments to gather myself. My mind and lips fought to push out all the tumbling thoughts roaming around inside my head. "About last night..." There. I'd said it.

"What about last night?" Noble's wicked smile made my cheeks flush.

"Noble!" I dropped my hands to my lap and shook my head. His playfulness helped me shed another layer of anxiety.

"What?" He held his hands up. "Last night was amazing. I mean..." Noble's eyes fell from my eyes to my lips, finally landing on my breasts. Each place he examined sizzled. "I could have performed a little better, you know..." The smile spread across his face again.

Better? He was capable of better? My stomach wrenched, but I was far from sick.

"No need to be so hard on yourself." I laughed nervously. "But that's not what I meant." I paused. "I don't want you to think I make a habit of sleeping with men I've only known for several days. That's all."

"Pfft! You're a grown woman, Holland. Who you sleep with and when you sleep with them is your business. I don't think any less of you. In fact, I consider myself lucky." Noble sat back confidently in his chair. Every move he made was draped in sexiness.

"Lucky?"

Noble leaned toward me and took my hand in his. Every cell in my hand was alive and aware of his touch. "Yes. *Lucky.*"

I watched the words fall from his gorgeous lips and pondered them for a moment. I felt lucky.

"Tell me more about you and your company."

Noble gently let my hand go, sat back, and tilted his head pensively.

"Coffee never kept me awake," he said, crumpling his napkin and balling it in the foil from his sandwich. "I could drink a cup and go right to sleep. In grad school, I worked two jobs and went to school full-time. I needed something for those all-night study sessions, so I'd mix up these different juice concoctions to give me energy. I'd add things like green tea, ginseng, and other secret ingredients." Noble grinned and winked. "If I told you I'd—"

"Have to kill me," we said together. Chuckling, I rolled my eyes. That would have been corny coming from any other man. Noble was incapable of being corny.

"My boy Ty asked to taste some and loved it. He told a few others about it and the next thing I knew, I was making batches, selling small containers to students. I called it The Notion." Chest lifted, Noble waved his hand like he was presenting the brand to me.

"The Notion?" I felt my face scrunch. Covering my mouth didn't stop the laughter from spilling through my fingers. "Seriously?"

"Yep." Noble's deep laugh wrapped around his words. "The *n* for Noble and it was my Potion."

"Cool story, but I don't know about that name." We both laughed. "Who came up with *Push*?"

Noble wagged a finger at me. "Everybody wanted The Notion. The name was changed to Push when we officially launched the company. Ty's uncle tried it and said we had a marketable product. Got some investors involved, and the rest is history. I never imagined myself owning a beverage company. I went to school for finance, so that helped with some of the business part."

"That's really cool. How did you come up with the recipes?"

"My mother was a great cook—always mixing ingredients and creating dishes. Made me her sous-chef. I'd get in the kitchen and create stuff with her all the time, so that part came naturally." Noble looked beyond me, suspended in nostalgia. "Yeah," he said after a while. "Cooking brings me comfort." Falling quiet again, his body was in the room, but his mind seemed far away. I let the silence settle between us.

"That's amazing," I said. *And a little sad.*

"Yeah. Push became my life." Noble's voice was low and serious. "When I saw that the company could take off, I put everything I had into building it. Did it for my mom. I wanted to make her proud, even though she wasn't here to see it. Felt like I owed this to her for all she sacrificed. Did it because I never wanted to struggle the way we had back then."

Not wanting to disturb the moment, I remained quiet. Several beats ticked by before Noble turned to me with a small smile.

I took his hand in mine. "I'm sure she's smiling right now."

Noble nodded and cleared his throat. "I wanted a degree in finance so I could understand money, because being poor sucked. I knew there had to be a better way. When I realized I could build an empire, I knew that could save me from my past struggles…" Noble lifted his chin. "Sometimes I wonder if I did too much. Other times I wonder if I didn't do enough." His laugh was low and skeptical. "Your mind ends up all over the place when you're unemployed. Too much time to think." Sitting back, Noble took a deep breath. "Not to mention, being unemployed is boring."

My laugh mixed with his, piercing the once-solemn moment unexpectedly. "Noble!" I chided.

"I'm bored as hell." He sat back and shook his head. "I haven't had this much free time on my hands since high school," he said, lifting the heaviness that settled around us. "And you?" Noble asked, peering at me with those knowing eyes. "What's your story?"

"Nothing as interesting as yours." I stood to clear the table. "I could sum it up in one sentence. I'm a typical small-town Southern girl who became a social worker so I could be there for young people feeling alone in the world." I'd said too much but continued anyway. Noble made me feel comfortable like that. "A girl who desperately needed a change and then unexpectedly ended up here." I waved around the room. "Hence, my first trip to New York as an adult. My life is a world away from yours."

"How so?"

"Well, first of all, I couldn't spend thousands of dollars in a few hours without wiping out the possibility of my eventual retirement." The hyperbole was fitting. I could only imagine how rich Noble was. I'd seen his home, got several glimpses of his lifestyle, and watched him spend more money in a half hour than I spent in months. "The cost of that dress could pay my rent in Charleston twice and leave enough to fill my fridge with groceries."

"We never had much," he said, "but after my dad left, life got harder all the way around. I used to tell my mother I was going to be rich so we would never have to worry about anything again. She always said that money didn't solve your problems. She called that one." He chuckled. "Now I have money, but there are things I wish I had that money can't buy."

"I didn't mean to offend you or imply—"

"You didn't," Noble interrupted. "And you don't seem typical to me." His eyes bore into me.

Had I imagined his voice being husky?

"Anyone special in your life?" I pushed the words out, nervous about asking, but still wanting so badly to know.

"Nope." Noble shrugged. He seemed…indifferent. Did he not want someone in his life?

As gorgeous as this man was, why weren't women knocking down his door? "Ever?"

"There were a few. None that worked out for the long haul." Noble paused. "Because of work, mostly. I spent a lot of time growing my company. Didn't leave a lot of time for dating or anything else, for that matter. At least that's what Ty says." He chuckled again. "And you? Anyone special?"

"No," I said, crumpling the empty foil from my unfinished sandwich.

"So we're both single," Noble said. "Interesting." His smirk was sexy.

We let that notion linger between us.

If circumstances were different…

I let that thought linger too. Who knew if I'd ever see Noble again after this trip was over?

I felt Noble's eyes on me, and after a few agonizing moments of silent scrutiny, I looked around at the work that awaited me to avoid his gaze.

"There's so much to do," I thought aloud and stood up, needing to break the hold he had over me.

"Then let's get to work." There was nothing sensual about Noble's words, but the way they dripped from his plump lips made me feel like he'd said "Make love to me."

I wasn't sure if the sweat pooling in the creases under my breasts was caused by the oppressive August temperature or the heat that emanated from my core with Noble so close to me—especially now that I knew what he was capable of in bed.

"Yep. Time to get to work," I said, pushing my chair in.

"Got a good playlist we could work to?" he asked.

"Of course. Need you ask?" I opened my music app and selected an R & B playlist from the early 2000s. Usher's song "Yeah!" flowed through my portable speaker. I cranked it up and danced toward the steps. Those boxes upstairs weren't going to fill themselves.

"Oh, this is a good one." Noble stood, executing a rhythmic two-step as he followed.

His moves were smooth. *Damn.*

"Where were those moves when we were line dancing at the gala?"

"Hey!" Noble pointed at me. "Line dancing is not my zone of genius."

I thought of one area of genius Noble could boast of. The memory of how he made me feel pulsed in my pelvis. A sudden shudder rushed through me. *Down, girl!* I hoped Noble hadn't noticed. How long would mental aftershocks rumble through me? It was like my body remembered and I'd blush in places I didn't know were possible.

Noble's muscles showed off as he moved furniture down to the first level while I packed boxes to the rhythms pumping from my portable speaker, separating my aunt's belongings based on their intended destination, St. Paul's or Charleston.

"Look at this." I stood, holding a stunning sequined gown up to me. "Aunt Goldie wore this at one of her shows," I said, turning to the mirrored closet door. "I remember it from one of her pictures." Twisting and turning with the dress against me, I fought back tears, feeling close to my aunt.

"Looks like it might fit," Noble said, breaking through my wavering emotions.

I started as if I were caught doing something wrong. "Maybe. You think?"

"Try it on."

"No need," I said, waving away Noble's suggestion and folding the dress. Noble had already seen me naked. I wasn't worried about undressing in front of him. But unraveling emotionally was the kind of exposure I wasn't ready for him to see.

Noble stood from his bent position over the box he was stuffing and gently took the dress from me. Standing behind me, he put the dress under my chin, letting it shimmer and fall. Tearing my focus away from the heat that surged between his body and mine, I looked at our reflection in the mirror. A serious sultriness filled Noble's eyes.

"Stunning." His words were a soft breeze against my ear. Shivers crawled down my back. "She'd want you to have it."

She would.

Noble's closeness, masculine scent, and throaty whisper had me flailing in a sensual abyss. The skinny straps of my tank exposed the skin of my shoulders. I wanted to feel his lips brush me there. The lump in my throat was unmovable, no matter how hard I swallowed. My pulse quickened and throbbed, and I heard the blood rushing through my veins.

"Try it." His voice grew huskier.

A shaky nod gave him the permission needed to lay the dress aside and turn me toward him. Noble pulled my tank top over my head and watched my bare breasts bounce and pebble under his scrutiny. He licked his lips and I wanted to feel the fire of his tongue on me. Lifting the dress over my head, Noble worked the material until it cascaded over my torso. He shimmed the material past my hips and stepped back, releasing a soft breath.

With eyebrows creased, a serious expression passed over Noble's face. "Stunning." Eyes pinned to me, he shook his head in apparent disbelief, making me anxious to turn and see for myself.

I spun, covering my gaping mouth before slowly moving my hand and breathing "Wow" as I stared at my reflection.

The dress hugged every curve on my body. Unable to look away, I studied myself, drowning in the beauty of the moment and awed by the fact that I was in a dress once worn by my great-aunt. Finally, I unglued my feet from where I stood and walked closer to the mirror. A perfect fit from front to back. Fingering the lush material, I traced the stitching while Noble's eyes devoured me, inch by inch.

I was unaware of my tears until Noble came and gently swiped them with his thumb. He lifted my chin in his hands until our eyes connected. I readied my lips for his, waiting to feel him. I ran my tongue across my bottom lip to moisten it. Noble's lips parted slightly in response. We stayed there, staring, breathing in the weight of each other's desire, wondering if we should allow our lips to connect. To kiss, to ignite the smoldering embers between us, just to be consumed by the inferno simmering beneath the surface.

"See," he said after several breathless beats. "You look stunning." His words were barely audible. "You could have worn that to the awards gala. You should keep it."

I nodded and tore myself away from the magnetic force binding us to one another. "Yeah. I'll do that."

I smiled, returning my focus back to the mirror. Exhaling, I closed my eyes, feeling so deeply connected to my aunt. Grateful to Noble for suggesting I try on the dress. Suddenly, I wanted to take my time going through her things instead of simply tossing everything into boxes for donations centers. These items were precious—priceless.

"Help me get this off," I said to Noble.

He helped lift the dress over my head and gently laid it aside. Anxious tension replaced the sizzling heat that enveloped us moments before. Bare breasted, I grabbed my tank and yanked it on.

"Back to work, buddy." I sounded like one of the fathers from those insurance commercials. I'd actually called Noble *buddy*. At this age, I still hadn't mastered escaping awkward moments without being a little weird.

Playfully, Noble rolled his eyes and we both dissolved into laughter.

While he finished the heavy lifting on the lower levels, I headed to my room to clear out anything I didn't need during the rest of my stay. Picking up my aunt's journal from my nightstand, I ran my hand across the worn leather cover.

"I've been a little busy, Aunt Goldie," I said to the book. "I'll get back to you tonight." Eager and afraid, I'd hesitated to get back to the journal, despite desperately wanting to learn more about my past.

"Holland!" I heard Noble call for me from downstairs.

"Coming." I traipsed down the two flights.

"The truck is here." When I reached the first-floor landing, Noble was opening the front door.

I greeted the men from St. Paul's and directed them to where they could start.

Over the next hour, they moved my aunt's bulky furniture, old lamps, and several boxes of clothing into the huge rig, blocking any traffic from moving up the street. By the time they were done, sweat made their dirt-stained shirts cling to their sculpted chests, compliments of the humidity.

Noble slapped both men high-fives, pressed tips into their calloused hands, and walked them out.

Inside, I looked straight through the partially emptied house and exhaled. With Noble's help, I was making great progress, shaving several days off my workload. He'd helped me clean out dishes from the china closet. I could tell from all the old chafing dishes, leftover bottles of bourbon and brandy, brass liquor carts, and fancy serving ware that my aunt had loved to entertain. Closing my eyes, I imagined her prancing around in expensive muumuus with champagne flutes in her hand, or slapping cards on the oak table during the bustling Friday night parties Ms. Elsie told stories about.

I packed several closets' worth of coats, shoes, and dresses, setting aside what I planned to keep or get assessed. A few of the items would be perfect for consignment shops. I couldn't wait to tell them these things came from my semi-famous aunt.

All the furniture in the living room, basement, and bed-rooms—except mine and hers—had been emptied and loaded onto that truck. I hadn't decided what to do with her bedroom furniture yet. Sending it with the others made sense, but my heart wasn't ready to let it go. A thin layer of guilt added to my conscience with every item I marked for that truck. I knew I needed to get rid of it all, but the more I went through her things, the closer I felt to her.

A sudden breeze brushed past me and I looked around. The window and door were closed. The rickety ceiling fan hadn't offered that much air since I'd been here. I wasn't the esoteric type, but felt confident that breeze was a nudge from my aunt. Closing my eyes, I wrapped my arms around myself and said to the air, "I feel you, Aunt Goldie."

Goldie started as nothing more than a distant next of kin who I was willing to investigate to fill in the blanks about my past. The house started as an old piece of property I needed to clear out and sell. Now, both were slowly becoming so much more. My aunt's love reached through time and the grave to touch my heart. The more I learned about her, the more I wanted to know. Who knew you could so deeply mourn the loss of someone you had never laid eyes on? Despite Ma's doting, I always felt like an orphan—like I was floating through space, untethered—belonging nowhere. Afraid that when she left me, I'd have nothing left, because she was old.

Getting to know these women who shared my doe eyes and blood through this house grounded me. I finally belonged somewhere. The three of them laughed and loved here. Through pictures, rooms, and clothes, I got to share the space they existed in, take in the subtle scent of them that lingered, and surround myself with the warmth left behind—a living, breathing monument set aside just for me.

My eyes moistened. I shook my head to bring myself back into the reality before me. I still had a ton of things to do, like mailing boxes of stuff to my apartment in Charleston, meeting with my aunt's financial advisors, closing out accounts, making the appointment with the real estate agent, and bringing in cleaners to prepare for the open house. I was still days away from being completely done. That also meant I had several more days with Noble before I had to return to my life—and possibly never see him again. And because of him, I'd have more time on my hands to explore. Then, there was Ma. At some point, I'd have to squeeze in a trip back home so we could have a serious talk. All of this before starting my new life in Charleston in a few weeks.

"Feels like you finally made progress?" Noble broke into my thoughts, startling me. I didn't hear him come back inside.

"Yes!" I smiled, genuinely happy. "Thanks to you." Our voices echoed through the mostly empty room.

"You're welcome."

"I'll get to that overgrown backyard by the weekend." The yard had the potential to be quaint, if it weren't for the overgrown weeds, cracked concrete, and bald patches of brown grass.

"I've got a guy for that too. I'll take care of it for you," Noble offered.

"You're a real lifesaver, Noble. What would I do without you?"

"Probably stay an extra week to get through all this stuff. Ha!" Noble's laugh sailed across the room right into my heart. I loved the sound of it.

"Hungry?" I asked Noble. Hours had passed since our breakfast. The least I could do was feed him after all the help he'd given me.

"Starving." Noble rubbed his tummy.

"What would you like?" I looked toward the kitchen. "Ah man, we packed up all the dishes. We'll order in. What do you feel like having?"

"Food."

I laughed. "What kind of food, silly?"

"The edible kind," he said with a straight face while I fell apart laughing. Then he joined me. His expression was as funny as his words.

I shook my head at him.

"There's everything around here. We can do Indian, Asian fusion, Caribbean… There's a cool Mediterranean place."

"How about Indian or Mediterranean. I don't get that often back home."

"We'll get something from my favorite Indian spot."

"Okay. My treat." When I saw Noble about to object, I said, "I insist."

He shrugged and pulled the menu up on his phone. We perused the selections before placing an order for delivery on my app.

Using the deep window bay as seats, we continued listening to music and swapping stories about our childhoods. Both raised by single moms—Noble and I were more alike than I thought. When our food came, we sat at the table, the last standing piece of furniture on the first floor. I figured I'd need that until I left.

Noble watched as I took a forkful of the butter chicken I let him order for me, wanting me to taste his favorites. After tearing off a piece of garlic naan, I dipped it in the sauce, popped it in my mouth, and moaned.

"Mm. This is delicious."

Noble smiled. "Told you."

Seeing him smile made me smile. This man…

"Taste this." Noble pushed his fork toward me and I tasted his dal, rice, and paneer.

"That's good too," I said while chewing, forgetting all form of manners.

Not many words were uttered while we picked from one another's take-out containers. Words weren't necessary; I enjoyed just sharing space with Noble. He made me feel comfortable, like I was used to being around him. Now and then, I'd steal glances or find him looking at me. He'd wink and I'd wink back or smile. Watching his mouth move as he ate reminded me of how he'd savored me in his bed. I wanted to feel him on me and in me again.

Sitting back, Noble, pushed his empty plate aside and patted his stomach. "That was delicious."

"It was."

"I guess I'll get going," Noble said, gathering up his trash.

I yawned. "Whew! Sorry." It wasn't even close to bedtime and I was exhausted. I didn't want him to think I was trying to get rid of him. If it weren't for the fact that the only beds that remained in the house were my twin bed and my aunt's queen bed, I would want him to stay. "I'm pooped," I admitted.

"Yeah. Me too."

When I stood, we faced each other but didn't move. I felt his eyes rove my body just as mine did his. These moments were the hardest to get through around him. Knowing what he could do to my body didn't make it any better. If Noble swept me off my feet and carried me up to my twin bed, I wouldn't protest. Instead, we politely danced around the desire bouncing between us like static. I couldn't help but see the longing in his deep brown eyes or notice the strong jut of his chin.

"See you later," Noble said, still not moving. Huskiness drew his voice down several octaves.

"Yeah." That came out breathlessly. I cleared my throat. "Good night."

Noble stepped closer to me, eliminating any space between our torsos. My chin lifted on its own volition. Defying my will, I stood before him, eyes closed, lips parted, desperately wanting to taste him again. Noble's masculine fingers found my chin, shocking my skin with his personal brand of electricity. His lips covered mine and fireworks exploded in my brain again. Flames radiated to the edges of my skin. We kissed and kissed. And then kissed some more. Cupping the side of my face, Noble pulled me closer, deepening the kiss. Our tongues danced as we took each other's breath away.

Noble looked at the ceiling and groaned. Resting his forehead on mine, we panted synchronously.

"You have no idea how…"

"I think I do," I whispered. But tonight, I refused to ask him to invite me to his bed. I was still reconciling that I'd completely given myself to him the night before. My head wasn't on right when Noble was around. I had thinking to do and a life to figure out.

"I'd better go." Noble stepped away.

Reluctantly, I agreed. "Yeah." I watched Noble walk out my front door.

Once he was on the other side, I leaned my back against it and stayed there for a clarifying moment.

After a cool shower, I filled my water bottle with ice water, climbed in bed, and grabbed my aunt's journal, picking up where I'd left off the other day.

March 17, 1997

After a whole week, Calvin and I came up with nothing. We visited hospitals, checked with authorities, knocked on doors, and combed every corner of Aiken and all the bordering towns. There was no Patricia or Holland to be found anywhere. Her neighbor said that one morning Patty was just up and gone. She hadn't seen her since. And the authorities weren't helpful at all. They never took our missing kids seriously. Hopefully, the investigator I hired will find them. Right now, I can't even cry anymore.

They didn't just disappear. They couldn't have. I know it in my soul.

Calvin may have been done, but I will never stop looking for Holland.

I didn't realize I was crying until fat teardrops plopped onto the page, darkening the script. The journal shook in my hands. I couldn't get enough air into my lungs, no matter how many shaky breaths I drew in. I tossed the covers off, jumped to my feet, and paced with a thousand questions stampeding through my mind.

"No. No. No. No. No." Aunt Goldie couldn't be right. I marched in circles.

I grabbed my cell phone, jabbing at icons and names with blurred vision and quivering fingers.

Ma picked up after the first ring.

Knots formed in my chest. Dragging in more gulps of air, I tried to unclog the path from my chest to my mouth, but couldn't get any words through my lips. I grunted, mad that I couldn't coherently translate my frenzied thoughts into words.

"Holly?" I heard Ma through the phone.

My mind spun.

"Holly? Say something."

The pain in my heart was physical, banging violently against the walls of my chest, snatching my breath away. I grasped at my shirt, gathering handfuls. There had to be a logical explanation.

"Are you there? Can you hear me?"

Tears stung my eyes and somehow, I found words.

"Did you kidnap me?" I shrieked. Ma's only response was a silence that lengthened and deepened into a quiet so loud it screamed in my head. I squeezed my eyes shut. "Answer me!"

"It's not what you think, baby girl." Her voice shook. "Please, j-just let me explain." I tossed the phone across the room and crumpled to the floor.

Eighteen

Noble

"Noble." Dan, the chairman of the board of directors, stood, extending his hand to me. Stout, with wiry gray hair, he studied me with piercing green eyes, a sincere smile, and added, "I'm so glad you were able to join us for dinner today."

"Me too." I smiled at the two men and one woman seated at the table in the Italian restaurant.

"This is John, Margo, and Scott," Dan said, presenting the three individuals from the board of directors' nominating committee.

I nodded and shook each of their hands. The board was diverse in every way but age. Tim had said they needed a fresh perspective. I see now that was a code word for *younger*.

"Thanks for taking the time to meet with us today," John said, his skin so bronze his silver beard seemed to glow. John looked like he'd graced the covers of *GQ* magazine back in his heyday. I remembered my dad reading that when I was a child.

"Let's get the waiter over so you can order. We understand you're a busy man, and we'd love to get right down to business," Margo said, her voice raspy, like she smoked cigarettes for breakfast every day. Margo's jet-black hair and large black eyeglass frames gave her a hip vibe. She raised her hand. "Dawn, darling," she said once she captured the waitress's attention. "Noble, what would you like to drink?"

The waitress retrieved a bottle of sparkling water for me and quickly returned for our lunch orders.

"I'd love to hear more about the mission of the organization and your needs on the board," I said, feeling good about this meeting even though it was just getting started.

Margo started with the organization's goal to get teens adopted into healthy and loving environments and their new mentorship program to help support the teens and their new families.

"As you see, we're all—" John looked around the table and chuckled "—people of a certain age, and our board is really in need of fresh perspectives."

"Yes," Margo said. "We don't want our board to age out and not have the support it needs to remain sustainable. We were very excited to hear of your interest. Tell us more about that."

"Mentorship is something I'm passionate about. I've been wanting to get more involved for a while now. I wouldn't be where I am today if it wasn't for the support of my mentors— especially Tim," I said. "As a little boy, I didn't have much. My mother and father eventually broke up when I was in my teens, and after that, I lost her to cancer. I wasn't adopted, but I know what it's like to feel alone and unsupported, and I'd love to get involved with an organization that fills those gaps for young people. I can easily see myself in them and would love to help."

Each of them smiled.

"Sounds like you'd be a great fit," Margo said.

As we ate, the quartet filled me in on all that would be ex-

pected of me as a board member. Making and securing donations, being an ambassador for the organization and the kids.
They shared some success stories and invited me to join them
at the next meeting. This felt right, and I needed to plug into
something meaningful. Hopefully, it would also prevent me
from being bored while I looked for another job.

"I look forward to…" I paused. The words *being useful* came
to mind, but I didn't want to say that aloud. "Serving," I said.

"Fantastic," Dan said. "Look for an email with a contact
form that we'll need you to complete."

"I look forward to working with you," John said, standing.
The others followed suit.

"I'm ready to get to work." That was the truth. The more
I listened to all the great ways the agency changed the lives
of young people, the more excited I was to join.

Maybe I could even be one of those mentors they were
looking for in the new program. I decided right then that I
was going to make a hefty donation to the cause as soon as I
got back home. Several business colleagues sat on boards of
nonprofit organizations. Tim always said it was a good look.
By the end of my meeting, I understood why they dedicated
so much of their time to these charities. I hadn't even attended my first meeting, and I already was moved and ready
to get involved.

On the way back, I called Tim to thank him.

"Like you said, I think this will be good for me in more
ways than one."

"Good. Did they mention doing any media outreach to an-
nounce your appointment?"

"Sure did," I said, but I felt like that no longer mattered. I
just wanted to help.

"How's everything else going? Your dad?"

I cleared my throat before answering. "Good, thanks."

"And your beautiful friend. The one you brought to the gala? She seems nice." Tim stretched the word nice into two syllables.

"Holland is good. Just a friend, though," I said, despite the smile that spread at the mention of her name.

"Yeah. I dance like that with my friends too," he joked.

I couldn't help my laugh. I was so lost in Holland on that dance floor, I forgot we were in a public venue. "Anyway," I said, chuckling. "I had a great call with a recruiter this week. I also set up a few lunch dates with some folks from my network. It's time to see what's out there."

"That's great news, Noble. I'm glad you're sounding better these days. Think it might have something to do with your friend."

It did, but I wasn't ready to admit that to Tim.

"I gave myself enough time to sulk. It's time to move forward and make some things happen," I said, despite how much I still missed everything about Push. Holland made things seem not so bad. I'd forgotten what it was like to have a life outside of the job.

It was going to take time for me to get used to someone else taking the reins of my company. I hoped it wouldn't be a tyrant who'd ruin the family-like culture we'd built. And what would happen to Ty? Would he feel comfortable staying? I didn't want to talk about this anymore. I was feeling too good. "Gotta run, Tim. I'll keep you posted on everything."

"Please do. I know this isn't easy. Trust that you will land on your feet and be in a better place than you expected."

"Yeah."

"Take care, Noble."

On the way home, my thoughts volleyed between Push, Holland, Ty, and the board of directors I'd met with. I'd been out all day and hadn't seen Holland. I found myself wondering how her day had gone. The past weeks had been hectic for both of us, and I was learning that having someone there for you and *with* you through challenging times softened the blows life delivered.

I pulled in front of the house and saw Holland sitting on her stoop.

"Hey!" I got out and waved, clicking my key fob to set my car alarm.

"Hi." Holland still sounded deflated.

"Are you okay?"

Holland dragged in a breath, placed her hand on the back of her neck and rolled it, working out the kinks. "Not really."

Without waiting for an invitation, I sat beside her on the stoop. The street light illuminated her pretty face. Holland had been crying again. Or perhaps she'd never stopped.

"I'll be fine," she said, her voice barely above a whisper. "Just needed some air."

I took her response as code for "I'm not okay, but I'm not in the mood to talk about it." I recognized that language.

"Have you eaten?" I asked, hoping she'd say no. That would give me an excuse to spend more time with her. I didn't want to push and hoped she'd return to my bed soon. Before Holland, most of my intimate time with women included sex. Though the sex with her was crazy good, I craved being around her in any way I could get.

"Not hungry." Holland offered little conversation beyond her short answers. She rested her elbows on her knees and placed her chin on her fists.

I pressed, unable to leave her looking so sad. "Want to go for a ride?"

"Rain check?"

I didn't know what was wrong with Holland, but the pain it caused her was evident in her bloodshot eyes and the way her shoulders hung, like gravity's pull was solely trained on her. I wanted to take her into my arms again. Maybe make love to her, slow and deep. Let her lose herself in the decadence our bodies created together so she could forget her woes. But I wanted to know what she needed from me.

Whatever bothered her wasn't something I could offer distractions to help lift her mood. She'd closed herself off emotionally. I understood. Even without sharing, having someone be there helped. Despite the humidity, I felt the coolness emanating off her as I stood on the outside of the wall she'd erected.

"Listen," I said. She looked up at me with tearstained cheeks. How long had she been crying? "I'm in for the rest of the night. If you need anything—and I do mean anything, I'm right here. Okay?"

Holland managed a small smile and nodded. "Thank you."

I headed home, hating every step as I walked away, but knowing I needed to give her space.

Inside, I peeled off my clothes, damp from the humidity that robbed the air of comfort. With my mind full of Holland, I showered, wishing I could do something about the sadness that stabbed at her heart. I wanted to know what made her cry like that. Who had done it? My mood grew somber.

Stepping out of the shower, I caught a glimpse of myself in the mirror, staring squarely at my reflection. Who had I become? My ego was tattered behind steely eyes and a hard exterior. After losing my position, I became a fraction of the person I was a few weeks before. Something had happened to that alpha dude who built an empire. The man who went after what he wanted and got it, despite all obstacles.

Displacement and imposter syndrome had bruised my confidence. I wondered why would anyone want me to address a room full of business leaders when I no longer had a business to lead? Those were the thoughts that had plagued me since the layoff.

"You built one of the largest beverage companies from scratch, that's why." I heaved in a deep breath as I dried my body in the steamy bathroom. That was something to forever be proud of.

I was becoming a new version of myself. Credit was partially due to Ty, Tim, and even Holland. They'd said I needed to live a little. But Holland made me remember what it was like to feel something besides the quick adrenaline shot of pride that came with work accomplishments. I still battled dark thoughts about my value, but I felt myself changing.

I rummaged through my drawers for comfortable sweats and then looked at the numbers glowing red on my nightstand as I pulled them on. It was after nine at night. Normally, I would have been just leaving work.

Flopping on my oversize king bed, I pointed the remote at the television. The screen illuminated. Muting the sound, I continued the dialogue in my head. Didn't I have a social life once? I rifled through my mental files and realized every event I had recently attended was on behalf of Push—golf outings, conferences, lunches, and dinners. Besides Ty, I didn't have lots of close friends. He understood my drive and shared in my successes. Yet, he still managed several relationships.

I couldn't recall going on a date after being with Piper. I picked up my phone, tapped, and swiped my way to Piper's Facebook page. A reel started with a clip of her hand sporting a massive diamond with undulating letters that said "I said yes," then faded and swirled through pictures and videos chronicling her journey from her engagement through her wedding day.

When Piper and I started dating, we frequented all the popular restaurants and lounges, but after a while, I'd crash at her place after work or she'd come to mine. There were no "baecations."

My cell phone rang and Dad's number lit the display. I wasn't ready for him yet, so I listened to the trill until he went to voicemail. Dad required a level of emotional sturdiness that I wasn't ready for. Guilt compelled me to text Tanya to ask how he was healing.

Slowly, she texted back.

Thanks, I responded.

My phone chimed. I tapped the app for my security camera. Holland was at my front door. Holding down the microphone icon, I announced, "Coming."

Remembering I was bare-chested, I grabbed a T-shirt from a drawer and tugged it over my head while I jogged down the steps to the door.

I knew the probability of dating Holland on an ongoing basis was close to nil, but if I had the chance, I'd give her as much time and attention as she needed, regardless of work. Her magnetic pull drew my undivided attention when she was present and commanded my focus in her absence. How was that possible in the short time I'd known her?

"Hey," I said, pulling the door open.

"Mind a little company?" she asked without looking at me.

"Anytime." I stepped aside for her to come in. "Long day, again?"

Holland dragged in a breath. "And then some."

I held the door open, thrilled that she was there. Holland stepped into me and laid her head on my chest.

"I didn't want to be alone."

Pushing the door closed, I wrapped my arms around Holland in the foyer. I let her settle there, feeling her body quiver from her tears. Then I walked her to the couch, where she folded herself against me, nestling into the crook of my arm.

I didn't ask questions. Didn't offer a listening ear. I let her cry herself into a fitful sleep right there in my arms. I did it for her, not me for a change.

I could learn how to prioritize the right woman and be the man I needed to be—especially this woman.

Nineteen

Holland

The security camera's chimes interrupted my early morning listening routine from my bed. I'd grown accustomed to taking in the sounds of the neighborhood, the hum of engines, the clicks of heels, and the chatter of people walking by. I enjoyed the symphony of kids crying and laughing, music blasting and fading as cars drove by. It had become the background rhythm that filled the space around me like a steady grounding presence, reminding me I wasn't alone.

Then the doorbell rang. Noble usually texted before showing up, and Ms. Elsie yelled my name from the moment she entered the gate.

Who was at my door so early in the morning on a Saturday, when 9:00 a.m. felt like 6:00 a.m. because I'd hardly slept? Not wanting to be alone, I'd gone to Noble's house for the past few nights and lay in his arms before returning home just before dawn to continue tossing and turning. My mother's words—*Let me explain*—constantly churned in my brain, robbing me of focus and sleep ever since. *Exhaustion* wasn't a strong enough word to describe how tired I felt. My eyes were puffed from crying, making me look like I'd been punched.

Luckily, my phone hadn't shattered when I had tossed it. I grabbed it and headed downstairs. I'd never connected to my aunt's security app, so the only way to see who was outside was to look out the window. I froze.

Willing myself to move, I took steady steps to the door and swung it open.

"Ma?" All my breath escaped in that one word.

I blinked, as if the image of her standing on my porch dressed in all black was something my fatigue had conjured up. Clearly, she was real. Her near eighty years curved her forward, making it seem like she was always leaning in to get a closer look.

Ma. Patricia. The two options vacillated in my head. What was I supposed to call her now?

"What—"

"Can I come in?" she asked, her voice low and even.

I couldn't find the words to respond.

"Can we talk?" a beat passed before she added, "Please."

I wanted to say no. Wanted to shut the door in her face. But she was still my mother—the woman who raised me. My upbringing wouldn't allow me to be so rude. I stepped aside. That was all the welcome I was able to give.

Carefully, she let herself in, filling the entrance with a tension as stifling as smoke. It choked me, and from the way she looked, it made her eyes water,

Ma looked around the empty space and huffed. She pursed her lips and pinned me with a pleading gaze. I loved her. I was angry with her. But more than anything, I was crushed by her betrayal. All of those feelings had me conflicted.

I walked away, not wanting her to see me cry. She didn't

deserve any more of my tears. Folding my arms, I left her in the entry and sat in the window bay.

Ma closed the door, turned the lock, and stepped farther into the house. The old wood floors creaked under the weight of her footsteps, breaking the silence between us. She scanned the emptied first floor from the front window where I sat, to the kitchen in the back, and turned toward the stairs. Dragging in another breath, she let it out slowly.

Setting her purse and small overnight bag on the floor, Ma came to me.

"I can explain," she said, just above a whisper.

Hot tears pooled in my eyes. I swatted at them before they could roll down my cheeks. My bottom lip trembled, so I pulled it inside my mouth. Instead of completely falling apart, I focused on random things outside the window, but I could see her wringing her hands in my periphery.

"I..." she started and paused.

"All this time." I sniffed. "You knew all of them." Words rushed from me, quivering and soggy. "And you said nothing. *Nothing!*"

She looked at me, eyes moistening. Then, she reached out, but drew her hand back. I faced her, biting my bottom lip, my face wet with tears.

"Please. No more lies." My voice sounded so small. "I deserve the truth."

She swallowed thickly. Walking to the window, she sat facing me and took my hand in hers. I pulled my hand back.

"The truth. Please." I wiped the wetness from my chin.

Ma looked down at her hands. She was wringing them again. "You needed a home, so I—"

"Don't do that!" I yelled. "Don't make this about me needing anything. Why did *you* do it?" My heart slammed against my chest.

Ma closed her eyes and swallowed again. "You'd lost your mother. Not even a year later, your grandmother died from the same kind of cancer. I was a widow. Couldn't have children. I wanted one so bad. Just one." A sob erupted from her, and she covered her mouth, letting the emotion tumble through her. She returned to wringing her hands and then continued. "I used to babysit you all the time. You were the sweetest child." She sniffed and wiped the tears from her face.

Silence wrapped around us. The weight of our emotions sucked the air from the room.

Pulling herself up, she sat straighter. "Goldie was always on the road. Her own family wouldn't see her for months. Lying in that hospice, Clara worried about dying so soon after your mother. She wondered how Goldie would be able to take care of you. Would she have to drag you on the road with her? Would she have to quit show business? Singing was all she knew how to do. She had never worked a real job."

I looked at the ceiling, trying to stop myself from crying.

Ma continued. "Goldie stayed at Clara's house for a while after the funeral. But then she had to go on the road again. She trusted me, and asked if you could stay with me until she got back. Of course, I said yes. Then, you got sick one day, and I tried to reach Goldie but she was out of the country. So I…" The faster she wrung her hands, the faster she talked. "I just… I got so upset…thinking." She huffed. "I understood why Clara was concerned, I…you…before she got back," Ma rambled. She stood, facing me, crying out her words. "I thought I was doing the right thing, giving you a stable home—Goldie couldn't." She sniffed. "I was so lonely. I needed you. So—" she stopped talking abruptly. Her chest heaved, and then she blurted out, "I left." The words tumbled from her lips hard and fast. Her mouth quivered.

I shot to my feet. "No." I scoffed. "You *kidnapped* me. You took me away from the only family I had." Even filled with sobs, my words were sharp enough to slice through her. A part of me wanted the pain to cut her to the core. "Left me with *nothing*. I could have known her. I missed a lifetime with her because of you."

Ma dropped her head into her hands and wailed. Sobs shook her entire body. "I never meant to hurt anybody."

I ached, watching her in pain. I wanted to hug her and wrap my arms around her, like she had done with me so many times, but I wrapped my arms around myself. I had to hold me up.

Her cries filled the room until silence once again settled between us again, with only small sniffles as interruptions.

I sat back down in the window. "You robbed me of so much." My voice was surprisingly calm. "I never got to know my aunt Goldie. It feels unfair that you know more about my family than me. I have no memories to savor."

Ma sat in the window with me. "I am so sorry. I wanted to give you a good life. I hope one day you'll understand and can forgive me."

I turned away so I couldn't see her in my peripheral. We sat that way for a long time before she got up. I felt her hesitate before walking toward the entrance. She grabbed her purse next to her overnight bag, rifled through it, and pulled something out.

"This is where I'm staying." She placed a card on the window bay. "I'm here until Wednesday if you want to talk. I can stay longer if you..." She let the words fall into silence.

I wouldn't look at her. I couldn't.

Slowly, she gathered her bags and let herself out. I sat in the window weeping, watching her leave. Watched the woman who mothered me walk away, too hurt not to let her go. This loss, I had participated in, and it ached. I was so tired of losing.

Twenty

Noble

Productive meetings and great workouts always made me feel better. I started my day with both. As expected, my "fresh perspective" was indeed a code word for *younger*. As one of the youngest members, I'd been tasked with joining the committee for the next event and attracting more potential board members my age. I was up for the challenge. The first person I thought about asking was Ty. It would be a good look for him too.

I spent the afternoon at the agency, getting to know the leadership and staff, and even met a few of the young people they helped.

Brayden, a lanky thirteen-year-old with twists and a slight dusting of facial hair was one of the first young men I met. His large brown eyes didn't conceal the grief he grappled with from losing his parents in a car accident. A few minutes with him reminded me of the lonely boy I'd once been, solidifying my desire to do as much as I could for this organization and kids like him. I no longer cared if being on this board was a good look or not.

As I left Chosen Alliance that evening, my mind shifted to Holland. She hadn't come to me the past few nights. When I checked in on her, she was still upset, but kept to herself. I didn't want to impose, but I needed to make sure she was okay.

In my home office, I checked my emails to see if there were any responses to my recent job interviews. That didn't take my mind off Holland so I texted her.

Me: Hey

Holland: Hi Noble.

I was glad she responded right away.

I smiled, of course. It had become my immediate reaction when it came to Holland.

Me: Are you okay?

Holland: I've had much better days.

Me: How about a great distraction?

Holland: Lol. Like what?

Me: Just say yes or no.

Holland: Your house or mine?

Me: Mine.

Holland: Be right there. Thanks, Noble.

I pumped my fist like a kid conquering the next level in his favorite video game. After shutting down my computer, I strutted out of my home office and headed downstairs to get ready for Holland's arrival.

I plopped on my leather couch, grabbed the remote, and pointed it at the TV. It still felt odd being home in the middle of the day on a weekday, but I was finally feeling better about my situation. I'd have to give Holland credit for that. She'd become the brightest part of my days. It was time for me to return the favor.

The doorbell rang and I hopped up.

"Hey!" I pushed the door open. She didn't look like she was feeling any better. "Come on in."

"Hey, Noble." Her quiet response made her accent deeper.

"You made any more progress today?" I asked, leading the way to the kitchen. "Something to drink?" I inquired, tossing the words over my shoulder.

"Yeah. Packed up most of my room and then swept and mopped all the empty rooms now that the furniture is gone. The place still needs a paint job. The real estate agent is coming tomorrow. Thanks to you, I'm ahead of schedule." Holland sucked in a breath and exhaled with a sigh. "What do you have to drink?"

I halted. "That sounds like you may need something stronger than soda."

"Humph!" Holland released a small chuckle.

I pivoted. "I've got you covered." Heading back to the living room, I pulled open my cellarette. Scanning the shelves, I announced the options. "It's five p.m. somewhere. How strong do you want to get? I've got scotch, wine, rum…"

"A glass of wine would be nice."

"Red? White?"

Holland twisted her lips and looked up. "Do you have any chocolate?"

"Yep."

"Then I'll take red. Got a good Cab in there?"

"Cabernet and Snickers coming up."

Holland fell over laughing. "What a fancy combination."

I pulled a bottle and glasses from the cabinet and carried them to the kitchen. Holland climbed onto one of the stools at the island. On the opposite side, I took two Snickers out of the fridge and, just for the heck of it, cut them into bite-size pieces and plated them. I filled our glasses hallway and pushed the combo in front of Holland. "Voila!"

Holland held her glass in the air. I delicately tapped mine against hers, and she laughed. Together, we said, "Cheers."

"Are you this luxurious with all your lady friends?" Holland raised her brows in mock amazement.

"Oh. It gets better. Back when I got my very first apartment. I had just started dating this girl. My company wasn't making enough money for me to get paid yet, so I barely had two nickels to rub together, but I knew I had to do something for Valentine's Day. Dinner at a nice restaurant was not in my nonexistent budget. The only furniture I had besides a bed was a folding table and two chairs. I went to the dollar store and grabbed anything I could find for a floor picnic. Ha! We had place mats, wine glasses filled with beer, and Chinese food. I thought it was pretty cool." I puffed my chest out.

"What did she say?" Holland grinned behind her glass.

"She thought it was *creative*. Needless to say, the relationship didn't last."

"Aw," Holland chuckled. "But that was so cute. I would have given you an A for effort."

"Thanks. I was proud of my struggle picnic," I said, popping a piece of Snickers in my mouth.

Holland's laughter faded, and sadness filled her eyes again. Despite her solemn expression, she was still beautiful. I watched her work her jaw around the chocolate and couldn't help but think about being in bed with her again. I decided to figure out how to keep seeing Holland.

I'd never been to Florence or Charleston but didn't mind going. It would be even better if she stayed in New York.

"Feeling any better today?" I said, pouring more wine into my glass.

Holland cupped her glass with both hands, like she was holding a mug filled with cocoa instead of a glass of wine. She set her eyes on the countertop and sighed. Then she lifted her head and grunted. "I'm not sure."

"Want to talk about it?"

Holland took a long sip, nearly finishing her crimson elixir. "I'm finding out way more about my past than I imagined, and it's not all good."

I rounded the island and sat closer to her on one of the stools. "Families are never perfect."

"My mother was here over the weekend."

"Oh. All the way from South Carolina? That's cool."

"Is it?" Holland gnawed on her bottom lip.

"Oh?" I sat up straight, giving her my full attention.

Holland dragged in a breath. "I'm discovering things about her that I never knew. I feel blindsided and betrayed." Holland blinked rapidly and took a long sip of her wine. She carefully placed the glass back on the countertop and a single tear slid down her beautiful face. She wiped it away and cleared her throat. "Sorry."

"No apology necessary. If it helps any, I have a pretty difficult relationship with my dad too."

"Yeah?" Her eyes held pity, and her voice was soft.

Taking a breath, I contemplated whether or not I should share the darkest part of my past. Somehow, I knew I could.

"During my sophomore year in high school, he left us. Cheated on my mom. When she refused to take him back, he started drinking. He'd been a decent father up until that point, but the drinking changed everything. He stopped coming around and when he did, he'd be drunk and would stand in front of the house, yelling for me and my mother to come out. He moved in with the woman he'd cheated with and didn't help us financially. My mother was fighting cancer while dealing with my dad's infidelity, but never told us. By my senior year in high school, he had left and she could no longer hide her sickness. She spent the next few years in and out of treatment and was gone by the time I started grad school. I was alone and Dad got worse."

Holland's gasp was barely audible. "I'm so sorry to hear that." Gently, she placed her soft hand over mine and a warm flame inched up my arm, feeling more comforting than sensual.

My father abandoned me twice. First with his infidelity. Second, when he wasn't there for me after losing Mom. I used to be mad at Tanya, but realized it wasn't entirely her fault. She was the one keeping me updated about Dad all these years. His drinking had been a thorn in their marriage since day one.

No one knew my story besides Ty and Tim. Now Holland did. I wanted her to know everything about me. And I wanted her to know that she wasn't alone when it came to family trauma and what it felt like to be alone.

"If you don't mind me asking, what kind of cancer did she have?"

"She died of breast cancer and a broken heart. She only told us when she knew she could no longer beat it. The shock of finding out just when we were about to lose her was the hardest thing I ever lived through."

A familiar tightening balled in my belly. I exhaled slow and steady, the way my old therapist told me to.

Mom's death deepened the fault line between me and my

dad, permanently setting our relationship on shaky ground. Despite marrying Tanya, he numbed his sorrows with alcohol. I numbed mine by filling every moment with work and college studies, leaving minimal time to dwell on the feeling that I'd lost both parents. Leftover anger warmed my chest. My jaw was set so tightly it hurt. I reminded myself to breathe again.

I looked into Holland's eyes, moist and soft with pity. She drew her mouth downward into a frown. There was something familiar about the way sadness darkened her eyes before she cast them to the floor. "Sorry to hear that," she said. Holland knew this pain personally.

"I found pictures of my mom." After a few silent moments, she added, "Learning so much made me curious about my dad. I'd love to find some information about him too."

What was worse? Being strangers with the dad you knew all your life, or never knowing your father at all?

"Family." I laughed to myself, still surprised about revealing some of my most painful memories to a woman I had known for less than a month.

Silence entered the conversation again, but it didn't feel awkward or sully the atmosphere with anxiety. With her hand over mine, it was comforting.

I didn't want to push Holland if she didn't feel like talking. Her head hung low. I watched her shove the chocolate around on the plate, wishing I could somehow erase the things that caused her pain.

"Yeah. Family," she said after a long while—her words drenched in sarcasm and melancholy.

I felt that deep in my soul and let it marinate.

When enough discomfort had passed, I said, "You've been working nonstop since you've been here, only stopping to shop and go to the gala." I got off the stool and stepped closer to her. "It's time for a reprieve. That's why I called. Let me take you out. It's not a date. It's two people needing a break, getting out, and leaving the parts of life that suck behind for just a while."

Holland's eyes roamed as she pondered my suggestion. "I could use a break." Her small smile knocked on the door of my heart.

"Let's go," I said, grabbing her hand and leading her to the car before she changed her mind.

Inside, I selected a playlist on my phone with a smooth vibe. Holland exhaled. Her shoulders lowered and she sat back. Both of us bobbed to the beat floating from the speakers.

"This is Isaiah Falls, right?"

I nodded. "He's got a chill vibe."

"Yeah. I like his music."

"Who else do you like?" I wanted to know everything about her.

"Besides old school?" She tilted her head, tapping her chin as she thought. "I like Lucky Daye, Muni Long, Drake, and of course, Beyoncé. Throw in a little bit of Taylor Swift, here and there."

"You're a Swiftie?" I asked, struggling to keep my eyes on the road instead of her.

Holland giggled and it sounded better than the music.

"Not exactly. Nor am I part of the BeyHive, but I like some of their songs. Growing up in the church, I also listen to a lot of gospel. Love me some Tasha Cobbs and Koryn Hawthorne."

"Okay. Those are all good. I have to admit, I haven't been to church much since my mother passed."

"Hmm. I may have to drag you with me one Sunday."

"I'm cool with that," I agreed, unable to mask the smile that eased across my face. The idea of any kind of plans with Holland kept me hopeful. I knew she was here temporarily, but the more time I spent with her, the more I wanted her to stay.

"What about you?" she asked, breaking through my thoughts of her.

"Well, you already know I love old school too. Some of the artists you named are cool. I'll add Frank Ocean and Chase Shakur to your list, and I like vibing to jazz."

"We have an amazing jazz restaurant back home. You'd love it. The music is great, and the food?" Holland groaned and rolled her eyes toward the roof. "It's delicious."

"But is it better than mine?" I winked.

"I can't lie. You've got skills in the kitchen."

"Outside the kitchen too." I smirked, knowing she would blush.

As anticipated, redness blossomed across Holland's pretty face. She closed her eyes and shook her head.

"You're bad." Holland swatted my arm.

"Oh so bad, baby!"

Holland threw her head back and laughed. The sound riffed through the air like smooth jazz. I held the wheel with both hands to keep from crashing. The sexy lines of her neck begged for me to kiss her there. Her sound, scent, and gestures could be bottled and sold.

"Hrs & Hrs" by Muni Long came on and Holland cranked up the volume. "I love this song!" She crooned into her fist like she was holding a microphone.

To my delight and surprise, she had a beautiful voice—a songbird. As if I needed another reason to fall for her. Holland sang the entire song and I wished it would never end.

I'd had my pick of women over the years. All of them were extremely attractive. But none of them gripped me the way Holland had. It wasn't just the sway of her hips, the natural sexy fullness of her breasts, her pretty face, or the full head of wild hair that I enjoyed running my fingers through. There was a depth to her. An inner beauty that resonated from her—a warmth that I wanted to sink into. When Holland looked at me, I felt like I was the only person in her world—like I was soaking in her attention. I never knew I longed for such a thing.

We continued on the musical tip, singing, laughing, and swapping favorites as routine traffic on the Belt Parkway gave me time to enjoy her. Holland passed her imaginary microphone for duets with artists like Drake. I hadn't had fun like this with a woman in years. I pointed out landmarks and the lines separating the boroughs.

"Queens looks different than Brooklyn," she said, noticing the changing landscapes.

Minutes later, I pulled up in front of the St. Albans Greatest mural on Linden Boulevard in St. Albans.

"This is amazing!" Holland said, hopping out the second I finished parking. "Can we take pictures?" She handed me her phone before I had a chance to answer.

With big toothy smiles, Holland posed in front of Billie Holiday, Ella Fitzgerald, James Brown, and others. I snapped picture after picture, like she was a supermodel in a magazine photoshoot, enticed by the way she maneuvered in front of the images.

"Come take some with me." She waved me over, taking the phone. "Smile!" she said, snapping selfies.

She took a few with the two of us smiling and holding up two fingers, then made a silly face. Teasing, I raised a brow at her silliness. She snapped those too then poked me with her elbow.

"Come on," she chided. "You have to make a face too."

"No, I don't." I waved her off.

"Mr. CEO too cool for funny face pics?"

I twisted my lips at her. She challenged me with those pretty eyes.

"It will be just between you and me, I promise." Holland pouted and dammit, I obliged.

"Just one!"

I crossed my eyes and stuck out my tongue. Cackling, Holland tilted her head, scrunched her nose like she smelled something foul, and then snapped a bunch of shots.

"That's it. I'm done." I stepped aside.

Holland opened her photos, swiped through the pictures and bent over laughing.

"Let me see." She turned the phone to me and swiped. I had to admit the pictures were pretty funny. Not many women could have gotten me to do that. I was learning that for Holland, I'd do almost anything.

"Ever heard of A Tribe Called Quest?"

"Of course. I'm an old-school-music lover."

We rode down Linden Boulevard to 192nd Street to see the A Tribe Called Quest mural painted on the side of the cleaners. Together, we sang the chorus of "Can I Kick It?" while taking selfies next to the artists' faces on the wall.

The light returned to Holland's sad eyes. The frown she'd been sporting was now a smile that showcased her pearly white teeth.

Back in the car, I cruised through my old neighborhood, showing her the places I frequented growing up. Told her how close-knit our blue-collar community used to be, and how doctors, teachers, bus drivers, and those who struggled to make ends meet like my family all blended together seamlessly.

I swung a left off Linden Boulevard, maneuvered through the side streets, and slowed as I passed the skinny duplex we lived in before betrayal and heartbreak slithered in like a snake in the night and desecrated our happy home. My father lived there now, having moved in with his new wife when I decided not to return to Queens after I had graduated. It no longer felt like home.

I slowed as I passed, seeing his pickup was in the driveway. Tanya's car was parked behind his.

"Who lived here?"

"I did." I didn't bother saying that Dad was there now. It wasn't the time to go into those details.

Holland studied the home. "Cool."

We made one more stop before heading back. A few blocks away, I pulled in front of a bodega with a few teens with their pants hanging below their waists decorating the storefront.

"Come inside with me," I said before getting out and rounding the car. I opened her door and reached for her smooth, soft hand, and then led her inside the store.

"What! Look-at-whah-the-cat-drug-in," Oscar practically yelled in a thick Puerto Rican accent, smashing all of his words together. Growing up, the neighborhood kids called him Papi.

Coming down off his stool behind the counter, Papi limped toward me with wide open arms. Age slowed his gait, tinted his hair gray, and creased the lines around his lips and eyes.

"What's up, Papi?"

His long arms swallowed me in a fatherly embrace.

"Long time, Noble. Long time." Papi looked over at Holland and grinned. "And who's this pretty lady?"

"My *friend*," I said, stressing the word *friend*. "Holland."

Smiling, Holland held out her hand, "Nice to meet—"

Before she could finish, Papi pulled her in for a hug. "A friend of my boy Noble is a friend of mine," he said with a wide grin. "He be nice to you? If not, I beat him up." Papi held up his fists then wrapped his strong arm around my neck to fake-choke me.

"He's been really nice," she said with a smile. "I'll let you know if he needs some straightening out."

Papi roared. "Oh! I like this one." His belly shook when he laughed. "We got your drink over here." Papi pointed to one of the refrigerators filled with Push Beverages. I didn't have the emotional capacity yet to explain to him that I wasn't with the company anymore. "The young ones love it," he continued. "They know it's yours." Papi looked at Holland. "Noble used to work here. Sure did," he added, as if she'd questioned the validity of his statement. "Stocked shelves, ran the register. Never had to run him out for stealing like those other knuckleheads," he said with a deep nod.

"Oh, he was a good one, huh?" Holland said, looking at me with a sideways smile.

"It's great to see you, Papi. We need to head back to Brooklyn though," I said, cutting the visit short before Papi launched into stories about me being popular with the girls in the neighborhood.

He'd taken an interest in keeping me off the streets like the other knuckleheads, as he called them. Said he saw something in me. Knew I was going to make it big.

"Leaving so soon?" Papi frowned. "Don't take so long to visit next time."

"I won't," I said, guiding Holland out by the small of her back.

"Nice meeting you," Holland said, waving.

"Let me know if you need me to punch him out. Ha!" Papi's laugh bellowed, reaching the aged ceiling.

We said our final goodbyes as he walked us to the car parked in front of the store.

"Ready to head back?"

"Sure. This was great," Holland said. "I feel like I'm getting to see the real New York. My cousin Amy would be proud."

Traffic on the Belt Parkway was predictably heavy on the way back to Brooklyn, giving me more time with Holland.

Inspired by our mini music session while visiting the A Tribe Called Quest mural, Holland became the self-proclaimed car DJ, sending us down old-school memory lane.

"You know this one?" Holland played "The Rain (Supa Dupa Fly)," by Missy Elliott.

"Ha! Of course. Let that one play." I tapped the rhythm into the steering wheel.

Holland sang every word, chair dancing and snapping her fingers. She closed her eyes when hitting the higher notes, and shimmied to the beat. I enjoyed the show and Holland's rich, soulful voice. The raspy quality was sexy. She had the kind of voice that got inside of you and made you feel things.

"You've got quite a voice there."

Holland stopped singing, and blushed. "Thanks."

"Oh, don't get shy on me now."

"Not shy, dude. The song is over," she chuckled.

"Then sing something else for me."

Holland looked at me incredulously. "Like what?"

"Hold on. Let me think." I wanted to challenge her. "Mm. How about 'Hello' by Adele."

"That's one of my favorite songs. It's so beautiful and incredibly sad."

"So. Let's hear it."

Holland turned her body toward me. "You really want me to sing?"

"Yep."

She huffed. "All right. I sang in the choir back home at my church." She cleared her throat and then moaned the first few chords. Even her moans were soulful and perfect. Holland closed her eyes and sang the first verse, increasing the intensity. She belted out the chorus, her voice powerful and deep.

"Holy shit!" My words surprised me. I moved my head to the beat she snapped with her fingers. I wanted to close my eyes and feel every note, but I was driving. She gave me another thing to like about her.

Holland kept her eyes closed seconds after she finished her last harrowing note. She brought every emotion in the lyrics to life, reminding me of what heartbreak felt like. I took a deep breath.

"Whoa! That was…" I couldn't think of an adjective that would do her justice. I settled on "Incredible."

She smiled. "Thanks."

"If you were my girl, you'd have to sing to me all the time. Like, 'Breakfast is ready, baby,'" I said in my worst possible voice, which was basically my true singing voice.

Holland laughed, slapping my arm playfully. "You're so silly."

"I'm so serious. Amazing. Just amazing. I guess singing runs in your blood."

"I guess it does." I wanted to kiss her right on her flushed cheek.

"You hungry? I know this amazing Italian restaurant over in Sheepshead Bay. New York has the best Italian restaurants."

"I wish I could. I have something I should handle this evening."

"Oh." *Damn*. I wasn't ready for our time together to end.

"Noble?"

"Yes?"

"Thank you for this." Her voice was calm. Serious. "It was just what I needed. You make New York feel cozy and not so big and scary."

"I'm glad you enjoyed it. I needed it too. I'll be around for the rest of the night if you need anything."

I dreaded pulling up in front of our houses. Holland kissed my cheek, thanked me again, and headed inside her house. I missed her immediately.

Twenty-One

Holland

I'd never seen Ma—I mean, Patricia—look so broken. I was still angry with her and didn't want to call her, Ma, but she was the only mother I'd known. A good mother, at that. Yet, I needed time to reconcile everything that I'd learned.

"I want to know everything. Is there anything else you've kept from me?" I said the second she opened her hotel room door.

Her inhale was sharp and her exhale deliberate. "Come on in."

I marched past her, through the narrow room with a king-size bed monopolizing the space, and straight to the window. Night had descended on us, and the view of the lights twinkling in the city landscape was halfway obstructed by the building next to us.

"C-can I get you anything?" she asked nervously.

"No," I said, and threw in "Thanks" as an afterthought. "Please, just tell me about my family." Folding my arms across my chest, I shifted my weight onto one foot and anxiously tapped the other. I had no idea what I was about to hear. "And don't leave anything out."

Pulling her robe closed, Ma sat on the bed and brought a cup of tea to her lips. She was stalling. I waited. I had all night, and she wasn't due to leave until the morning. She looked at me, her expression pleading.

"This was why you never let me go anywhere when I was younger, why you wouldn't let me go away to college, wasn't it?" I couldn't handle the silence. "You were always afraid I'd find out."

Ma turned away, resting her eyes on the mess of sheets on the bed. She smoothed a random section.

"Your grandma, Clara, was my best friend growing up. When your mother was born, she made me her godmother."

I tried to catch my breath, and blinked back the stinging in my eyes. I didn't want to cry, but my emotional barricade couldn't stand against the blow she'd just delivered with her confession. And she was just getting started.

"You were like my own grandchild. I was there when your mother got sick, then your grandma. Goldie was never around. When she ran off to be with that singing boy, Clara and I were only around twelve, maybe thirteen." She shrugged her shoulders, trying to recall the age. "The family barely saw her at all. Then Jonah died. His band broke up and one of the girls started singing for bigger acts. She got Goldie a gig and that changed everything for them."

I remembered from the journal that my aunt Goldie's mother threw her out because she sang "the devil's music." She couldn't come back.

"No more bars," Ma continued. "They were big-time, singing backup for the biggest rhythm and blues stars at places like the Apollo. She came home a few times a year. That was it. When Clara's mother got sick from her diabetes, I helped Clara take care of her. Not Goldie. She was…" Ma looked up at me. My eyes met hers squarely. "Gone all the time." She stood and slowly walked across the room. "We did everything without her. Y-you needed somebody—" She stopped abruptly.

The way Ma spoke of Goldie like she wasn't family made my blood run hot. I couldn't stand still any longer, so I paced the small patch of carpet by the bed. But I understood Goldie. She wanted, no, *needed* more than a small town like Aiken could offer. Her desire to leave had been even bigger than mine. Only she was brave enough to leave her small nest, which made her an outcast in her own family.

"Then Clara met Charles. He ran off when she told him she was pregnant with your mama. Yona was a beautiful child." Ma shook her head slowly, smiling at the memory of my mother. She remained quiet for a moment.

"I'd gotten married, but that didn't last after we found out I couldn't make babies right.

"Clara was right there to help me through my grief when I kept losing my babies." Tears trickled down her cheeks. "The doctor told me not to try again. Everything was all messed up down there. I made money babysitting for the working people in the neighborhood. I guess all those babies being around all the time was some kind of reminder. He left. Moved North for work."

Ma sat back down and huffed.

"Your mother went off to school up in Virginia. She came back pregnant in the middle of her junior year, had you, and finished her schooling at home."

"Where was my father?" The words rushed out.

"Somewhere up North. He didn't know. She refused to tell us who he was. Said she could take care of her baby on her own just like her mother took care of her. A few years later, she was diagnosed with breast cancer. That's when she finally gave Clara his name. Told your mother that he moved out of the country but later said, his big dreams didn't include an unexpected baby and she didn't want to stand in his way. By then, the only thing Clara could focus on was taking care of Yona, but it was too late to save her. Clara's cancer came back too, but after losing Yona, she didn't try to fight it. The illness and heartbreak took her out less than a year later."

Streaming tears pooled under my chin. I didn't bother to wipe them away. So much loss, sadness, and grief.

She huffed. "I thought I was doing the right thing by Clara by not letting you go to New York. You'd spent more time with me than your aunt, and you had already lost so much. You knew me better than her. Goldie came around on holidays and special occasions. Until your mother got sick, you were at my house almost every day."

Ma turned to me with pleading in her eyes. At first, I couldn't speak, and then I was able to mumble, "And then what?"

"I went to Florence, moved in with my cousin, Amy's ma, and changed my last name. Had a friend help me register a new name and start over—become somewhat untraceable."

I stepped closer to her. "So when that letter came from the lawyers in New York, you knew what it was about."

Tightening her robe, she looked away. "They found us. It was time."

My body trembled from the dangerous cocktail of rage and anguish whirling inside of me. A damn broke in my chest, and I crossed my hands over my stomach as if I could hold in the pain thundering in my gut.

I cried for my mother, Grandma Clara, and Aunt Goldie. I cried for the father I never had a chance to know. I cried for the love, loss, and grief that was a constant presence in their lives. I even cried for Ma's lonely, dejected existence and the fact that the only family she could claim was one she had to steal.

Ma held me. Slid to the floor with me. We cried together.

"I'm so sorry, Holly. I never meant to hurt you." She sobbed. "Please forgive me."

I wanted to tell her how much pain she caused me—scold her about everything that she took from me. But I knew she already understood. I was the one thing she was able to hold onto, until now. It was no wonder I'd felt like I needed to break out of the life I'd been living. I thought about my sister Patience. Was she stolen too?

I sat up and wiped the wetness from my face. "What about Patience?" I locked eyes with her, to see the truth regardless of what she said.

"Patience is different. She was a foster child. I adopted her through an agency. Legally," she added. "I love her. I love you. You're my babies. All that I've ever really had that loved me back."

I unfolded myself from her and got up from the floor. Pacing, I ran my hands through my hair. My emotions were a tangled mess of yarn. If I tried to pull at one string, I would completely unravel.

It was time to go.

"Bye, Ma." Her quiet sniffles followed me to the door.

When the Uber rolled up in front of my house, I wasn't ready to go inside. I didn't want to be alone.

I found myself walking up to Noble's door. I rang the bell and tapped my feet nervously until he came to the door. No shirt. Just sweats. The light from the television flickered behind him, bathing him in a halo. I could have used the company of an angel.

Life as I knew it was a lie, but the way Noble made me feel was real. I wasn't disillusioned by my pain. I wasn't trying to bury it with a vice. I knew exactly what I was doing. He had been a salve these past few nights, and I desperately needed soothing right now.

"Hey," he said, with lips molded perfectly for kissing.

My eyes locked with his. Noble raised both brows. I didn't bother with greetings or salutations. I stepped in, snaked my hands around his neck, and pulled him to me. My elixir. I moaned into his mouth. I saw the fireworks and felt the explosion. Numbed the pain. Noble squeezed me in his arms, deepening our kiss with a hint of desperation. I pressed my body against his and felt his erection blossom immediately. A heat wave swelled around us.

Noble lifted me without breaking our kiss, wrapping my legs around his muscular waist. He steadied himself and then kicked the door shut, closing off the sounds of the living city. My back against the wall gave Noble leverage. Clinging to him, I lifted my chin to catch my breath. He kissed my neckline and then found my lips once more.

"Baby," he panted. "Holland." He was breathless. "Are you—"

"Shhhh!" I put my finger to his lips. "I just need you."

Noble's erection became a boulder. I swirled my hips against it.

Securing me in his arms, he carried me to his bedroom. Laying me gently on his bed, he sucked my lips. I yanked my tank top over my head and shimmied my shorts down. Standing, Noble grabbed a condom from his side table and reappeared in front of me so fast that it seemed like he had never moved.

Handing me the condom, Noble slid his sweats down, letting them fall to his ankles. He pulled down his boxer briefs, his erection springing free. My breath hitched.

I tore open the wrapper and smoothed the condom over his

shaft. He groaned toward the ceiling. Heat and desire twinkled in his brown eyes when he looked down at me.

I scooted back on the bed, making room for him. Crawling toward me with the grace of a panther, he captured my nipples between his teeth. First gnawing, then licking, and finally suckling, he continued until they pebbled against his tongue.

Ready to feel him inside, I wrapped my greedy hand around his stiffness, relishing in the girth.

"No," he whispered. "I want to take my time with you."

His words were deliciously agonizing—torture to my burning desire to have him inside me. Noble started his kisses at my lips, then moved down to my navel. Steam rose from every kiss, leaving a sultry blazing trail from my neck to the inside of my thighs, while his hands massaged my breasts. He left no parts uncharted. Noble kissed, sucked, nibbled, and licked me everywhere.

I writhed and ached with need, squirming under his fiery touch until I could no longer stand it.

"You okay?" he breathed.

I loved that Noble checked on me. I nodded vigorously, wanting him to hurry back to what he was doing.

"Ready?" he asked.

I wrapped my hand around his rock-hard erection and guided him toward the slickness waiting between my legs. That was my answer. Noble hissed, lifted my legs over his shoulders, and entered slowly, filling me up with friction so delectable, tiny bombs burst throughout my body. I drew a breath so sharp, it nearly choked me.

"Mm," I groaned. "Ahh!"

Noble swallowed my cries into his mouth. His strokes were deep and deliberate, each driving me further into euphoric bliss. He released my legs and cradled me in his arms, burying himself even deeper inside of me. His moans were baritone and guttural.

I'd never felt pleasure this profound. Noble found my lips again. He reared back, gazed into my eyes, and kissed me again. Tears pooled in the corners of my eyes, trickling down the sides of my face. Our moans were drumbeats. Our loving—rhythmic. Raising our hips, we collided in sync until we lost our rhythm and control. Noble bucked against me. The most ferocious release I'd ever felt exploded over him. Suddenly, I felt weightless. Noble gathered me in his arms and held me for the longest time. He gave me just what I needed. And then I wanted more.

Twenty-Two

Noble

"How did the interview go this morning?" Tim asked.

I stood up from the desk in my home office to twist and stretch. I'd been sitting in front of my laptop since I came back from the city.

"Seems like it went well. Felt more like an interrogation. There were six board members on that interview panel. I tried to use my usual charm," I said, trying to keep it light. "But I felt like I was in front of a firing squad."

"They can be intimidating," Tim agreed.

I was rusty at interviewing. Selling and charm, I had that in the bag, but I hadn't interviewed for a job since I was in grad school. The stakes were way higher, and imposter syndrome had entered the room uninvited a few times. I had to concentrate hard to decipher who was really talking, members of the panel, me, or my imposter syndrome. I reminded myself of my accomplishments with Push and felt a little better. My work there was unprecedented. I was proud of that.

"You have another one this week."

"Yeah. I feel good about them. One is a start-up. They're really interested in me helping get things off the ground. They got huge backing from an angel investor."

"Sounds good. I have another friend I'd like for you to meet. Can you do lunch on Thursday?"

"Let me check my calendar. Still empty! I'll be there," I joked.

Tim's laugh was small and unsure.

"You can go ahead and laugh, man," I said. "I've gotten past the woe-is-me stage of getting fired. And the time I've been spending getting to know the work at the agency has been great. I've met several of the kids and families we serve." I thought of Brayden and wondered how he was doing. I made a mental note to ask about him the next time I went by the office.

"I don't know if I would call what happened getting fired. The package you got was pretty awesome. I know because I made sure the board made it as sweet as possible." Tim laughed for real this time. "I'll send you the details for Thursday. I'm looking forward to seeing you."

"Me too. How's Ty doing as interim?" I really wanted him to succeed.

"Good. You've taught him well."

"Are they considering him for the position permanently?"

Tim took a moment to answer.

"No," he finally said. "They're looking for a seasoned leader. Ty's doesn't have that level of experience. He's never held the title himself."

"Yeah. I get it." I felt bad for Ty. He'd worked as hard as I had all these years. And I was pretty sure that when the new CEO took the position, they'd probably bring in a whole new leadership team. I hated to think it, but Ty's days were likely numbered too. That's how these things worked.

"Gotta run, Noble. See you Thursday."

"See you then,"

I wanted to call Ty and warn him, but refrained. I could bring him with me wherever I landed.

I returned to my email. One came in from one of the positions I wanted. Clicking the subject line, I opened the email. It took the wind out of my sails. It was yet another *While your qualifications were impressive…blah blah blah… Unfortunately…*

I shut my laptop. No need to finish reading. I didn't feel bad, though. I realized I needed a life more than I needed a job. Financially, I was well-off. All the other parts of my life were out of sorts. The further away I got from the dreadful day I was asked to leave, the more clarity I got about who I was and what I wanted. I'd never say leaving Push was good for me, but it forced me to reflect in a way that wouldn't have happened otherwise.

For the first time in ten years, I was thinking about myself, and I was finally excited to discover the things I truly wanted before stepping into my next role. I'd make room for life *and* work next time.

Holland came to mind. Actually, she stayed on my mind. Even better, she'd stayed in my bed the last several nights. Being with her made me realize there was so much more to life than just working. She shed light on the places I had ignored for so long. I hated watching her leave, but we both had things to take care of. We both had very separate, very different lives. Holland showed me what I was missing. Something that could lead to love. A partner who could be there for you when life tossed darts at you and they stung—bad.

I knew she was only here to sell her aunt's house, but I wished she was here to stay. I wanted Holland in every way. She wasn't impressed by my title. She couldn't care less about how much money I had. Hell, she hardly wanted me to spend my money on her. Holland was Holland, and when I was with her, I was Noble—not a CEO. My awards and credentials didn't matter. She wanted me just the way I was, unemployed and all.

I'd become successful by going after what I wanted. I wasn't going to stop now.

I texted Holland.

Me: Hey! Day going well?

The bubble with the three dots appeared briefly and disappeared without a text. I waited, and they came back.

I guess. Another bubble. Just a lot on my mind. Decisions.

Me: I get it. I've got some decisions I'm grappling with too.

Holland: Yeah. And I'm still figuring out what to do for my birthday.

Your birthday? I sent the shocked-big-eye emoji. When is your birthday?

Holland: Next weekend.

Me: We should celebrate before you leave. Italian restaurant?

Holland: Sure...

I'd never been in a long-distance relationship before, but I was willing to try. I just had to make the rest of Holland's time in New York memorable.

Twenty-Three

Holland

"Keep your eyes on the road!" I scolded Amy. We were doing our FaceTime ritual. She'd call me on her way to work or when she was heading home, and we'd yap the entire half-hour ride.

"Did you just say you canceled the meeting with the real estate agent on Saturday? Why?"

I huffed. "I don't know if I want to sell anymore."

"Mm. Okay. What happened to change your mind?"

"So many things. Ma came this weekend."

"She did? I didn't know. Patience didn't say anything, neither did my mom. How was the visit?"

I groaned. "I'll give you those details when you get to the house. There's a lot to this story. I wouldn't want you to crash."

"Holland! What kind of tea are you about to spill?" The rise of her tone told me she was concerned.

"Hot and potent."

"You scared me for a moment. Okay, I'll be there in five minutes. I'll call you when I get inside."

Minutes later, Amy called back. "I'm home now with a glass of wine in my hand. Now, what does your mother have to do with you selling the house?"

I braced myself with a deep breath. Emotionally, I was all over the place. I didn't know which emotion would trump the others once I got into my story.

"Let me start with this. I never imagined myself living in New York. Even when I first came, I thought this city had too much going on and everything moved too quickly. It was dizzying. It just seemed big and cold." I huffed. "I don't feel like that anymore. Noble, Ms. Elsie, and this neighborhood feel alive and cozy in a way I've never experienced. I've been slowly falling in love with it. Most importantly, it's the house. I feel at home. I feel my mother, grandmother, and aunt here, like a big hug. I love it more every day. Well, not the big rats part of the city, but the vibe."

"Wow, Hollz."

"I know. And…" I thought of Noble and my stomach fluttered. "I'm falling for this…place." *And Noble.*

"So you're staying? What about your apartment in Charleston?"

"I know. I have to figure this out. Here's the biggie. This house is the only thing I have left connecting me to my real family and I don't want to let that go. My mother, grandmother, and aunt walked these halls, slept in these rooms, and cooked in this kitchen. If I sell, I'll have nothing left of them besides some boxes of pictures, documents, and memorabilia. My room is here, all fixed up just for me. Ma's visit solidified my decision. I want to be here."

"Hollz. What happened with Aunt Patty?"

I closed my eyes and breathed again, trying to steady my emotions before continuing.

"I was never supposed to be with her, Amy."

"What? What does that even mean?"

I told Amy the entire story. On the screen, her mouth opened and closed as she listened. Tears welled in her eyes. She shook her head disbelievingly and covered her mouth, not saying a word until I finished.

"Holland. I can't believe this. I'm so sorry. Who knows about this? Does Patience know?"

"Patience doesn't know. No one knows. I assume Ma will have to tell her now. She got back home Wednesday evening."

"I don't know what to say."

"I know. But now do you see why I can't let this house go? It's all I have. I belong here."

"So what are you going to do?"

"I don't think I'm going back to Charleston. I'll have to get my things shipped and see if I can get out of my lease. I need to call the school and let them know I'm not taking the job, and then I'll have to find work here. My aunt didn't leave much money behind, but it's enough to get me by until I land something. The house is completely paid for, so having no mortgage or rent is helpful. It just needs work. Lots of work to make it mine. I was looking for a change. This is way bigger than what I expected, but it's good for me. I feel like I've found my wings."

"Well, that's good to hear. I'm going to miss you so much."

My heart throbbed. "We'll still talk all the time."

"Yeah, but I can't just jump in the car and come see you without packing a bag."

"I know. I can't wait for you to come visit though. I can show you around. There's so much to see and experience here."

"If staying makes you happy, then do it. Is this a rash decision or the right decision?"

"It feels right." And it did. "One more thing."

"My heart can't take anymore."

"I think I'm falling for the man next door."

"Girl, the man next door? That's so damn cliché!" Amy laughed. "But that's the kind of tea I like. Tell me more."

I laughed. Talking with Amy always made me feel good. "And you won't believe this," I said.

I purposely hesitated.

"Girl. My heart can't take this. Tell me!" she whined.

"I slept with him." I covered my face.

"Oh! Oh! Oh! *Girl*. Was it good?" Amy's face was so close to the camera, I cackled.

"Felt like fireworks."

She clapped and giggled at the same time. "You're coming out of your shell, little butterfly."

I threw my head back and laughed again. Thoughts of Noble brought me joy.

"I'm not going to be naive about this. We just slept together, but I hope we can still be friends."

"You're really feeling him, huh?"

"I am, which is un-freaking-believable. He makes me feel safe, beautiful, sexy, and seen." I groaned. "It's in the way he looks at me like I'm a snack. And not in a creepy way. He's fun, caring, and let's not forget, packing!" I sang the last word.

"Oh! That part. Because *that* matters!" Amy declared, snickering.

"Girl! Yes!"

"What did y'all do this weekend besides…" Amy left her question hanging in the air.

"We did plenty of that," I said, admitting to all the sex we'd had. "But besides that, he was there for me in a way that I've never experienced with a man."

"Oh, girl!" Amy squealed.

"We talked for hours. He literally drowned me with attention. He's this amazing mix of hard and soft, manly and nurturing."

"He got any brothers? I didn't know they made them like that in New York."

A sharp bark of laughter burst out of me. "Neither did I. At first, I kept questioning myself, wondering should I be doing this. But I heard you in my head, telling me to live. Speaking of you, guess what else we did?"

"What?" Amy's excitement crackled through the screen.

"Watched episodes of *Up and Vanished*."

"That's my show." The sounds Amy emitted sounded like a screaming pack of hyenas. It was too infectious for me not to fall over laughing with her.

It had been bold of me to show up at his door like that, but I'd needed him, and he'd filled that need repeatedly.

We had spent the entire weekend and most of the week absorbed in each other, Noble feeding me food and filling my desire with incredible, mind-numbing sex. Despite the anger I harbored, being with him was magical enough to make me forget the pain, even if it was for just a moment. That's what I imagined relationships felt like. I'd never had that before, and I wanted more.

"Does he know you're staying?"

"I haven't told him." Honestly, I wondered if that would douse the sizzle between us. The pressure of limited time made what we did more interesting.

"Wow," Amy sighed. "In a matter of weeks, your entire world has changed. I'm excited for you, Hollz. Just be careful. What are you going to do about Aunt Patty?"

I'd felt like a balloon had burst and I was flying uncontrollably around the room when she mentioned Ma.

"I don't know. I can't talk to her right now."

"You're going to have to deal with it sooner or later. Find

it in your heart to forgive her. Don't carry that anger around. You've got too much living to do now."

I said nothing. Instead, I walked in circles around the colorful area rug in my small room. The pain was too fresh. I didn't want to make promises that I couldn't trust myself to keep.

"Hollz. I know you hear me," Amy said. I still didn't respond. "I know this revelation is hard to swallow, but she *did* raise you, love you, and willingly make every sacrifice a single parent could. You know your mom. I believe Aunt Patty really thought she was doing the best thing she could for you. Give yourself time to grieve, be angry, and deal with whatever emotions you have to. It's all okay. But don't allow this to hover and linger—especially when you're learning to be free. Find a way to let it go."

I huffed. "I will."

I stayed quiet for several moments, absorbing the weight of Amy's words.

"Have you decided what you're going to do for your birthday? Will you be in New York or Charleston?

"Not sure. I was supposed to start the job in Charleston two weeks from Monday. I still have to tell them I won't be taking the position. Then there's the apartment and I'll need a job here."

"Patience and I could come to celebrate with you. I've never been to New York."

"I'd love that." I yawned, exhausted from all the sleepless nights over the past few days. Partly because of Ma and partly because of Noble. I grinned, thinking about the Noble part. "I'm gonna jump off this phone now. I have a new life to plan and a house to decorate and furnish. Decisions, decisions."

"Okay, homeowner," Amy said teasingly.

"I like the sound of that. Bye!"

It felt good to let everything plaguing my mind out on Amy. Weights were removed from my shoulders.

Feeling empty, I picked my cell back up to check out options for dinner when the doorbell rang. "Holland." Ms. Elsie's voice floated through the cracked open window.

"Coming." I skipped to the door. "Hey, Ms. Elsie." I stepped aside to let her in. There was no place to sit except the window bay so I led her there.

"Haven't seen much of you lately, so I just wanted to check on you."

"Aw, thanks. I'm okay." I sat and patted the space beside me, inviting Ms. Elsie to join me.

"That's good. Now, when are you heading back again?"

I felt the excitement of the words roll through me. "I've decided to stay."

"Oh!" Ms. Elsie clasped her hands together. "That's wonderful. Your aunt would be so happy."

I looked around at the space. "It will take some work to get this place together, but I'm up for the challenge. Nothing a few coats of paint wouldn't fix."

"And a couple of chairs," Ms. Elsie laughed.

"Yes. This window isn't very comfortable."

"Let me know if there's anything I can do to help. I am so excited."

"Actually, Ms. Elsie. I'll need a new job. If you know of anything, can you let me know?"

"What do you do?"

"Social work. I'm a counselor. I mostly worked with kids."

"I might know of something. Let me get back to you." Ms. Elsie patted my thigh and lifted herself off the window. "I'm so happy you decided to stay. You'll love it around here."

"I already do." I walked her to the door.

I watched her walk out of my gate and up her steps. Instead of closing the door, I looked over my new street. It was alive with its usual playlist of kids, people, voices, and cars—no longer overwhelming. I imagined Aunt Goldie sitting on her porch, taking in the beautiful brownstones standing tall like soldiers.

I went outside and sat on the stoop. My neighbor Niquel pulled up and waved as she exited. "Hey, Holland," she said as she stepped out before opening the passenger side to let her cute little doggie out. Together, they traipsed up the steps and disappeared behind the neat facade of her home.

I could do this. Couldn't I? It was as far away from Florence and all it represented as I could get. A country girl at heart, I'd go back, but not for a long time. Even Charleston seemed too close.

I thought back to my cancer scare, which started my whole journey to figure my life out and wanting more.

Cancer. My hands flew to my mouth. Remembrance clicked in my brain like a missing puzzle piece. My mother, grandmother, and aunt all died of breast cancer. I needed to call my doctor and let him know. When he had asked about my family history, I couldn't give him any information. I pulled out my cell and added a reminder to call him first thing in the morning.

Twenty-Four

Noble

"Hello." I turned down the music flowing from my speakers.

"Noble Washington?"

"This is he." I don't usually answer numbers I'm not familiar with, but with all the jobs my recruiter recommended me for, I didn't want to miss anything.

"Great. Hello, Mr. Washington. This is William Levy, from the EMD Group. We're a consulting firm for midsize business leaders. I sent you a few emails but figured I should call."

That's what I got for using the same phone for work and personal use. This guy had called about the email I'd been avoiding.

"Are you there?"

"Uh. Yes. I'm here."

"In case you didn't get to read the email, we have a conference coming up in a few weeks and have been looking for a dynamic speaker. You came highly recommended. With your success in growing Push, we believe you'd have a lot of insight to offer the CEOs attending the event. And with your age, presence, and charisma, you're just who we need. There's a fairly large honorarium, and your travel accommodations would also be covered."

I leaned against the stool at my kitchen island. "Tell me more about this conference."

By the time William, or Bill, as he eventually told me to call him, finished filling me in on the details of the conference, I was sold. They wanted me. They really wanted me, and from what he described, it was just the kind of energy I needed. They surveyed attendees to see what type of leaders they wanted to hear from, and the overwhelming interest was in me and how I was able to make Push so successful while still being so young.

And the conference was in San Diego. At Tim's suggestion, I'd thought about a quick getaway to get my mind together. This could be it.

"Thanks, Bill. Please send me the details, and I'll get back to you with a final answer ASAP."

"Thanks, Noble. It was a pleasure speaking with you, and we hope to work with you soon. You're an inspiration to young professionals everywhere."

His words made me feel like the Grinch when his heart started growing. "I appreciate you considering me."

I ended the call, clapped my hands, and spun around. "You're back, baby!" I thrust my fists in the air. This was the kind of press I needed while trying to land my next role. Why had I ignored his emails?

I called Tim and then Ty to let them know about the opportunity. Both thought it was great.

"How's it going at the office?" I asked Ty. He'd been on my mind since my conversation with Tim.

"It's okay. Everyone is still trying to get used to you not being here."

"Let me ask you a question."

"What's up, bruh?"

"Would you want to be the new CEO of Push?"

"I…" Ty huffed. He didn't answer right away. "I would to preserve what we built. It would be difficult without you."

"What do you really want, Ty?"

"What do you mean?"

"If Push wasn't part of the equation, what would you want to do?"

"I guess I never thought about it. What makes you ask?"

"Just curious. I've asked myself the same question lately and I'm starting to understand more about me as I explore the answers. And I listened to you."

"Interesting."

"Yeah. Think about it and let me know."

"Will do, man, thanks."

There may be an opportunity for Ty and me to work together again. I looked at my watch. It was time to get going.

I headed next door to pick up Holland. She'd agreed to let me take her out to celebrate her birthday. Wanting to expose her to more New York flavor, I had grabbed a pair of tickets to a matinee and an early dinner at Carmine's. This would be Holland's first time attending a Broadway show.

"You went shopping?" I asked, seeing her in a nice black dress that hugged her curves and low heels. She came to New York ready to work with her luggage filled with tanks, sweats, shorts, and leggings.

"Yep. My whole outfit only cost about eighty dollars." She snickered, taking a dig at my elaborate spree for the gala.

"And you still look like a million bucks," I said.

"Thank you."

I loved making her blush.

I ordered a car to take us to the city, arriving early enough for her to take in Times Square's throngs of people and bright lights.

Holland wore a perpetual smile. Her neck should have been tired from constantly swiveling, trying to take in all the sights.

Holland sat at the edge of her second-row seat during the entire show.

"That was amazing," she said when it ended.

"It's a great show."

"You saw it before?"

"Yeah," I said, remembering that I had attended a special screening with several other CEOs when our company sponsored their opening-night reception. If it hadn't been for Push, I probably wouldn't have seen it.

"And you didn't mind seeing it again?"

"Seeing it with you made it better."

Those pretty cheeks flushed again, and I felt excitement in my groin. *Down, boy.*

"Up next, Carmine's. A Broadway staple, tourist attraction, and pretty decent restaurant."

Once inside, we were seated fairly quickly. Most people were still at work, so the restaurants didn't get crowded until the after-work crowd descended.

"So how did you like everything?" I asked as we waited for our meals.

"It just gives me more to love about New York. I was so overwhelmed when I first got here. But I've fallen in love with the vibe."

"I told you my city was lit."

Holland threw her head back when she laughed. I wanted to plant a string of kisses on her neck.

Holland sipped her Coke with lemon. "How's the job search?"

I bobbed my head. "It's going? I'm not as stressed about it as I used to be."

Holland tilted her head, giving me a pensive look with those pretty eyes. "What changed?"

I thought for a moment. "A lot. I'm no longer angry about having to leave. Having time on my hands forced me to pay attention to my life. I realized what had been missing, and figured out what mattered the most. My priorities have completely shifted. I joined a board of directors for this charitable organization." I shifted in my seat, excited to talk about the organization. "They do amazing work. I'm seeing life from a new perspective. Things have more…meaning now."

"I love that for you, Noble. Seems like we've been on a similar journey."

Yeah, it did, and I hoped we would continue on the same road together.

"Why don't you just start a new company?' Holland said, taking a nonchalant sip of her drink, as if she hadn't dropped a mind bomb on me.

I'd been so wrapped up in wallowing, I hadn't thought about starting another company. What kind of company would it be though? Push was my best idea.

"If you did it once—" she broke into my thoughts "—you could do it again."

Completely unaware of the impact of her words, Holland smiled at the waiter and leaned back while he placed appetizers on the table.

"I guess I could."

"What would it take?"

"An idea. Investors. A team."

"How hard could that be? I saw how much people admired you at the gala. It's obvious that you're brilliant. Just come up with something else."

Those were the sexiest words any woman had ever uttered to me. I didn't think it was possible, but Holland managed to score even more points. This was what I was missing. Someone in my corner, without an agenda. Someone who wasn't afraid to tell me like it was.

"What about you? How much longer are you staying?"

Holland finished her sip and swallowed. "About that."

My curiosity was piqued.

"I've decided to stay. I need to get my things from Charleston and have them shipped here."

Did she say she was staying? I repeated her words in my head to make sure I heard them right. I wanted to get up and run through the restaurant. Instead, I calmly asked, "Why?"

She sighed. "The short answer is, I feel connected to my real family here. I love that I'm in a place where they laughed and lived. I've grown to really like New York. It's not as big and scary as it first seemed. This city has so much to offer. The food, people, variety…my neighbors." She smiled at me. "Plus, it's the change I didn't anticipate but needed."

"Glad to hear that, neighbor." I flashed my wickedest smile. She blushed again.

"That means more sleepovers?"

"Noble! Stop." She laughed and popped a piece of fried calamari in her mouth.

"I'd love that."

Holland's smile faded, locking eyes with mine. I felt my heart beat in several parts of me. Sparks flashed in her eyes.

"I don't want to seem opportunistic," she said, her tone turning serious. "I've never slept with anyone so soon after meeting them. You're a big-time city dude. I'm a simple Southern girl. I don't know what you thi—"

I held my hand up, stopping her midsentence. "I think you're amazing. I like you, Holland. A lot."

Her smile, small and demure, lit up her face.

"I'm feeling you. I want to continue getting to know you. I want to see where this can go," I added.

"Guess there's not much you haven't seen."

Both of us laughed. I loved how perfectly witty she was.

I raised my brows. "And I like what I've seen."

"Noble!" She swatted at me. She snickered again. "I have to make some changes to make that house home for me, you know."

"I'm happy to help."

"Thanks, but I can do this on my own. I have to. I need to."

"I'm right next door if you change your mind."

Our food came. Holland scooped some of the salmon, veggies, and pasta onto her plate.

After a forkful of pasta, she said, "Ms. Elsie called someone about a job at a nonprofit organization for me. They have an open position that would be perfect, and they're looking to get someone in the position fairly quickly. I have an interview tomorrow. Wish me luck."

"You've got that in the bag. We'll celebrate that along with your birthday. Now, can we have one of those sleepovers tonight?"

Holland gasped. "Noble!" She burst into laughter. When I didn't join her laughing, she stopped. "Are you serious?"

"As a pandemic." I widened my eyes, holding back my smile.

"Well." Holland pushed the food on her plate around with her fork and looked up at me seductively. "I guess I should thank you for such a wonderful afternoon."

I raised my hand and called, "Check, please!"

The sweet sound of laughter erupted from her. I couldn't wait to get her back home.

Holland and I barely shut my front door before we started peeling off each other's clothes. An entangled trail of shoes, pants, underwear, and her dress led to the bed. I kissed the laughter from her lips.

Holland expertly worked my erection with her hands. She

knew me now. The intensity made me jerk and hiss. I couldn't wait to feel her.

I buried my face between her big, beautiful breasts, then flicked my tongue against her nipples until they pebbled.

"Mm," Holland moaned.

"You like that?"

"Yesss."

I sucked her nipples again, then inserted a finger inside her, feeling her clit swell against my thumb. Letting my hands do the work, I tweaked, massaged, and caressed her bud, while kissing her deep until she bucked and gushed all over my fingers. I swallowed her screams in more kisses.

Holland grabbed my ass and pulled me to her. I pulled on the condom and entered her to the hilt. Her eyes rolled back. She closed them and licked her lips—her face plastered with pure bliss. Watching her pleasure almost sent me over the edge. I was determined not to come too quickly, but the way she suctioned my erection with her inner walls made me weak. I unraveled fast. Holland parked her hands on my chest, opened her eyes, and stared right at me. It was bold, intense, and so damn sexy.

"Ahh!' My eyes rolled back. We found our rhythm, molding to one another. Our bodies remembering which maneuvers brought the most pleasure.

We were perfecting our dance until we were ready to explode. I tried to focus and hold on to my composure, but Holland lifted her hips, cushioned her sweetness around me, and met me stroke for powerful stroke. Within seconds, every muscle in me spasmed as pleasure ripped through me. I exploded in torrents, core clenching and unclenching until I'd been emptied. Holland flopped back on the bed, pretty caramel arms sprawled across my white sheets. A satiated smile curled her beautiful lips. I couldn't kiss them enough.

When my breathing returned to normal, Holland turned

to her side to face me. She traced the curves and ridges along my stomach and chest.

"Holland," I whispered, staring into her pretty face.

"Yes," she said, her voice still husky.

"This is what you look like when you come." I opened my mouth and widened one eye, making an exaggerated funny face.

"No, I don't!" Laughter bubbled from her sweet lips and she swatted me.

"How do you know? You ever seen your own O-face?" I teased.

"Well, this is what you look like." Holland made a sillier face and grunted like a gorilla.

"Nah, I look cool. Like this." I raised a brow like The Rock and hit her with a smolder fit for the cover of a magazine.

Another laugh rumbled through her. This time, she swatted me with a pillow. I grabbed it, tossed it aside, and rolled on top of her, kissing her laugh into submission.

"Want." *Kiss.* "Me." *Kiss.* "To show you." *Kiss.* "What I look like." *Kiss.* "So you'll remember?"

Holland giggled. "Yeah. I think I forgot."

She was already wet, so I entered her again. This time taking it slow and deep until she grabbed fistfuls of sheets, groaning with the rise and fall of her climax.

We showered together, then lay in bed naked, binge-watching another crazy series, and nibbling on snacks and each other.

Holland was still beside me when I woke the next morning. She must have been too tired to leave after our sexual acrobatics the previous night. The more rounds we went, the more creative we got, and the more fun we had.

After waking up to find her next to me for the next few days, I knew she was truly comfortable.

Twenty-Five

Holland

Noble and I spent the week settling into the rhythm of this thing growing between us. We hadn't named it. Didn't need to, but enjoyed every moment. I craved him when he wasn't around.

Noble sent me off to my first day of work with good wishes, good kisses, and a firm pat on my ass.

Ms. Elsie came through. I aced my interview and was offered a job with the foster care agency on the spot. I couldn't wait to start—until my new boss arrived. Janet Higgins marched in, fanning away beads of sweat popping across her forehead, courtesy of her frequent sudden hot flashes. Dirty-blond hair lay slick against the weathered skin of her face. She pinned dark eyes on me and tossed me a flippant, "Good morning."

"Good morning," I replied, sounding way too cheerful in contrast to her monotone greeting.

"Follow me," she instructed.

I closed my eyes to keep from rolling them. This was the

woman I would be reporting to every day? She differed sharply from the pleasant woman who'd first interviewed me for the position. I didn't know if she was having a bad day or if this was how she was all the time.

Janet introduced me to the small team I would be working with. The three of them welcomed me with warm smiles.

"And this is your office." Janet pushed a door open and waved me in. "You can put your stuff here. Get settled and meet me in my office next door in about thirty minutes."

"Sure," I said to Janet's back as she marched off.

I took a deep breath, grateful for the job and Ms. Elsie's help. Surviving Janet would be something different. As program manager, I was responsible for executing the programs they had to support foster kids through the adoption process—a cause that was close to my heart.

I put my stuff down and went to the cubicles just outside my office to talk to the women I'd just met.

"Thanks for the warm welcome," I said.

"Absolutely," said Paige, the oldest of the three.

The others smiled and nodded. Paige stood and walked closer to me. She looked down the hall toward Janet's office, and then in the opposite direction before leaning closer to me.

"We do great work here. Those kids jump right into your heart once you meet them. Just do your best to stay out of Janet's way. She may not be the most cheerful person you'll ever meet, but as long as you do a good job, you'll be fine. She's a real stickler when it comes to rules, so learn them and stay out of her crosshairs the best you can. Remember, we're here for those kids."

The other ladies nodded in agreement.

"Oh. And she's deathly afraid of the board," Paige added. "Let me know if you need help with anything, okay?"

"Will do. And thanks."

Paige's comments gave me insight into dealing with Janet. I knew it wouldn't be easy. When I got to her office, she slapped me with a list of do's and don'ts before explaining that we had an important meeting the next morning about an upcoming event.

"The board members will be in attendance," she said. "If you have any questions, ask me directly after the meeting. Don't ask anything in front of the board members."

"Sure," I said, thinking about how odd her directive was.

I pegged Janet as the type who was intimidated by higher-ups, carefully guiding her interactions through all the proper protocols. This was going to be interesting. I went home that night, reminding myself to stay out of Janet's way, knowing she would never be described as being a "pleasure to work with."

First thing the next morning, the conference room filled with people. I stood near the back, away from Janet—away from everyone. I wanted to observe. I heard a voice that made me turn my head so fast I risked whiplash.

"Holland." Noble came to me and kissed my cheek. "Don't tell me your new job is with Chosen Alliance?"

"What are you doing here?"

"This is the agency I was telling you about. I'm on the board. They asked me to be the chair of the committee planning the event. I didn't realize this was the nonprofit Ms. Elsie hooked you up with."

I laughed. "It all happened so fast. You have got to be kidding me. What are the chances? Does Ms. Elsie know you're on this board?"

"I don't know. How didn't we realize we were talking about the same agency is beyond me." Noble and I laughed together.

"You two know each other?" Janet's accusing tone scraped

into our conversation like nails on a chalkboard. Her beady eyes narrowed suspiciously.

"Yep," Noble said, smiling, unaware of how her glare bounced between us. "Janet, right?" he asked.

"Yes, sir." Janet's nod was so sharp it resembled a military salute. She turned to me. "Holland. Can I speak with you outside?" Before I could answer, she turned to address Noble again. "Pardon us, Mr. Washington." Without another word, she marched out of the room.

I followed close behind, leaving Noble looking as confused as I felt.

"You should be aware that we have strict rules against fraternizing with coworkers, leadership, and especially board members."

"Janet, Noble is a f—"

"*Mr. Washington*—" she chopped into my sentence, correcting how I addressed him "—is a new and very important member of the board. It would be best if you dealt with him accordingly. Do you understand?" she scolded, leaving no room for debate.

Oh. I understood, all right. The words on my tongue were unprofessional, so I swallowed them. I needed this job as much as I wanted it. It was perfect for the kind of life-changing work I wanted to do. Plus, I didn't want to make Ms. Elsie look bad for referring me.

"Of course," I said.

Janet blinked hard, turned, and walked away as abruptly as she'd arrived, leaving me bewildered at how curtly she'd dealt with me. I breathed deeply, returned to the conference room, and sipped on the horrible coffee as the executive director called the meeting to order. I took a seat as far away from Noble as possible. With brows knitted, he looked at me quizzically from across the room. I kept my expression blank. When I turned my head, Janet was peering right at me.

I texted Noble and told him I'd explain later. As soon as the meeting ended, I left before Noble could make his way over to me.

I went to the bathroom, hoping he wouldn't come out of the meeting looking for me. One of the other managers came in as I washed my hands.

"Don't worry about Janet. She's way more bark than bite," she said to me. "She's a stickler for performance, but she'll back off if you're great at getting your work done."

"Thanks," I said, noting that this was the second person who talked about how much of a stickler Janet was.

"You're welcome," she said cheerfully, missing my slight sarcasm.

I had to remind myself that this job was paying way more than I made in South Carolina, and thousands more than the school in Charleston offered. My house may have been paid for, but I still had utilities and renovations to cover. I'd had difficult bosses before. I'd have to suck it up for a little while, making the best of it.

I hightailed it back to my office, hoping to avoid running into Noble. I spent the rest of the day out of Janet's way, completing training videos. Five o'clock couldn't come fast enough.

Noble was waiting on his stoop when I got home. He met me at the gate and walked with me into my house.

"What a day," I said.

"Wanna talk about it?" he asked.

"Not really. Once you showed up at the meeting..." Shaking my head was my way of finishing my sentence.

"Janet is your boss?"

"Yes. Unfortunately."

"She's a stiff one, huh?"

"You know, she scolded me for calling you Noble. I tried to tell her we were…" I paused. "Friends." That wasn't exactly true. I didn't sleep with friends or crave their touch when they weren't around.

"Ah." Noble was about to brush it off.

"Noble." I got his attention with my serious tone. "How often are you going to be in the office?"

"Once a week until the event in a few weeks. Why?"

"Do me a favor. When you come to the office, let's keep our distance." I hated to ask that.

Noble's brows furrowed. "Are you serious?"

"Yes. I don't want any issues at work. Janet was pretty adamant about letting me know that no fraternizing was allowed." I mocked her tone.

Noble waved away my concern. "That doesn't make sense." He threw his hands up. "We knew each other before you got there. Do you want me to talk to someone?"

"Absolutely not!"

Noble reared back, surprised at my response.

"I need my job. That certainly wouldn't go over well with my boss."

"I was just—"

"Trying to help." I completed his sentence. "I know."

"Okay. Okay." Noble backed down, holding his hands up in surrender. "I get it. I don't want to make trouble for you at work. I'll stay away from you whenever I'm in the office."

"Thanks."

Awkwardness charged the atmosphere. I'd never felt so uncomfortable in Noble's presence.

I hung my bag on the banister and sat in the window. Noble sat beside me.

"How's everything else at work going?" he asked.

"Okay. It's perfect for me, but I didn't anticipate having such a…" I searched for the right word. "Spiky boss."

"Look. I didn't mean to upset you."

"I know."

This was our first disagreement—sort of. There was so much for me to take in all at once: my new family—or lack of, a new city, a new home, a new job, a new…friend. It felt overwhelming. The interaction at the office made me wonder if I should put a hold on things between Noble and me. Relationships were complicated enough.

I got up and walked aimlessly around the living room, my thoughts grappling with the events of the day.

I looked over at Noble. He was studying me. Normally, I would have shared what was on my mind. Not this time. I needed space. My mind swirled with too many conflicting demands.

"I'm exhausted." My voice was smaller than I intended.

Noble looked down at his hands, pursed his lips, and nodded. Slowly, he stood. He walked to me, lifted my chin softly, and kissed my lips. His touch was as titillating as always. I was still learning how to bridle my body's response to him. Just as slowly, Noble left, giving me the space I desired. I missed him the second he walked out my door.

From the first moment we had touched, his presence besieged me. It was a feeling I couldn't shake off. His voice, melodic and entrancing, tested my resolve. Every part of me became aware of him whenever he was around. I fell into his bed without an ounce of resistance.

If this job situation did anything for me, it showed me that I needed to hit the pause button. I should have put Noble on the back burner, but he was so irresistible. Too many areas of my life required my attention. Falling into his bed probably wasn't the best way to deal with everything. It brought us closer, but I needed space to adjust to all that was happening in my life. The last thing I needed was a trauma bond.

Telling him I needed space would be the hard part. First of all, he lived next door. Second, our bodies oozed chemistry and attraction. It sizzled in the atmosphere around us. I was drowning in it. We couldn't hide it if we tried. If I wanted to keep my job, I had to shut it all the way down.

I craved a shower, not just for the cleansing, but to clear my mind and dampen my feral emotions into submission. Previously, I'd done my best thinking under the spray of a showerhead. I stayed in there until the water cooled and then went to my room and grabbed my aunt's journal for an escape, but was too distracted to focus on the words. I turned off the lights and got under the sheets, hoping sleep would settle my mind.

Twenty-Six

Noble

I knew how to touch Holland in ways that made her tremble uncontrollably and scream my name in ecstasy. I knew she was a soul looking to find her place in the world. The one that would make her feel like she finally fit in. I knew her sweet scent when it lingered in a room long after she had left. Being around her and acting like I barely knew her was agonizing, but this was what she wanted.

The executive director and chairman had asked the other new board members and me to spend a few hours at the agency to get a deeper perspective of their work. I looked forward to it until I saw Holland's fleeting horrified expression when they announced to the staff that we would be around for the entire afternoon.

I hadn't taken it seriously when she'd said we needed to cool things down now that she was working at the agency. I thought it was a little ridiculous until I told Tim about it. He was resolute in his response.

"You mean that woman you brought to the gala. You

haven't known her that long anyway, right?" Tim asked when I mentioned it.

My jaw clenched when he referred to Holland as "that woman." It didn't matter how long we had known each other.

"Yes. Holland Davenport," I said, putting respect on her name. I couldn't claim her—yet. But I needed Tim to understand that she wasn't just some woman out of a ready pool of prospects. She felt more like *the* woman.

"Oh. Okay?" He looked confused. "So are you guys dating exclusively?"

Tim had me there. She wasn't technically my girlfriend. We had never established what we were. "Not exactly."

Tim raised a brow. "Well, if you guys are serious, then maybe you could notify the organization to keep things clean. Otherwise, you might want to do her a favor and keep your distance if it could cause her problems on the job—especially since she's new."

Tim was right. I had no claim on Holland and didn't want to embarrass her by going to leadership to say she was my girlfriend, because she wasn't. I needed to talk to Holland.

My mind reentered the conference room when the executive director called the meeting to order. Holland's boss glared at her when they announced that several of my fellow board members and I would be actively engaged in the event planning. Janet's scowl transformed into a tight smile when she realized I was looking right at her. I was beginning to think that scowl was her default expression.

Janet's sneer made me think of Tim's warning. I'd hate to contribute to Holland having a hard time around the office or having people think there was some scandal going on. It was important for her to prove herself.

My fellow board newbies and I had already spent time with a few other departments, leaving the heart of the organization for last—programming. It was Holland's domain and the last day of a grueling first week. Janet gave an overview of how their work drove their mission and asked each staff member to introduce themselves and explain their role.

Holland's turn came and I forced myself to look at everything in the room but her. I was so distracted I didn't hear her explain her position and refused to ask questions like my colleagues. I glanced at Janet, who stood against the door frame, tight-lipped, arms crossed. She'd watched Holland closely as she spoke, as if she were waiting for her to look my way.

Holland said she was just a harmless stickler, but to me she was more like a thorn pressing into Holland's side.

"As you see, our program managers all have master's degrees in social work, because their credentials and experience are critical to their work. Any questions before we talk about our role at the event?"

I chanced a glance at Holland while Janet addressed the room. She sat, stiff-necked, with her eyes locked on her boss.

Janet answered my colleagues' inquiries and then led the group back through the office. I hung back, letting Holland and her team lead the way.

"Well, my work here is done. I'll leave you with the managers," Janet said before heading back to her office.

Holland led us into her small office and walked us through some of the logistics assigned to their department leading up to the event. Her scent teased my nostrils. While she addressed us directly, I recognized her passion for the work, as she explained her part in helping kids find loving homes and ensuring they had the right support along the way. This was where she belonged. Janet was a thorn, but nothing too prickly for Holland to manage.

When we were done, I headed to the conference room to check my email. I texted Holland to see if she'd like for me to wait around so we could head home together. She texted back that I should go ahead. She'd see me at home.

People were saying their goodbyes. I hung back, making small talk with the executive director until I saw Janet head for the elevator. I slipped across the floor and into Holland's office. The sound of the door closing startled her. She looked up and froze.

"Noble!" Despite the door being closed, she looked around. "What are you doing in here?" She marched over, cracked the door, and poked her head out. "I told you I'd see you at home."

"You've been avoiding me all week."

Averting her eyes, Holland folded her arms across her chest. "I've been busy."

"Starting your renovations?" I craned my head into her line of sight.

She sucked her teeth. "Preparing for them."

I pressed my lips tight in disbelief.

"You shouldn't be in here. My boss…"

"Is crazy."

"She's still my boss, and this isn't a good look if she comes knocking on my door."

"She's gone." I smiled. Holland didn't.

She dropped her arms, looking exasperated. "Well, someone probably saw you come in here. What do you want?"

"We've hardly spoken all week," I repeated.

"I know." She walked over to her desk, adding space between us. "I need you to understand."

"What kept you from answering your phone or texting me back? Is this really about your boss? This job?"

"Unlike you, Noble, I *have* to work," she spat.

My eyes widened. I opened my mouth to ask what her comment was about, and thought better of it. I closed my mouth and pinned my eyes on her. The question in my eyes had to be evident, but this wasn't the place.

Holland didn't apologize, but she relented with a full-bodied sigh—her chest and shoulders dropped, and she looked away.

I let the dense silence linger.

"I—" She paused.

I folded my arms across my chest this time, waiting for the apology.

"Need to go." Holland grabbed her purse from her desk drawer, hustled around me, and walked out the door.

I stood in her office, trying to figure out when everything between us went left.

Instead of wrestling with the other commuters on the subway, I opted for a quieter ride in an Uber. The extra time it would take us to navigate rush hour traffic gave me time to think.

I didn't like the wedge that was widening between us. There had to be a way around it. At the beginning of the week, Holland and I were on the same page, it seemed. Not anymore. Had I done something wrong? How could I respect Holland's situation without losing her completely? How had I become so entwined with her that distancing myself felt like I was stripping away parts of me?

I wanted all of Holland, not swatches of her. "What burned between us was too potent to play nice," I said aloud.

"Sorry?" The Uber driver looked back. "I didn't hear you," he said, responding to my mutters.

"I was talking to myself."

"Oh. Okay," he said and set his focus back on the bumper-to-bumper traffic.

And how did Holland really feel about all of this?

I shook my head. Through the window, I watched people shuffling along the crowded sidewalks—moving around each other like an orchestrated dance. Ears plugged with their chosen distractions, they were oblivious to everything around them.

We pulled up in front of my house. My jaw ached from how tightly I'd ground my teeth together. It was becoming painfully obvious that while I wasn't always used to getting what I wanted, I wasn't interested in settling.

Twenty-Seven

Holland

I woke to several Happy Birthday texts, including one from Ma, which was surprising. It said *I love you*. I appreciated that she hadn't called, since I wasn't ready to speak to her yet. I texted back Thanks.

The doorbell rang. I took off down the steps, and yanked the door open before asking who it was. Amy would have been so upset with me. On the other side, a scrawny delivery person was hidden behind a massive array of balloons and flowers.

"Holland Davenport?" he said, craning his neck around the bouquet.

"Yes, that's me."

Struggling to hand me his tablet, he said, "Sign here for me, please."

I did and relieved him of the beautiful display. He looked grateful.

"Looks like somebody loves you. Happy birthday, miss." He pointed at me and winked. I made the mental note that New Yorkers used *miss* the way Southerners used *ma'am*. I liked *ma'am* and vowed to continue to use it. I had to hold on to some things.

"Thank you!" I wondered who'd sent them.

With nowhere else to place them, I put the bouquet in the window and fished for the card.

Wishing you the happiest birthday. Your Neighbor—Noble.

"Oh! How sweet." I brought one of the lilies to my nose and savored the scent.

I was grateful—happy even. But this reminded me of how hard it was to banish Noble to the friend zone. My body was already invested, and if I was completely honest, a small part of my heart was too. That's why it had to be all or nothing. Making my way in New York was too important. My job was vital to my plan.

I looked through the window at the reason I'd run to the door in the first place. Amy and Patience were coming through the gate.

"Woo!" I burst through the door before they made it to the stoop.

"Ahh!" Our screams harmonized in a high-pitched chorus.

They dropped their bags and we hugged, jumping up and down together.

"I can't believe you're here!" I grabbed Amy's bag. "Come on inside."

"Happy birthday," Noble's voice broke through our reunion and radiated through me like bass.

"Hey, Noble. Thanks." His smile was my kryptonite.

Amy and Patience looked at me with wide eyes. Amy flashed a knowing smile.

"Sis, is that your neighbor?" Patience's whisper wasn't a whisper at all. She scanned Noble from head to toe. "Hey, *neighbor*," she said and her megawatt smile was bright as sunlit diamonds.

"Girl. Come on inside." I nudged her forward.

"Mm," Patience strutted up the stoop. "Girl. If that man lived next door to me..."

There was no need for her to finish her sentence. We all knew I had already done what she was going to say she would do. Whether it was at home or work, it didn't matter. I couldn't escape Noble. At the office, I found it hard to concentrate if I knew he was in the building. I felt him before I saw him. I tried not to look at him. Janet seemed to be watching every time I snuck a glance.

Seeing Noble and keeping my distance was torture. I missed our playful banter, long talks, and the meals we shared. I missed feeling cared for when he cooked or checked in on me to make sure I was okay. Every part of me longed for him— the sound of his laugh, the safety of his arms, and the pleasure of his bed. But I needed to cool this thing down between us. I wanted this city, this house, this job—and Noble. I thought about still seeing him at home and just ignoring him at work, but I couldn't seem to manage that. I was drawn to him in the most deliciously troubling way. It had to be all or nothing.

I had no business going so far so fast with him in the first place. Noble was an adventure—a fun, rule-bending, wild ride that made me feel truly alive for the initial weeks I was staying in New York. Falling for him wasn't part of the plan and my decision to stay in New York had raised the stakes. Relationships were a complication I didn't need while I was figuring out who I was.

When I snatched a glance at him before I entered my house, Noble was grinning and shaking his head. His parted lips and the sound of his laughter made me want to run to him. Instead, I mouthed, *Thanks for the flowers* and followed the girls inside.

"This is nice!" Patience said, slowly taking in the place. "But where are we supposed to sit? That little table and chairs are all you've got in here?"

"Renovations start next week," I said. "I took some equity from the house. I'm gonna redo the kitchen and baths and get some furniture. You two have your own rooms on the second floor complete with very comfy air beds."

Simultaneously, Amy and Patience scrunched their noses, looked at each other, and said, "*Air beds*."

"Hey!"

"Girl, we're just joking," Amy said. "Come here." She wrapped her arms around me. "I missed you so much. How are you really doing?"

"Okay." I nodded.

"And," Patience said with a colorful acrylic-tipped finger in the air. "Can we just go ahead and address the big ol' elephant, so we can get on with the night?" She flipped her long braids behind her shoulder. "I don't want it hanging over our heads and spoiling our fun this weekend."

I cut my eyes to the ceiling.

"She wastes no time," Amy said. "But she's right." She folded her arms over her chest.

"I know you may not want to hear this, but Ma is distraught. She's been crying every day since she got back. Granted—" Patience popped her lips "—she *should* be upset, what she did was…not good, but this whole thing is tearing her apart. All of us." Patience's eyes softened. "But, Hollz, she loves you with everything in her, and she wants to make it up to you—when you're ready, of course. Just remember, these past twenty-five years, she's been an amazing mother. You were her special one. You still are. No matter what, we're still a family."

"She's right, Hollz. You have to find a way to forgive her. Don't carry this. It's too much to hold on to. You've got a whole new start and a lot of living to do."

"I hear you."

My phone rang just in time. I was done with the conversa-

tion. I retrieved it off the window bay and declined the unknown number for the third time that morning.

"Let's get your bags to your rooms."

Lugging her bag up the stairs, Patience said, "I can't wait to
get out. One thing I know for sure, the men here are freaking
gorgeous. That New York Swag is a real thing. Your neighbor has it. I can tell."

After a brief tour of the empty rooms, I took them to my
room.

Amy's hand went to her mouth. "Oh! This is an adorable
blast from the past. How sweet. Now I wish I could have met
Aunt Goldie."

"Dang. It looks like this room was designed by a six-year-
old Disney princess. It's cute, though," Patience said, smack-
ing gum.

"After I renovate, I'll move into my aunt's room on the
second floor. Right now, I'm enjoying the cute pink throw-
up room." We all laughed. "Get situated, so we can go eat.
I found a place that has an amazing brunch. I can't wait to
show y'all around."

My phone rang again as I left the girls to get situated. It
was the same unknown number. Curiosity got the best of me,
so I picked up but remained quiet a moment to see if it was
computer generated.

"Holland Davenport?"

"Who's asking?"

"Kenny Robertson." Silence filled the line.

Who was Kenny Robertson?

Several beats later he said, "I believe I'm your father."

Almost dropping the phone, I backed my way to the window and sat, thinking my knees might give at any moment.

"H-how did you get this number?"

"From a Patricia Davenport."

Ma, I mouthed. "What did she say? How did she find you?"

"She emailed me and we arranged to speak. She was quite convincing, so I wanted to explore this and confirm that it's true. Yona Reeves was your mother, right?"

"Yes. How did you know Yona?"

"College." I could hear the smile in his voice. "We attended Hampton University together."

I stood, then sat back down. "I don't know what to say." Too antsy to stay still, I kept moving, feeling the blood course through my veins.

"I'd like to meet so we can talk. I'd love to confirm if you are my daughter." He paused. "That is, if you want to..."

"Sure... I...um... When would you like to meet? Where are you?" The questions fell fast.

"Queens."

"New York?" I asked as if I didn't know where Queens was.

"Yes. I teach in Manhattan. I could meet there too. Whatever works for you."

"I'm in Brooklyn," I said, the shock fading.

"I'm happy to come to you. Just tell me when. Evenings and weekends work best for me."

"Sure. Um, there's a coffee shop nearby," I said.

"Great. I'd love to do this sooner rather than later."

Amy and Patience came down the steps and watched me circle the living room as I talked. Unspoken questions knit their brows.

"Okay," I said. "Can I reach you at this number?"

"Yes. This is my cell."

"All right. I have to go," I locked eyes with Amy. "But I'll check my calendar and get back to you."

"Looking forward to it. Good talking to you, Holland."

"Yes. You too."

"Who was that?" Patience asked, finally clearing the bottom step.

"And why do you look like you saw Casper the Possibly Friendly Ghost?"

"Y'all. That was my—" I paused before saying "—father."

"*What?*" they said in unison.

"Yeah. And he wants to meet."

"Whoa!" Patience spun around. "Why is your life a whirlwind right now? That's crazy."

"How did he find you?"

"Ma."

Patience and Amy swapped knowing glances.

"Enough about this. I need brunch and bottomless mimosas," I said and headed upstairs to get dressed.

Twenty-Eight

Noble

"Looking forward to it," I said to the recruiter and pumped my fist as I ended the call. "Yeah!"

It had finally happened. Tim was the first call I made after being offered the position of CEO for a wine and spirits conglomerate much bigger than my own company. The compensation package was astronomical.

"I got it!" I yelled as soon as Tim picked up.

"That's great news. See? You kept your nose clean, we controlled the narrative, the award, the charity board. All of that made a great package."

"I thought it was because I was charismatic?" I joked.

"And smart, right? Smart ass," Tim teased. "I'm proud of you. I knew you'd land on your feet. I'm almost surprised you haven't started a new company yourself."

I was about to say that Holland said the same thing. The blow of losing my company had shaken my confidence. But they were right. I had started and successfully grown one company. I could have done it again.

"Thanks, Tim, for being here through all of it."

"We should celebrate. And let me know if there's a spot on the board of directors. I'm thinking it might be time for a change for me as well," he said.

"That's not a bad idea." It would be great to have Tim join my new board. "Just don't fire me again." We laughed.

"Speaking of boards. How's it going with yours?"

"Great! This organization is really changing lives. I'm glad to be a part of it."

Except for the fact that Holland put me on ice because of it just when things had heated up between us.

"I'm glad you stuck with that. Board involvement is important. Companies look for that in leaders."

"The recruiter mentioned that. He also said the company wanted to lock me in before someone else snatched me up. Apparently, I'm a good look for their hip new rebrand. How's the job search going for Push?"

"We've got a few great candidates, but don't want to rush into a decision. Push is a strong brand. Lots of people are vying for the position. We're going to take our time to find the right fit."

I thought of Ty. How long would my friend have to hold on just to end up getting his walking papers?

"Let's get dinner on the calendar so we can celebrate," I said.

"Send me a few dates that work."

"Will do."

I contemplated calling Ty but waited. Instead, I called Holland, prepared to leave a message, since I knew she was at work. I was getting used to her cold shoulder treatment. And she had to be exhausted after partying with her sister and cousin all weekend.

"Hey." Her voice was low.

"Is this a good time?"

"Um. I have a few minutes. What's up?"

"Seems like you had a great birthday weekend. Did you enjoy your company?"

"I did." Her smile was evident in her words.

"Great. I landed a new position." I told her about the offer.

"How cool. That's my favorite wine. They're here in New York?"

"The headquarters, not the vineyards," I said.

"Oh, that makes sense. Congratulations. I'm so happy for you, Noble."

"Thanks. Um, I need to talk to you. Will you be home tonight?"

"Yeah. Everything okay?"

I'm hoping it will be. "Sure. What time works for you?"

"How about seven? I'll probably be asleep by nine. I obviously didn't get a lot of sleep this weekend with Amy and Patience around." She chuckled.

"Okay. See you at seven."

"Okay. Um." Holland paused. I could hear faint voices in the background. "I need to go," she whispered. I imagined her shrinking into her chair.

"See you later," I said.

I wished time away, wanting it to be seven o'clock already. Despite all the work I had to do—filling out documents for the new job and handling board stuff for the agency—the day didn't move fast enough. Around five, I threw together a pasta dish and chilled some white wine. This conversation was going to require a full belly and something more potent than soda. From six to seven, I checked the window every few minutes.

Holland arrived right on time. She stepped in wearing her fatigue like bad eye makeup yet was no less beautiful. I hugged her. I'd missed the feeling of her in my arms. I took her light sweater and laid it on the back of the couch.

"Hungry? I made dinner," I said nonchalantly, as if penne alla vodka, kale salad, and freshly roasted garlic on French bread was something I threw together every day. "I have wine too. White or sparkling?" I asked, holding up the bottles.

"Sparkling would be nice." Holland wasn't wasting words. I wanted the funny, sweet, Southern-accented version back.

I could tell by the way she watched me move about the kitchen that she wondered why I'd called her.

"Let me make you a plate and we can get down to why I asked you to come by."

"That sounds good," she said and continued to sit quietly, hands folded in her lap.

After plating the food, I placed hers in front of her with a glass of prosecco.

Holland lowered her head and said a silent grace. Eating a forkful of pasta, she closed her eyes, shaking her head slowly.

"I missed your cooking."

"You didn't have to."

Holland exhaled and put her fork down.

"Noble." She wiped her mouth with her napkin. "I need you to understand something." She took a deep breath. "Life came at me like a fastball. So much happened in such a short time that I felt like I was drowning. Some good. Some…not so good. Suddenly, I had all these decisions to make. It was hard to focus. Being around you made it hard for me to think straight. I got the job, and felt like things were finally coming together, but now there's so much at stake. I needed space… to think straight."

And I couldn't think straight without her. When had I fallen so hard for this woman? "I get that. Which is the reason I asked you here."

"Is this about my job?"

I put my fork down and looked directly into her eyes, needing her to see my sincerity.

"This is about us."

Holland looked down at her plate. "I can't—"

"Let me finish." I held my hands up.

Her eyes met mine. She dragged in a breath. "Okay."

"I'm going to leave the board."

She looked alarmed. "Because of me? No! You love being on the board."

"Absolutely. I believe in the mission, but more importantly, I believe in what's possible for us. I want this," I said, pointing between us. "I can support the agency without being on the board. I can serve on other boards. I want to give us a chance. With me off the board, you don't have to worry about your boss or job. It's been hard trying to keep my distance."

Holland blinked. Her mouth dropped open, but she didn't speak.

"Say something." I stood, rounded the island and took her hand. "You can't tell me you don't feel this thing between us. There's no ignoring it. I want to seriously give us a shot. With you, I've learned there's more to life than work. I can love work and have a life at the same time. I want that now—with you."

"Noble." She looked confused. "Are you sure you want to do this?"

"Do *you* want this?" I tossed the ball back into her court. My stomach knotted as I waited for her to respond. No woman had ever made me feel this way. Holland's hooks were deep inside of me.

"But we've only been, you know, for a short time."

"I don't care about how much time has passed. I know what I feel."

"Noble. I don't know what to say."

"Say you'll give us a shot."

Holland looked away. Her beautiful bosom rose and fell with every breath. I heard my pulse in stereo through the dense silence. Every second took forever.

"Talk to me, Holland."

"Noble. I need to think about this. We're from two different worlds. My life is a tornado right now, spinning out of control, picking up new shit to toss into the mix all the time. I need time. You…" Holland's mouth opened, but she kept her words inside. She tossed her head back, stared at the ceiling, and sighed. "I just can't right now."

I let go of the breath I'd been holding. That wasn't the answer I wanted to hear. Hiding my disappointment, I cleared my throat and picked up my wine glass. We stewed in the heaviness of the moment as Holland pushed the fork around on her plate. I finished my wine and poured another glass. My appetite dissipated.

"Sorry, Noble."

With that, Holland got up and left.

Twenty-Nine

Holland

I fussed with my shirt, yanked it off, and tried another. Two pairs of jeans and one pair of leggings later, I turned in front of the mirror, and decided to keep on the cargo jeans, tank top, and cropped jacket to guard against the unpredictable coolness of a late September afternoon. Good thing it was Sunday. I'd had most of the afternoon to be indecisive—something I'd become very skilled at, because there were too many decisions to manage at once. Overthinking was my new pastime.

Did I want Noble? Of course I did, but did I want him bad enough to allow him to walk away from a board position he loved? He found his work at Chosen Alliance as meaningful as I did. It was evident in the way he showed up extra early for meetings, talking and greeting everyone as if he were the executive director. People marveled at the way he remembered their names, which none of the other board members bothered to do. When it came to the youth we served, he always made time to get to know them. I couldn't live with making him walk away from that.

Did I want to stay friends or cut things off with Noble completely? How could I be friends with a man whose bed I wanted to crawl into every night? And how could I cut off the man I enjoyed spending time with the most?

Would dating Noble distract me from my journey of rediscovering and redefining who I was while I was still learning so much? Was our connection a result of shared trauma? Should I forgive my mother? Was I truly ready to meet my father? This tornado of decisions was already all-consuming. How could I focus on being Noble's girlfriend when I had so much to focus on in my own life?

Questions stalked me day and night, flooding my thoughts and stealing my focus. Would I even make a decent girlfriend? It had been so long. Besides, I wanted to be the priority in my next relationship. How could I demand that of Noble, when he would be one of many things I had to split my focus on in life? I had never been so indecisive. Then again, my life had been so much simpler in Florence. Even though I could never see myself going back there.

I pulled a pair of flats from the closet. What did one wear when meeting their father for the first time? I slipped my feet into the crisscross sandals and grabbed my purse. Having no idea what he looked like, I'd created an entire persona based on him being an English professor and HBCU grad. I imagined him as a well-read, proud intellectual who spent time in coffee houses and traveled extensively during school breaks. Polished and published. How would he be dressed? Maybe in a tweed blazer, smart trousers, and loafers.

I picked up my phone and looked up his LinkedIn profile. Why hadn't I thought of that before? His headshot revealed a bald man with a salt-and-pepper beard, caramel-colored skin, and prominent cheekbones like mine. Staring at the picture, I tried to distinguish other similarities between us.

Bearing such a strong resemblance to my mother, I couldn't see anything else that confirmed that this man was my father. I scrolled through his feed. Like me, he didn't post much. I checked Facebook and found a few posts and pics of him with a pretty, espresso-skinned woman with striking gray hair that was short on one side and fell over her eye on the other. They had twin college-age girls. My sisters. Potentially.

If I stayed in my room another moment, I would probably change my clothes and my mind again. I stopped myself from pacing aimlessly and took a deep breath, let it out, and took another.

Then I pep talked myself down the stairs. "You've wondered about your parents all your life. This is your chance to meet your father. You can do this."

I let the map app on my phone guide me to the coffee house, walking past the stores and shops I now frequented. From inside, familiar faces of owners and customers waved at me. They knew my name.

Several blocks later, I entered the coffee house looking for the man from LinkedIn and Facebook. Settling in one of the comfy chairs by the window, I people-watched until I saw him get out of a Jeep Wrangler Rubicon. He was fit and walked with rhythm, like he was stepping in time to music only he could hear. While he adjusted his dark aviators, I took note of his tennis shoes, black jeans, and a black T-shirt with the words Black Designer T-shirt scrawled across the front. I stifled a chuckle and stood as he came through the door.

"Ken—" I realized I didn't know what to call him. Addressing him by his first name felt wrong. I waved until his head swiveled in my direction.

He smiled, walked over, and opened his arms as I reached out to shake his hand. Dropping his arms, he reached out to shake as I opened my arms to hug him. We laughed, shook, and then hugged.

"It's very nice to meet you," he said, exuding warmth with his smile.

"Nice to meet you too…um." I rubbed my hands together, not knowing what else to do with them.

"You can call me Kenny." He stared and shook his head. "You are the spitting image of your mom. But those cheekbones, I guarantee, came from my mom."

I laughed nervously. "You think so?"

"I know so. Can I get you something?" He angled his body toward the barista.

I realized I was wringing my hands. "Sure." I followed him over to the counter.

When I ordered a medium chai latte with oat milk, cinnamon, and a shot of espresso, he laughed and said, "We'll have two of those." We both picked something from their eclectic sandwich menu and headed back to the comfy chairs by the window.

"What would you like to know about me?" he asked, unwrapping his sandwich.

"Everything."

"Ha!" His laugh was deep—the kind that made women blush and giggle. I could imagine the younger version of him wooing my mother. He must have been a mess in his heyday.

"I grew up in Queens, with my parents and sister. Went to Hampton. That's where I met your mother. She didn't play hard to get. She *was* hard to get. That woman gave me a run for my money." He laughed nostalgically.

My heart swelled, hearing about my mom.

"I finally snagged her by the end of my sophomore year. We dated until I left in the spring of my junior year to study abroad in Spain. At first, we kept in touch, writing letters back and forth. Long-distance calling was expensive, so we never talked on the phone. Then she just stopped writing. When I returned, I looked for her, and everyone said she'd left school. I never heard from her again."

"What year was that?"

Kenny leaned back, lifting his head as he thought. "The year before I graduated, so it was 1993."

The year I was born.

"I thought about her for a long time—wondered what happened to her. Then I ran into one of our classmates a few years ago and learned that she'd passed." He fingered his cup mindlessly for several moments. "I liked her a lot. Even then, I felt like she could have been, 'the one.'" He sat back. "She was tough—mysterious. That's what drew me to her. She wasn't like the other girls. She told you what she wanted you to know, and that was it."

"Then what?"

"I went to grad school at Hunter College, and then Columbia for my PhD. I got a gig teaching at Hunter and have been there ever since. Met my beautiful wife, Heather, at a party, got married, and had two beautiful daughters." He smiled at the mention of his wife and daughters. I smiled too. "Not too much else to tell. New York born and bred." He stopped talking and looked at me like he was proud of me. His smile was warm.

"Thanks for sharing," I said, taking a sip of my chai latte.

"Your turn," he said, making it sound more like a question.

I took a deep breath. "All of it?"

"Every last detail. Or whatever you're willing to share."

"The woman who found you is my adoptive mother." I started with that and shared the journey leading me to sit with him, sipping twin cups of chai lattes.

"How old are you?"

"I was born September 1993," I said, answering his real question, minus the math. "The day you called was my birthday."

Kenny raised his brows and nodded. "Wow. Happy birthday. That seems to add up."

I wrapped my hands around my empty cup, holding back tears, not sure what else to say.

Kenny covered my hands with his. "It's okay."

My lips trembled and plump tears rolled down my face. I lowered my head and let the emotions roll through me. I cried for the memories I'd missed being a part of, for not getting to know my mom, and for several exhausting weeks of discovering more than I had ever imagined about myself.

"It's okay," he repeated over and over. "We can move at whatever pace works for you. I'll tell you one thing. You're my daughter. I know it. And once we confirm it, I want you to meet my family, but only when you're ready."

I grabbed the napkin and wiped my eyes. "I'd like that."

"Good. Let me know when you're ready."

"Oh, I'm ready," I said, sniffling. What sense did waiting make?

"I'll take care of everything."

Once I gathered myself, Kenny and I eased into lighter conversation. We both loved music; he admitted to singing in his church choir as a kid. He told me stories about my mother and how she had him wrapped around her finger.

"Why do you think she kept her pregnancy from you?"

"I wish I knew."

"What would you have done if she'd told you back then?"

"I would have been your father sooner."

I pressed my lips together and blinked back fresh tears.

Thirty

Noble

"Do you think I'm going to lose my job?" Ty looked to me for an answer.

I paused midbite, put the buffalo wing I was about to consume down, and sighed. "The real question is, what's your backup plan if you do?"

Ty took a long swig and placed his beer on the coffee table. "I need to figure out something quick."

"Yeah. You know how these things go. New CEOs clear house and bring in their own teams. I'm already thinking about the team I'm inheriting. I'm hoping there's a spot for you there."

"Thanks, man." Ty sipped again. "It was hard enough with you leaving. I know there will be a slew of changes once the new person is in place. Not sure I'll make the cut."

"You probably won't." I thought about my conversations with Tim. "What would you like to do? What do you want for you?"

"I'm figuring that out now."

"What if we started something new?" I blurted before giving it more thought.

Ty's eyes widened. "Like what?"

"I don't know. We did it before. We could do it again. And now we know so much more."

Ty shook his head slowly. "You're right. Finding investors wouldn't be an issue."

The more I thought about starting a new company, the more I liked the idea. If other companies thought I was a great fit to recharge their brands, why not recharge my own?

"We need to really think about this." Ty's smile returned, brighter than before. "Figure out what's marketable, start-up costs, systems, et cetera. Maybe do something new altogether." Excitement was building.

Ty was doing what Ty did best, strategizing. I was the dreamer, the visionary. Ty put details together like a puzzle to make the vision happen. We made a great team. I was confident that whatever we decided to do, it would be successful. Now I was energized.

"Let's meet, map some things out, and bring in Tim to get his take."

"Let's do it."

"Yeah, boy!" Ty said as we high-fived.

I was too excited to focus on the game. I texted Tim about my idea to start a new kind of beverage company, and he responded within minutes.

"Tim is in. Said he's available for dinner Tuesday to hear more," I told Ty, my fingers tapping across my phone screen. "That good for you?" I asked him.

"I'll make it happen," he said. Seconds later, we were confirmed at Brooklyn Chop House—a favorite that I'd been missing lately.

Ty sat back. "What's up with the girl next door? She sold the house?"

Muscles clenched in several parts of my body at the mention of Holland.

"Uh. Nah. She's staying."

Ty sat up. "For real?"

"Yeah." I tried to be nonchalant.

I felt Ty's eyes on me, and when I looked over at him, he had one brow raised.

"What?" I laughed.

"You know what. You're feeling her."

"Nah... I..." I waved away Ty's comments and the rest of my sentence.

Ty twisted his lips. "You can't lie to me, bruh." He laughed.

And I couldn't lie. "I tried, dude. We got off to a good start." I told Ty about the job, Holland's boss, and about me offering to leave the board. "She put me on ice."

"So you're going to just let her go?" Ty shook his head. "I haven't seen you this into a woman since..." He tilted his head pensively. "Since forever. And I have never seen you want something and *not* go after it."

I waved Ty off again and turned to the television. "Nooooo!" I screamed at the running back's fumble.

Ty was on his feet, punching the air. It was the perfect distraction. We refocused on the game. The Giants were still losing, but I was too excited to be upset. Ty and I yelled at the referees' calls and judged the coaches from the couch. All of our would-haves, could-haves, and should-haves weren't going to help the Giants win this one. It was a regular part of our football Sundays.

My phone rang. With eyes glued to the television, I picked up and answered it without looking at the screen.

"Yo."

"Noble!" The way Tanya cried my name made my blood curdle in my veins. The anguish pierced the excitement like a pin in a balloon.

Suddenly, I was only aware of two things: the wails coming through my phone and the sheer fear that my heart had stopped beating completely.

"Tanya!" I shot to my feet. "Where are you?" My heart found its rhythm again, beating ferociously.

Ty stood beside me, eyebrows knit in concern.

"He... I...the ambulance... I found him..." Tanya could barely push words through her cries.

"Just tell me where you are," I repeated as calmly as possible.

"H...home."

Ty moved with me as I paced, catching the words as they fell from my lips. As soon as I said "I'm coming" he pulled his keys from his pockets and said, "I'm driving."

"The ambulance..." Tanya managed.

"What hospital?"

"L... I... J," she sputtered.

"Northwell!" I commanded to Ty, referring to the official name of the hospital. He was already walking to the door.

"We're on our way."

Tanya sobbed into the phone. I didn't hang up. I let her cry until I overheard the commotion from the EMTs' arrival. Their questions came fast. Tanya finally managed full sentences, explaining that she'd come home and found him curled up on the floor, unconscious, with blood crusting his lips. I felt comfortable ending the call once the ambulance hauled my father away.

Ty broke every traffic law from Brooklyn to the hospital on the Queens and Long Island border while I scolded myself for every call I'd ignored. Fear rendered me unable to sit still. I rocked back and forth the entire ride.

I'd forgotten how to feel before Holland came into my life. The sizzle of her touches awakened my sensibilities, and now I ached with feeling. I was a boy again, wanting to see my dad the way I did when he was still my hero. We reached out to each other just enough to make sure we were still alive, both craving more, but not knowing how to say that. Just like with Holland, I wanted more—needed more from my dad. This estrangement was suddenly exhausting.

I silently prayed, *Please. Don't take him yet.* He wasn't perfect, but he was all I had.

We burst through the emergency room doors. Ty retreated to the waiting area while I searched for the bay the woman in intake directed me to. I saw Tanya. She crumpled in my arms, crying into her hands.

I called his name. Dad reached for me. The attendants preparing to wheel him away stepped aside. I placed my hand in his. He squeezed it and shut his eyes tightly. A tear spilled down the side of his face to his ear. When he let go of my hand, I marched through the emergency room, past Ty in the waiting area, and out the door. Outside, I sucked in air, hard and fast. My chest felt like it would burst. I pressed the palms of my hands to my eyes and heaved.

Moments later, I managed to calm myself. Turning back toward the emergency room door, I spotted Ty. He nodded and went to sit back down. Tanya was inside.

The doctors explained that he needed emergency surgery to repair the severe damage to the lining of his stomach.

"Thanks for driving me, Ty. You can go. I'll find my way back." There was nothing more we could do besides wait. I wasn't leaving that hospital until my father was out of surgery.

"Nah, bruh. I'll be right here."

I was too choked up to say thanks. Tanya stood by, shifting her weight from one foot to the other. Her eyes, swollen and red, had dark circles underneath.

"Have you eaten anything?" I asked.

"No," she said without looking up from the ground.

"Let's grab something." I wasn't hungry, but she looked like she hadn't eaten in days.

The sun had long since tucked itself away and the hospital cafeteria was closed. The easiest option was a diner several blocks away. Inside, the three of us drank coffee and pushed half-eaten meals around on our plates.

"Your father is so proud of you."

"Yeah." How would she know?

"He talks about you all the time," she said as if she heard my thoughts. "Made sure all his friends knew you were the founder of Push." She looked down at her plate, pushed more food around. Then she looked at me, over to Ty and back at me again before opening her mouth, but said nothing.

Ty took the hint. "I'm gonna make a call. Be right back."

Whey Ty was out of earshot, she addressed the elephant in the relationship. "I know you never liked me."

"I never said that."

Tanya pursed her lips. "Who likes the person who breaks up their home?"

I said nothing.

"I was enamored with that man." Tanya's small smile was nostalgic. "We were all enamored. He was one of the guys that all the girls in the office crushed on. None of the electricians wore wedding rings at work. We never knew which of them were married. I'd watch him come and go every day and one day, the weather was horrible. My car broke down, and he offered me a ride home. That's how it started. That was my chance. I flirted with him so I could go back to the office and brag to the girls. I didn't know he had a wife and kid until I'd fallen hard enough not to care. I never knew your mother was sick."

My jaw tightened. I swallowed the brick in my throat threatening to cut off my air.

Tanya looked at me. Her eyes were soft but intense. "I'm sorry."

No one spoke.

"My dad was a grown man," I said after a grueling span of silence.

Tanya looked relieved. "He drank a lot when we first got together," Tanya continued. I wanted her to stop talking. "It wasn't so bad—the drinking, until…" Tanya's eyes flitted to me and back down to her plate. "She died. Your mom, I mean. After that, he drank all the time. A few years later, he started having stomach issues. By the time he tried to stop drinking last year, it was too late. He's been getting sicker ever since."

Tanya finally stopped talking, taking in the voices and clinks of forks against plates around us. Finishing our coffees, we let the waiter take our barely eaten meals, and headed back to the hospital, and parked ourselves in the waiting area for a few hours.

It wasn't until Tanya nudged me awake that I realized I'd been sleeping. I blinked away the haze, remembered where I was, and stared at Tanya until she came into focus.

"He's in recovery," she whispered. "They said we can go see him."

I got up, stretched, and righted my clothes. The clock said it was after one in the morning. Ty sat in the corner, head against the wall, still asleep.

"You go first," she said to me.

I nodded.

An attendant walked me through wide security doors into

the recovery area. I stood over my father, grateful that he was alive.

"Noble," he croaked and held out his hand.

I put my hand in his for the second time in over ten years. "I'm here, Dad." He exhaled as if he was glad.

"Thanks," he said, his voice still frail. "Men are stupid."

"What? What are you talking about?"

"Should have said this a long time ago." His words were labored. "I'm sorry."

I put my hands on his shoulder. "Don't worry about that now."

"No better time." He paused to breathe. "I need to...before it's too late." He took several slow and steady breaths. I squeezed his hand lightly. "I'm sorry and I..." He took a few more breaths. "I want you back. Can I..." He inhaled, rolled his head to see me better, and exhaled. "Try again?"

The tears I'd held back all evening fell relentlessly. I licked my lips and tasted the salt. "Yeah, Dad. I'd like that."

By the time Ty dropped me off, it was almost three in the morning. I turned the key in my door and paused. I looked back to Ty and waved, watching him drive off. I thought about his words when we were watching the game.

Closing my door, I walked out of my yard and into Holland's. This couldn't wait. I texted and rang the bell several times until Holland's beautiful sleepy face finally filled her door frame.

"Noble?" Holland covered her yawn, folding her arms over her breasts. "Are you okay?"

"Invite me in...please." My voice came as a whisper.

Thirty-One

Holland

A loaded plea, Noble's words went straight to my heart. I pushed the screen door open and knew I was opening myself to more than him entering my house.

Something was wrong. I could see that in his distressed eyes, but I recognized something else. Stress and loneliness had driven me to Noble's bed and he had effectively healed me in ways I could never have imagined. Noble needed that in return.

Noble stepped in, and I pulled him into my arms. His embrace wasn't sensual. It was needy and hungry, stripping away all ego and exposing the core of his soul. Noble held me as if his life depended on it. If he let go, he would fall into an abyss.

I held him tighter and rubbed circles into his back, feeling his anguish. I wanted to be there for him like he had been for me. Our desire had other plans, rising and floating around us like ribbons in a soft breeze—cutting through all denial.

Noble pulled himself out of our embrace to rest his forehead against mine. I caressed his cheek with my thumbs.

"What is it?" I whispered.

"My father."

I wrapped my arms around him again, understanding fully how he'd allowed me to use him to dull the things that hurt. I'd let him use me tonight.

I'd wanted to go to Noble after meeting with my father. I'd wanted to share that with him so badly, but I'd already told him in so many ways that I didn't want him, even though every part of me did.

I kissed Noble and released a flood. Fire blazed between us, leaving me hot and wanting. His fingers ignited my skin.

I pressed against him, feeling the swelling between his legs. Desire throbbed between mine. I took Noble by the hand, stepped around cans of paint, and led him up to my room. I grabbed a condom from the small pack I'd stuffed in my purse, and laid it on the nightstand.

Carefully, I undressed him, watching some of the pain seep from his expression. Removing his clothes gave me the advantage of touching every part of his hot body. I took Noble's hand and directed him onto the bed. He watched me drop my panties and pull my tank top over my head. His chest heaved.

Noble reached for me. Gently, I pushed his hand down. It was my turn to take care of him. He squirmed under my kisses, from his lips to his groin. When I lowered myself onto his sheathed erection, his back arched. His hiss was so heavy, I thought he would choke. Noble filled me so deeply it touched my soul.

I planted my hands on his chest and swirled my hips, suctioning and cushioning him. Noble squeezed his eyes shut and met me, slow, long deliberate stroke for delicious stroke. With his hands on my hips, I bounced on him, faster and harder. We collided with each other and ecstasy ripped through me.

I throbbed and gushed. Noble's groan swelled in his throat and erupted through his mouth.

"Ahh!" He looked dead into my eyes as his expression morphed from what looked like pure pain to pure bliss.

Noble threw his head back and bellowed as his orgasm thundered through him. I collapsed onto his chest. Soon after, Noble wrapped his arm around my back. He kissed the top of my head.

"Please tell me you want this as bad as I do," he whispered.

There was no more denying or running from the truth. My heart and body craved Noble, even when I distanced myself. I lifted my head so he could see my eyes when I said, "I want this."

I laced my fingers in his. We kissed until his erection swelled again, begging for reentry. We satisfied one another until the sun bathed us in its light.

And then, we talked—verbal intercourse that purged the fears and joys we were confronting. A clean slate as we harbored no more secrets.

Thirty-Two

Holland

My mother opened the door and froze.

"Hi, Ma."

My words were a switch, shifting her emotions from dejected to overjoyed.

"Holland!" she cried, throwing her arms around my neck and knocking me back.

She was wrong for what she'd done, but I couldn't remember when I didn't feel the fullness of her love while growing up in her home. I still daydreamed about what life would have been like had I lived with Aunt Goldie. They had both loved me.

"Holland?" Patience was suddenly behind Ma. "What are you doing here?" she asked, taking me in her arms when Ma finally let go. She pulled me inside the house and plopped on the living room's worn sectional.

"I had to meet the movers and turn in my keys. Now that the renovations are done, I wanted to get my furniture to

New York so I could finish decorating. We just drove here from Charleston."

"We?" Patience said, letting nothing slip by.

"Noble came with me."

"Who's Noble?" Ma asked.

"Her *boyfriend*," Patience said, the way one kid teased another.

I was still getting used to calling him that. Noble and I had been inseparable since he'd showed up at my door the night of his father's health scare.

"Where is he?" Ma asked.

"I needed to do this alone."

Ma's gaze shifted uncomfortably. "How about some chai?"

"Sure."

"In here," she said, walking into the kitchen.

Patience nodded her head in that direction. "Go on, sis. This is long overdue."

I hadn't been in that kitchen since July. It was the end of November. From the table, I watched Ma make the tea. She placed two cups on the table and sat directly across from me. The aromatic scent curled up with the steam. How many times had I sat at this table with Ma, discussing things over tea? As a kid, we sipped on sweet tea. In high school, we switched to hot tea. I fell in love with vanilla chai.

At that table, she had given me the you're-perfect-just-like-you-are talk when I bloomed late and the boys teased me. And again later, when I was uncomfortable with my large boobs when no other parts of me had filled out. She was the one who told me that men loved through actions, not words. I understood that clearly now.

Ma hadn't taken her eyes off me. She watched as I scanned the changes, noting the new curtains over the kitchen sink.

"I'm so sorry, Holl—"

"I forgive you."

Ma dropped her head. Her shoulders shook as she cried. I reached across the table and placed my hand over hers.

"And thank you for giving me my father back."

She lifted her head, curling her lips from a frown to a smile. She wiped her face with a napkin from the wood-block holder. "You sure?"

"The DNA test results said…" I put on my Maury voice. "He *is* the father!"

Ma put one hand on her heart and laughed. The sound was freeing, making the rest of the tension in the room dissipate.

"We talk every week. I had Thanksgiving dinner with them, met his wife and daughters—my sisters."

"Were they nice to you?" she asked.

"Yeah. They want to get to know me and asked if I could come by on Christmas. I told them I'd let them know." I paused. "So much happened in such a short time, you know?"

"Let them know the favorite-sister slot is already taken." Patience stood at the entrance to the kitchen, arms folded, just as pretty as she could be, with ginger-colored braids, a crop top, and sweats. I laughed. She curled her fingers together, making a heart, and folded her arms back across her chest.

I waved her in. Patience poured hot water in a mug and sat, dunking a tea bag.

"What about the other test results?" Patience said, blowing into her cup to cool the tea.

"What other results?" Ma asked.

"Since my mother," I said, distinguishing between Ma and Yona, "grandmother and aunt all died from breast cancer, I told my doctor. She was especially concerned because my mother died so young. She connected me with doctors in New York so I could do genetic testing there."

"And?" Patience said sharply. Both Ma and she seemed to hold their breath.

"And…the BRCA mutation gene *was* detected."

Ma blew out a breathy "My Lord!"

"Holland!" Patience's hand flew to her mouth.

"But!" I held my hands up. "I don't have cancer."

Ma sighed. Patience's head fell back. She closed her eyes and dropped her hunched shoulders. I'd come to terms with this reality, like all the other discoveries over the past few months.

"For preventative measures, I'll have to get mammograms and ultrasounds every six months, as opposed to annually like most people. Knowing is the best defense."

"Whew," Ma said. "You're right. It's half the battle."

"Wait!" Patience tilted her head. "Where's Noble?" She got up from the table. "I know you didn't have him sitting in the car all this time."

"He dropped me off. He's checking into our hotel."

"We got plenty of room," Ma said.

"Ma!" Patience's tone was incredulous. "And where is Noble supposed to sleep?" There wasn't enough space in Ma's two-bedroom ranch house. "We ain't got bunk beds no more, and I am not sleeping on that couch!"

All three of us laughed.

Amy burst through the front door. "I can't believe you crossed the county line without letting me know you were here!"

"Amy." Glad to see her face in person, I got up to hug her. "How did you know—" I stopped midsentence and looked at Patience. She averted her eyes and shrugged. "Guilty!"

"Noble and I were going to come by."

"Noble is here too?"

"Yeah."

"And how's…" Amy swirled her finger around the room. "*Everything*." She stretched the word conspicuously.

"Everything is fine," I said, smiling at Mama.

Patience walked over and put her arms around Amy and me. "We're all one big happy family again."

Thirty-Three

Noble

Ty and I guided Holland, Ms. Elsie, Ty's mom, Tanya, and our dads to the front of the historic brick building in downtown Brooklyn.

"Take your blindfolds off."

Ty and I chuckled as they looked at each other, confused.

"Where are we, and why are we here?" Ms. Elsie asked, pulling her coat closed against the brisk February air. Everyone laughed.

"Look at the sign," Ty said.

"Vive Brands?" Holland asked with her nose scrunched.

"You're looking at the new home of Vive Brands, makers of nonalcoholic wine and spirits!"

Holland's mouth dropped.

"You mean drinks that ain't got no liquor in 'em?" Ms. Elsie asked, making everyone laugh.

"That's exactly what it is, Ms. Elsie," I said. "For people who want to live it up after they give it up. Our wines and spirits are made with pure organic ingredients and elixirs, blended to make you feel good and have a good time, without the negative effects of alcohol or hangovers." I needed to practice our pitch.

Tanya's broad smile gleamed in my peripheral.

"Mocktails are a growing trend and a great time to enter the market," Ty said.

Still looking confused, Ms. Elsie planted her hands on her hips and said, "So you mean to tell me, I can drink as much as I want and won't get drunk?"

"Yes, ma'am," Ty said.

"Where do I buy it!" She clapped her hands. Her jolly laugh infected everyone around us.

"I'm proud of you young men," Ty's dad said, putting one arm around Ty's neck and the other around Ty's mother.

"So this is what you've been up to?" Holland said. She knew I was working on something, but didn't know what it was.

"You said I should start something on my own, so we did."

"That was a great idea, Holland. We just didn't know where to start. We did some research to figure out what made sense," Ty said.

"And for many reasons, this did." I looked at my dad. He winked. He'd been sober since his emergency surgery. "Let's take a tour."

Ty and I guided them through the lobby, our offices, and the area with all the shiny new machinery where the drinks would be made.

"I'm so happy for you, babe." Holland kissed my lips. The sweet scent of lilies wafted in the air around her.

From the moment Holland said she wanted our relationship as badly as I did, I'd done everything I could to remind her she'd made the right choice. She helped me through my reconciliation with my father, and I was there for her as she began to build a relationship with hers.

Wading through tumultuous seasons, we kept one another

together, weaving ourselves into the fabric of each other's lives. There was no doubt in my mind that Holland was the woman I wanted to build a life with.

Even bundled up in a scarf, double-wrapped, gloves, and a winter coat, she looked as sexy as ever. No one else had scarves and gloves. This was Holland's first encounter with a New York winter. It didn't matter that we told her how mild recent winters were compared to when we were kids. This was way colder than she'd experienced growing up in South Carolina.

"Babe." I grabbed Holland's arm. "Let me show you the executive office." Conspicuously, I looked left and right and tiptoed toward the large space designated as my office.

Holland twisted her lips. "Noble, what are you up to?" Still, she followed me without hesitation.

Inside, I closed the door and backed her up against it. Pressing my body against hers, I sighed. "What makes you think I'm up to something?" Before she could speak, I planted a series of pecks on her cheeks. "Do I look suspicious?" I kissed her breath away.

"I guess this *is* normal behavior for us," she whispered and then giggled. We could never seem to get enough of each other.

I descended on her lips again, grinding against her. Holland's hands roamed my chest. She slid a finger across my groin, and my erection responded. We got lost in each other, until someone knocked on my office door. We both jumped, looked at each other, and laughed.

"Coming!" I announced."

"You got that right," Holland snickered.

We straightened our clothes and opened the door.

"And this is Noble's office." Ty flashed us a subtle, knowing grin.

Our family and friends filed in.

"Mm-hmm," Ms. Elsie said when she walked in. "You two got lost, huh?"

Holland's caramel skin flushed with red undertones. She pulled both lips in, trying to hide her embarrassed grin.

"I can't help it, Ms. Elsie," I said with my hands up and shoulders raised.

"You sure do love that girl, don't you?" Ms. Elsie said and continued touring my office. "This is nice."

Holland's smile slid down her face. Her mouth opened, her eyes darting between me and Ms. Elsie. She recovered quickly enough, but not before I saw the question behind her eyes. Did I love Holland? Absolutely.

I turned to lock eyes with Holland and said, "I sure do, Ms. Elsie."

Holland's eyes opened even wider, her mouth slightly agape. Despite the others milling about, checking out the new office space, we were the only two people in that room. No one seemed to pay attention to us, but we were hyperaware of each other.

Holland wasn't huge on public displays of affection. Neither was I, until she came into my life. I couldn't keep myself from hugging her, holding her hands, kissing her face. I didn't care if the entire world watched. I loved touching her.

Holland had finally closed her mouth, but her eyes were still locked on mine.

"You love me?" she whispered.

"I do." I nodded vigorously. If she didn't hear my words, she'd see my answer. "I love you, Holland Davenport."

"I love you, Noble Washington."

Holland stepped closer, pulled me by my collar, and lifted her chin. I accepted her invitation and descended on her lips again. Neither of us cared that we were in the middle of a room full of people. This was our declaration to the world by way of the few family members and friends that were there. Holland Davenport and Noble Washington were in love.

★ ★ ★ ★ ★

If you liked Unlikely Neighbors, *don't miss these spicy romances from Karen Booth and Yahrah St. John and Afterglow Books!*

Swap and Smell the Roses

When Willow Moore's lifelong dream of music stardom goes bust, she's burned out enough to need drastic change. As in, she's trading her Brooklyn apartment for two months in the Connecticut countryside. Soon she's baking bread, spending Saturdays at the farmer's market and stopping to smell the roses…

But some things in her new #cottagecore life aren't so pleasant. Like her landlord, former chef Reid Harrell. As grouchy and reserved as Willow is chatty and outgoing, Reid is an annoyingly sexy keep-out sign.

If only Willow was good at staying away.

Going Toe to Toe

What happens in Aruba, stays in Aruba…

That's what former ballerina Lyric Taylor keeps telling herself. After all, now that the curtain has closed on her ballet career, and with the search for her biological parents stalling, she could use a little distraction. So when a lodging mix-up leads to an unexpected fling in paradise with her sexy bunkmate, Devon, Lyric takes the plunge.

Seven days of sun, sand and plenty of sizzle—and when it's time to go home, their no-strings sitch will come to an end… Right?

But nothing can prepare them for discovering Lyric is Devon's daughter's new dance teacher.